With Best

from

Jan

LOVE IN THE LIMELIGHT

By Jan Marsh

Cover Artwork by Jill Hobbs

Dedication

To Mabli

Without whose red pen this book would have been a dog's dinner

ODE TO A PROOFREADER

Without your aid

I would have made

Even more blunders.

But the wonders

Of your sharp sight

Have made things right

Or at least-*righter*.

And also many thanks to our Tiny Writers Group

KJ Rabane

Ron Powell

Pam Cockerill

Robert Darke

Iona Jenkins

For their invaluable support and feedback

And finally, to Dave for all his patience and hard work in the production and cover design of this and all my books.

Chapter 1

The smell of the man sitting next to her was almost overpowering, a combination of unwashed body, stale ale and dirty clothes. His coarse face, reddened by the cold and no doubt the drink, was turned towards the stage where the beautiful Miss Harrison as Juliet stood on her balcony looking down on Romeo. Silently Eliza mouthed the words, thrilled by their poetry and passion. Squeezed up to her on her other side was her sister Flora, wriggling and sighing, already bored and looking forward to the short comedy that would be performed after *Romeo and Juliet*. Eliza had bribed her with a length of green ribbon to come with her to Drury Lane, but Flora found the plays, especially Shakespeare, tedious and unfathomable. Eliza shot her an irritated glance and glowered at the man on her right who had belched loudly just as Romeo was reaching up to take Juliet's hand. But these were minor irritations to Eliza who was in the place she loved most in the world, a world of dreams and endless possibilities. The seats in the gallery may be the cheapest but perhaps, by some miracle, she might find herself one day on the very stage itself.

Several days later, Eliza was measuring out lengths of muslin in Mrs Bell's Emporium when the shop bell jangled and a tall distinguished-looking man entered. In commanding tones, he asked to speak to Mrs Bell who was sitting sewing in the back parlour, her custom during the quiet time in the afternoon, her feet up on a footstool, Rex the dog by her side and a dish of sweetmeats close at hand.

'Who shall I say it is, sir?' asked Eliza politely.

'Tell her it's Ralph Turnbull, m'dear. Come to talk about costumes.'

Eliza's heart skipped a beat. Turnbull. That was the name of the new manager at Drury Lane. And costumes? That must be to do with the theatre too. She hurried along the passage to Mrs Bell's inner sanctum.

'Mr Turnbull, ma'am, come to see you about costumes,' she announced after a peremptory knock on the door.

Mrs Bell's speed at presenting herself, in the shop, smiling and accommodating, was remarkable for one of her bulk, but she was complaisance itself as she showed him bales of cloth, trimmings, ribbon and lace, quoting prices that Eliza knew were vastly inflated then allowing him to beat her down.

'Oh, Mr Turnbull,' she simpered coyly, 'you will ruin me if I agree to these prices of yours.'

'Madam, this is not my usual role, you understand – master of the wardrobe – but I wanted to sound out a new supplier and your establishment is spoken of so highly.' He glanced at Eliza who was busy refolding some lace that Mrs Bell had flung extravagantly over the counter.

'And your assistant is so pretty – and your good self so charming,' he added as a quick afterthought.

'Pretty ... and star-struck, Mr Turnbull. She seems to spend all her spare time at that theatre of yours from what I gather. And she knows most of those speeches by heart.' Mrs Bell smiled fondly in the direction of her young assistant who was blushing deeply at the attention she was being given.

'Is that right? Do you like the theatre, m'dear?'

'More than anything, sir.'

'A pretty girl like you,' he mused thoughtfully, 'which is your favourite part?'

'If you please sir, I love the part of Juliet, but also the comedy roles too. Millament in *The Way of the World*.' Then she added daringly, 'I would like to be an actress sir, like Miss Newley.'

'And what do your parents think about than then, miss?' he inquired with amusement. 'Would they like to see you an actress on the London stage?'

'My ... my father is dead, sir, this twelvemonth ... but,' she continued hastily, 'he loved the plays, and he always said that he thought I had the makings of an actress. I have been reading for many years now and he always listened to the parts I had conned by heart.' The life and spirit in her voice had suddenly died, and she had become embarrassed and sad. 'I miss him,' she said and looked down at the lace.

'I'm sure you do, my dear,' declared Turnbull in a kindly voice, as he continued, 'I have been making some changes at Drury Lane since I took on this position ... new broom, eh, Mrs Bell? I'm always on the lookout for fresh talent. Only small parts at first of course. Why don't you come and see me tomorrow afternoon with a couple of speeches and I'll give you a hearing? What do you say, Miss ...'

'Grahame, sir, Eliza Grahame,' she supplied, unable to keep the eagerness out of her voice. 'At what hour would suit you?'

'At three then, Eliza. And Mrs Bell,' he continued in a business-like voice, 'I shall send Mr Noakes round for the materials we agreed on. You are a formidable lady to do business with, but your goods seem to be of a very high quality. Good day, ladies,' and, raising his hat, he made his exit, leaving both women delighted with the consequences of his visit.

Mrs Bell had agreed to give Eliza two hours off the next day to go to Drury Lane, but only if she worked on after the shop closed on Friday to make up orders. At two o'clock she set out for the theatre dressed in her best russet fustian gown; a dress she had made herself from material bought at cost from the shop. The night before she had curled her hair with papers, causing Flora, with whom she shared a bedroom, to ask all sorts of questions which she skilfully avoided answering directly, knowing that her sister would go running to their overworked and short-tempered mother with tales of Liza's vanity and ambition; Annie Grahame's view on life was that it was an unremitting vale of tears and any attempt to improve one's lot was audacious folly that was doomed to lead to disappointment.

The roads from St Giles to Drury Lane were narrow and needed careful negotiation, not only to avoid the mire and horse dung but to keep out of the way of carts laden with goods destined for the shops, hackneys, and even the odd sedan chair carried by flunkeys. The clang of iron wheels on cobbles, the shouts of street vendors and the smells emanating from pie shops and butchers all wove together into a rich gauze that was part of everyday life in a London growing in prosperity and importance.

As Eliza walked among the jostling crowds, in her head she rehearsed the speeches she had chosen, determined to be word perfect so that she could perform them in the most meaningful way. How proud father would be of her today she thought and gulped back a lump in her throat.

Eventually she arrived at the theatre, its impressive new façade designed by the Adam brothers, now facing Bridge Street and giving the building an elegance and importance that all avid theatregoers thought it deserved at last. Even now crowds were beginning to form ready for the opening of the doors for the five o'clock performance. Taking a deep breath, she spoke to a fellow who looked much at home at the stage door and asked where she might find Mr Turnbull and was directed into the auditorium where only a few of the candles had been lit, the seats were empty, and a carpenter whistled a tune as he made some last-minute adjustment to a piece of scenery. From backstage came the thin notes of a fiddle playing a few bars of a tune that was started and restarted many times.

For five minutes Eliza was Juliet Capulet, waking in the vault among her dead ancestors, only to find Romeo dead at her feet. Turnbull sat in an empty seat in the pit and heard her high clear voice cut through the everyday business of the theatre and was reminded in those five minutes of why he loved his craft so much. In addition, she was a pretty little thing with a good figure – not shown to best advantage in the fustian perhaps, and such an addition to the company would be no bad thing.

When she had finished her Juliet, she looked at him eagerly, ready to go on, but he raised a hand to stop her, noting the disappointment on her face. Joining her on stage, he laid a hand on her arm.

'My dear Eliza. That was truly excellent. Come and work for me here for three shillings a week. Please. You have talent, but there is much to learn in this business. I shall work you hard and you will often feel like returning to Mrs Bell with her silks and ribbons.'

'Oh no, sir, never … not if I can be here,' she exclaimed with wonderment, looking around the vast auditorium, magnificently redecorated with a soaring arched ceiling and sparkling crystal chandeliers. 'I'm so grateful to you,' her voice was breaking, 'you will never regret giving me this opportunity.' Despite her resolve to be grown up and business-like, she burst into sobs, thinking of how her father would now never see her on stage nor help her learn her parts.

The news of Eliza's triumph was not well received at home. Flora saw ahead of her many more tedious hours spent at the theatre. And there would be no support from her brother George who, at fifteen, thought the theatre a waste of time and money, the province of the fop and the dandy. Annie, Eliza's mother, did not relish the idea of her daughter as an actress.

'No better than they should be, so I've 'eard,' she sniffed, as she dished up the supper that evening. 'You'd be best off sticking to your job at Mrs Bell's. It's steady and clean and all girls like to be around pretty things, don't they? What'll you do when the theatre closes for the summer? There'll be no money coming in then.'

'We go on tour then,' asserted Eliza proudly. She'd never been outside London before and the thought of Bristol and Harrogate, Dublin even, filled her with excitement.

'Then how are you going to pay your keep here, my girl? You know how hard it's been since your father died. I need your wages and Flora's from the laundry and George's too to run the house. My money from the Crown don't go nowhere. When you're off touring with your plays, we'll be struggling here. And where are you going to meet a nice steady boy?'

She ladled the mixture of vegetables and scrag end of mutton onto their plates then tucked a wayward strand of hair under her cap. 'You'll be seen by plenty enough but they're not the kind to go offering to marry you, Eliza. You must know that.' She pushed the plate towards Eliza, her face set in an expression of discontent and worry.

'I ... I'll send you money when I'm away, Ma, I promise. Please let me do it, please.' Eliza's eyes were filling with tears, her food untouched. Flora and George had set about theirs promptly and George was chewing noisily and mopping up the gravy with hunks of bread, occasionally shooting malicious glances at his eldest sister who was now afraid that this wonderful chance would be taken from her.

Annie sat down heavily at the table, sighing and looking at Eliza. All her daughter's initial sparkle was gone from her, replaced by doubt, fear and anxiety. Annie's heart softened, and a smile formed on her lips.

'Let's see how you are getting on when it comes to the end of the season. We might have to think again if times are really hard. But eat up now or George will be after yours too!'

Four months later Eliza had learned much more about her chosen craft.

She now had her own candle and mirror in the ladies' dressing room with chalk lines drawn on the floor to protect her own tiny space in this chaotic, noisy room, full of the odours of women, sweat, perfume and milk. Several of the actresses had babies who they brought in to nurse or simply because they had nowhere to leave them. Hetty Ames's three-month colicky Charlie wailed and bawled through many a rehearsal and once or twice the normally tolerant Mr Turnbull would shout, 'For the love of God! Keep that child quiet someone. We've got a play to rehearse.'

Eliza's ability to learn lines was the talk of the dressing room.

'Pity he don't give you longer parts then, isn't it?' sneered Maggie Ford, a blowsy blond who had played every whore in *The Beggars' Opera* at some time or another and who resented Eliza's fresh-faced prettiness and sharp intelligence.

It was true she had never had more than three lines to speak as yet, but the repertoire was changing constantly. The company performed on average three plays in a week, two a night, rehearsing two and learning one.

'It's difficult to remember which play it is,' remarked Eliza to her friend Susan Turner, a pale and delicate-looking girl a little older than Eliza, with a strong and melodious contralto voice. 'Sometimes I have to think hard which character I am playing tonight,' confessed Susan, dabbing on powder that was the only makeup the actresses used. 'Am I Phoebe?' She put on a vacant silly smile in the looking glass, 'or am I just one of Macheath's harlots?' and she lowered the neckline of her bodice and flashed a saucy smile at her reflection.

Eliza loved it, the chaos, the panic about lost props, the gossip, the noisy audiences. There were royal visits (Queen Charlotte loved the theatre and the news that the Royal Family was in the house caused a ripple of anticipation backstage), and several of the actors sought to make a mark on the princes and their entourage of the great and the good. After all, popularity with the Royal Family could make or break a career.

The week before, Mr Turnbull had given her a song to sing in the farce after the main play and the audience had clapped and cheered her even though she didn't have a voice anywhere near as good as Susan's. Perhaps, she thought, it had something to do with the breeches and tunic she had been given to wear. The worldly Hetty obviously thought so.

'They love that, the men,' she said knowingly to Eliza as she sat and nursed the colicky Charlie. 'Love to see the shape of the leg, you see, dear. Under all the skirt and hoops, they can't tell what our limbs is like – not unless they're married to us, of course,' she chuckled. 'Put a pretty young thing like you in breeches now and they can fancy her to their hearts content.'

Eliza was disappointed. And she had simply thought they liked her performance of the love-sick country boy. Ned Rowley had said she was good in the part. He'd been hanging around a lot lately, Ned. Always very obliging and quite a good-looking boy too – well, a man really. He told her he was twenty-two. Tall and muscular, he had a commanding presence on stage, though his speaking voice didn't have the deep thrilling quality of Mr Jacobs's. Sometimes she stood in the wings, closed her eyes and just listened to the way Mr Jacobs's wonderful voice resonated in the theatre, making it possible to forget that he was quite short and had a big nose. And he was quite old. About forty, Susan said, though he still played Hamlet because the audience loved him. They heard that voice and they melted. Perhaps Ned could work on his voice and try to bring more depth and mystery to it.

Lately Ned always seemed to be on hand to offer to walk her home, an important consideration when rakes and drunkards were on the prowl late at night. Sometimes George came to escort her home, but he did it grudgingly, scowling and walking alongside her, hands in pockets, head bent low while she tried to entertain him with tales of missed cues, fluffed lines and muddled props. At least when Ned walked with her, she could take his arm and chat naturally to him, laughing over the current gossip. He treated her with friendship and respect and Eliza felt proud if one of her neighbours saw them.

But in this brave new world that Eliza had entered, no one had more impact on her than Sarah Newley, the *prima donna* of Drury Lane. Rumour had it that she was paid two pounds a week and would make as much as two hundred pounds from her first benefit in May. The King and Queen were enchanted with her, dropping into the green room whenever she was playing, and she was the darling of the public, from pit to gallery. Tall and fair, with an elegant figure, and a perfect profile, she was every inch the tragic Muse, though she had been less successful in comic roles. Her voice was sweet and clear, her movements on stage fluent and elegant, though Eliza had heard her cursing like a fishwife when things didn't go her way. People queued at the stage door to catch a glimpse of her when she arrived in her carriage for rehearsals, and flowers and notes were constantly being delivered.

'One day,' whispered Eliza to Susan as they watched her drive off with a handsome admirer, 'one day that will be me. I'll be just like her.'

'Only shorter!' giggled Susan who was down to earth and a realist. She had modest ambitions herself but loved the buzz of the theatre, the highs and lows. The fudging of appearance and reality that could transform an ordinary girl from St Giles into a lady or a shepherdess or a harlot. And rich and powerful men came to the theatre often, even made favoured actresses their mistresses, on occasion, their wives. Where would a girl from Shoreditch have the chance to meet a man who could keep her in luxury? At least as long as her looks and figure lasted. And by then the practical and provident Susan would have saved up a tidy sum to see her into her old age. At twenty-one, Susan had more wisdom and understanding of how life worked for women than Queen Charlotte and the Duchess of Devonshire combined.

Chapter 2

It was January and ice and snow slicked the streets making them hazardous and dirtier than usual. Although she was wearing pattens and holding up the hem of her gown, Eliza's skirts became dirty and draggled by the time she got to the theatre for the morning rehearsal. She and Annie had quarrelled that morning over a missing penny piece that Eliza knew George had stolen from his mother. But in Annie's eyes George could do no wrong, and Eliza was under suspicion. To add insult to injury, Mr Turnbull had given Susan the part of Margaret in the new production of *Much Ado about Nothing.* Eliza felt she could have played it well, but she was assigned the role of Ursula, and had just two lines. As she headed for the side entrance, head down, cloak pulled tightly around her against the sleety wind, she almost bumped into a man who was hurrying purposefully towards the stage door. He paused momentarily as she grasped the handle and must have stepped on the trailing muddy hem of her dress, because as she pushed open the door and stepped in, there was a loud ripping sound. She turned in embarrassment and annoyance, threw back the hood of her cloak and said, 'Well sir, now see what you've done,' pulling the material from under his foot and examining the damage and looking angrily at the perpetrator for the first time. He was perhaps in his late twenties, pale, with dark brown unpowdered hair clubbed with a black ribbon. He surveyed her from grey heavy-lidded eyes, his mouth twisted in a mocking smile.

'Madam, I apologise,' he drawled unapologetically. 'Had you not been so dilatory in opening the door and getting inside, we should not have collided so unfortunately.' Looking pointedly at the bedraggled and ripped skirt that she had now raised off the floor, he raised his superior eyebrows a shade and added, 'I cannot think the little misadventure has harmed your gown appreciably.' With a curt nod he pushed open the door and walked off briskly into the rabbit warren of corridors, leaving her speechless, which was not a state she found herself in very often. The insufferable coxcomb! To be addressed in such a way without even the common courtesy of a proper apology. And how could anyone keep a skirt clean in such weather?

Inside now, as she watched his elegant figure striding down the corridor, she was a little puzzled. She knew enough about clothes and fabrics to have spotted that, despite his swagger and his superior drawl, the dark green frock coat had not been of the finest cloth, the sleeves were a little short, the frogging a little worn. Although the claret waistcoat was meant to make a statement, it was an inferior copy of the Spitalfields silk that was the mark of a man unconcerned by the size of his tailor's bills. Not a careless young buck, then, of unlimited means, and probably not a titled admirer of Sarah Newley. A terrible thought crossed her mind. Had he come to audition?

As she hurried past Mr Turnbull's office, she heard laughter and voices through the half open door.

'Richard! Good to see you!' exclaimed Turnbull. 'Quite the dandy I see. How are we ever going to be able to afford you?'

Half an hour later they were on stage for *Much Ado about Nothing*, the scene where Hero was preparing for her doomed marriage, her women friends all round her uttering some quite immodest words. Eliza didn't understand them all, but she got the idea that it was to do with the wedding night and what would be happening then, so she tried to look worldly and knowing. As this banter went on, Eliza noticed a figure in a claret waistcoat come into the auditorium and sit down in the pit. The thought of him watching them in this early stage of the rehearsal unnerved her a bit and she missed her cue, for which she was duly reprimanded by Mr Turnbull. With burning cheeks, she tried to redeem herself but Sarah Newley, who was Beatrice, looked annoyed and spoke her next line with ill-concealed impatience. It was with a feeling of relief that Eliza saw the young man, Richard, get up from his seat half an hour later and leave the auditorium.

There were no further appearances of the ill-mannered Richard, a fact that Eliza told herself was a relief. She saw enough truculent male behaviour at home from brother George.

In March, the company was beginning to think of the forthcoming Easter holiday. It was traditional for the theatres to close for Easter Week, forcing everyone to take a holiday, which meant there would be no wages. Eliza had been saving a few pennies each week so that she could make her usual contribution to the family budget, but it had been difficult. In all honesty, she was dreading the week off because the theatre had become more like home to her than home itself; now she felt so distanced from George and Flora that it was sometimes awkward to be with them and this made her sad.

At rehearsal one morning Mr Turnbull had gathered them together to make an announcement. He looked pleased with himself, his broad face beaming, his wig a little askew and his hands full of papers.

'Another new play!' groaned Susan who always had trouble learning her parts. But Eliza was excited. Perhaps this time there would be something better for her, maybe a song, though she didn't want another breeches part even if it got her noticed.

'Ladies and gentlemen,' he began, 'I have today something very exciting to impart to you. A brand-new work, commissioned by myself for our venerable company (a few sniggers from the youngsters here) by a new up-and-coming playwright.' He turned to the wings where a tall figure stood in the half-light. Eliza's breath suddenly became more shallow and a sinking sensation developed in her stomach. Smiling slightly, wearing a green coat and claret waistcoat, stood the destroyer of the hem of her russet gown. He stepped forward to join Mr Turnbull onstage.

'Richard, right on cue. An impressive entrance. This is Richard Cavendish who has written us a play so original that it will not only make his name, but it will be guaranteed to run and run.'

There was a ripple of applause, though Sarah Newley's was noticeably more enthusiastic than that of the others. She was beaming at Turnbull's protégé and fussing with her hair in a quite unnecessary way. A big part for her, no doubt, thought Eliza, as Cavendish began to hand out copies of the script, consulting a list as he did so. When he got to Eliza, he looked up from the list into her face with a slight flutter of recognition in his eyes then brusquely asked, 'Name?'

'Eliza Grahame.'

Looking back at the list, he said flatly, 'No speaking part. You join the ladies at the ball in Act 3.' As he was about to move on to Susan, Eliza asked boldly, 'Do you have a spare copy of the script, sir? I like to study the play nevertheless.'

'You're not an understudy you know,' he replied in a condescending tone that suggested she must be an imbecile even to think so.

'Oh yes, I know that. But it would be an honour to be part of this new play of yours – even if I don't speak in it,' she said with deceptive sweetness and humility, adding with heavy irony, 'begging your pardon, sir.'

Unsure of how to take her words, he handed her a script that she accepted with a slight curtsy and smile.

'I'm learning my craft so well that I can say one thing and mean another,' she thought as she took it. Susan came over to her, her face shining with excitement.

'Look, Eliza, I'm a country girl come up to town, Miss Merit, in love with Mr Valiant – that's Ned,' she said giggling, 'I'm to sing a song of my own choosing in Act 3. And you?'

'No lines, just in a crowd at the ball.'

Susan looked disappointed for her friend. 'That's a shame. Miss Newley's part looks wonderful. I heard her tell Mr Jacobs that Mr Cavendish had written it especially for her.'

'I had rather sweep the stage and sew chemises than play a part that man had written for me!' exclaimed Eliza crossly, making her way offstage and back to the dressing room, clutching the script.

During Easter Week Eliza tried to help her mother by running errands, cleaning the house and preparing food so that Annie was able to work a few extra hours at The Crown and make some much needed money. She visited her old employer, Mrs Bell and told her some of the juicier titbits of Drury Lane gossip that delighted her so much she made Eliza a present of several yards of muslin.

'The weather is improving all the time now. You'll be able to make yourself something pretty for summer. There's a slight fault in the weave here,' she indicated it to Eliza, 'but you'll be able to disguise it I'm sure. You're such a clever one with the needle. It was a lucky day for you, was it not when Mr Turnbull came into my shop?'

'Indeed so, ma'am. I'm so grateful to you for the way you told him of my fondness for the theatre. When I am as famous as Miss Newley, I shall give you free tickets to see me,' and she kissed her old employer on the cheek and gathered up her muslin.

When her mother was at work at The Crown and Eliza had the house to herself, she began to read the new play by Richard Cavendish, *The Heiress*. It was an exciting experience reading something new and she was eternally grateful to her father John for the way he had insisted on both her and Flora having enough basic education to read well. Annie had thought him mad and begrudged the money he could ill afford to send them to the local dame school.

'What do they want with reading? I cannot read, and it's not done me no harm. George, of course, I can understand. But not the girls.'

John had sighed and shaken his head. 'Education should be for everyone, Annie. It will mean freedom for the likes of us in years to come.'

'You and your books,' she scoffed. 'We're free now, aren't we? You talk like we was slaves.'

He smiled bleakly and knew she would never understand. 'The girls will be taught, Annie. That's an end to it.'

So as Eliza read through Act 1, she began to see the shape of the play in front of her. The words came to life as she imagined them fleshed out by the actors – not herself of course, she thought bitterly. She could envisage the witty exchanges, the quarrels, the sudden switches of fortune, the happy ending. The words that he had given to Lady Heartfort, who would be played by Sarah Newley, were so witty, so deftly penned she laughed aloud on occasion. Would the Queen of Tragedy be able to give the dialogue the lightness of touch, the playfulness the part required? The scene with Sir Francis Digby was truly wonderful. Cavendish had used all the tricks of comedy such as disguise and mistaken identity with the villain being justly punished. The audience would surely love it. And all without having to put a woman in breeches! Much as she disliked the popinjay Richard Cavendish who considered her only fit for a ballroom scene, she admired his skill as a playwright.

As the week wore on, she found herself focusing on the scenes with Lady Heartfort, trying out the lines aloud, moving around the cramped rooms the family called home, as if in a grand salon or ballroom, delivering a withering riposte to Lord Digby as she peeled the potatoes and emptied the slops. On Friday afternoon she had quite forgotten the time and Flora came home from the laundry to find Eliza walking around the living room, script in hand, for all the world like a lady of the *ton* from Grosvenor Square. 'I declare, Sir Francis, the world knows but two kinds of women. I, however, am the third,' and nodding haughtily at the cat.

Rehearsals for *The Heiress* began after Easter and although she was involved in only one scene, Eliza watched as many as she could while playing in *Much Ado* and Violet in the farce. She had become used to the juggling act required to keep several plays in her head at one time; all the players had to do this except Sarah Newley who did not appear every night of the week.

Miss Newley was showing another side of her character since the Cavendish play had gone into rehearsal, thought Eliza. When the playwright was in the theatre, she was less of the *prima donna*, less inclined to have quarrels with her dresser, and less likely to send minions like Eliza on whimsical errands (Eliza had been sent off to

Catherine Street for oysters when she first joined the company). To Cavendish, Sarah was amiability itself, accepting his occasional criticism and agreeing without demur to small changes to the script. Eliza had never seen her smile so much. She had become Sarah Newley, the woman, instead of Sarah Newley, Drury Lane's leading lady.

As Lady Heartfort, she sparkled, but there was an extra brittle and bright quality to her performance when Cavendish appeared at rehearsals. The realisation began to dawn on Eliza that the incomparable first lady was in love with him.

'Do you see any signs that he is enamoured of her?' asked Eliza as she and Susan walked to the theatre one morning. 'To me it seems quite the opposite. He's polite, respectful, but I don't see any special warmth.'

'He's being discreet then,' responded the more worldly Susan. 'She, though, knows no discretion. Did you see the way she was flirting with him yesterday, laughing up into his face …?'

'… her hand on his arm,' added Eliza. 'Mr Turnbull didn't seem very happy.'

'Of course, Mr Cavendish is very handsome.'

'And very rude too,' countered Eliza whose repair of the ripped skirt had never been entirely satisfactory.

'He has a pleasing smile.'

'When he uses it, which is rare – except at the misfortune of others.'

'He is a clever man – you will give him that. Clever and witty.'

'In his writing, yes. I have never heard him say anything particularly clever. He obviously needs to work out all his clever remarks on paper first,' she added tartly.

'You are quite censorious, Eliza. Do you now allow him the fine figure, the dark curls, the grey eyes, the fine white teeth then? I find his presence at close quarters quite disturbing I own and he only an impoverished playwright too.'

'Dressed up to look wealthier than he is.'

Susan laughed and took her friend's arm. 'If Miss Newley has not succumbed to his charms, she must be made of ice. And from what Hetty Ames has told me about madam's love life, that is definitely not the case. Hetty said that she was Lord Hollin's mistress two years since, then Mr Gatley's, the Whig politician. She knows the ways of the world, and if she's set her sights on m'laddo, she'll have him.'

The Heiress was shaping up, but the long sessions spent rehearsing took their toll on the actors. Cavendish never seemed to feel the need to eat and drink when he was conducting rehearsals and it was usually Mr Turnbull who called for a break in the proceedings so that everyone could snatch a bite to eat.

Eliza had been helping out in wardrobe that morning but had returned to the empty dressing room where she was enjoying a rare moment of peace and quiet. Sitting in her bodice and petticoat, her long chestnut hair unpinned loosely about her shoulders, she was reading aloud the part of Lady Heartfort from her well-thumbed script.

Looking up with an expression of haughty pride on her face, which she was sure Milady would have at this point in the play, to her horror she saw the author himself standing at the door, a smile

19

on his face. A crimson tide of embarrassment spread over her neck and shoulders, and her hands flew up to try and cover her exposed flesh.

'It is customary to knock, sir,' she said in embarrassment.

'Apologies, Eliza.' He bowed slightly but the smile remained. 'My role seems to be that of the constant apologiser. But I see you are conning my work. Do you intend to compete with Miss Newley for the role? I hope not because Mr Turnbull and some others have a fancy for some pasties from the pie shop.'

He held out some coins to her, which she had to rise from her stool to take from him. Up close, the closest she had ever stood to him, she noticed just how white his teeth were and how the grey eyes sparkled, this time with fun, not sarcasm. Her small fingers grasped the coins from the palm of his hand where he pretended to imprison them in his teasing grip.

'My Lady Heartfort, four of Mr Elwood's best pasties if you please. And perhaps you ought to put more clothes on before venturing out.'

Chapter 3

Opening night for *The Heiress* was just three weeks away. Mr Turnbull's temper was shorter than usual. He snapped at missed cues, fluffed lines, and had even been heard to shout at Sarah Newley whose moods seemed in a constant state of flux. One day she was charming to all, patient with the youngsters, sweetness and docility personified, all of which made Eliza think that she had captured the heart of Richard Cavendish; the next day she raged about a late prompt, called Ned an imbecile and burst into tears during the rehearsal that the author was expected to attend, but did not.

Eliza thought privately that if being in love brought so much misery, she would be in no hurry to experience it. Yet, in all the plays she had seen and read, it was considered to be one of the most exalted of human emotions, transforming those who fell under its spell. It was certainly transforming Sarah. Dark circles appeared under her eyes, she had lost weight quite noticeably and was looking gaunt and strained. Satirical prints appeared in shops showing a scrawny haunted-looking Sarah with the caption "The End of the Run"? In the meantime, she played Beatrice on alternate nights and went home to her comfortable house in Gower Street. If Richard Cavendish visited her there, he was so discreet as to be invisible.

One Tuesday afternoon, two weeks before the opening of *The Heiress*, the cast was assembled for rehearsal, but there was no sign of Sarah. Cavendish was morose and irritable as the actors sat around and chatted in a desultory fashion waiting to begin.

Eliza was helping out in wardrobe as she had little to do in the play itself, and her skill as a needlewoman and sharp eye for putting together convincing costumes had become evident to Polly, the wardrobe mistress.

Suddenly, from Turnbull's office came a frustrated bellow that silenced the chatting players.

'What do you mean an accident? How? Is she hurt?'

Then a silence followed by, 'Sdeath girl … broken her ankle …? How in heaven's name …? She is not able to appear?'

Minutes later, red-faced and wig askew, Turnbull stood before the assembled cast, Cavendish, pale and strained, at his side. In a voice that was controlled and devoid of any emotion, the manager announced that Sarah Newley had broken her ankle having fallen downstairs at home. She had a severe fracture and would therefore not be able to play the part of Lady Heartfort. Mary Holland her understudy would now be playing that part.

Mary Holland, a striking girl with a graceful figure and a pretty singing voice, had been playing Hero in *Much Ado*. She looked shocked, put her hands to her face in disbelief. This was the chance that every actor longed for; a sudden move from relative obscurity to possible fame, the result of chance or Fate or what you will. Eliza, the chemise she had been altering still in her hand, experienced the bitter feeling of someone else awarded this glittering prize and swallowed hard then turned away back to the costume room. Half an hour later as she and Polly sewed and chatted, they heard footsteps thundering down the corridor, then two very angry voices.

'She doesn't know it, Turnbull!' shouted Richard. 'She hasn't learned it. She knows some lines then she simpers and pouts and tries to make up the next line. I tell you she will ruin the play. I will not let her do it.'

When Turnbull spoke, his deep voice sounded alarmingly controlled. Eliza knew that this should be a warning to Richard as the manager was at his most lethal when apparently calm.

'*You* will not let her! Let me remind you, sir, that I am manager here. It is not under your control. Besides, she knows she will have to be word perfect by …'

'I don't just want someone who is word perfect. A parrot can be word perfect. I want someone who knows the words so well that she speaks them as if they were hers. Someone who does not *act* Lady Heartfort but *becomes* her, someone pretty, charming, intelligent, seductive …'

Suddenly he stopped and spoke in a different, urgent tone to Turnbull. What he said made the hairs prickle on the back of Eliza's neck. Cavendish and Turnbull suddenly burst in on Eliza and Polly.

'So, Eliza, when I saw you that time in your dressing room with the script, you were trying to learn Miss Newley's part?'

'No sir, not trying to learn it. I know it already. I was trying to think how I would say the words.'

'Very well. Please come out on stage now and show us how well you know it.'

'Richard!' remonstrated Turnbull, 'Eliza has never had a role of any importance since joining us. You expect too much of her.'

Eliza flushed at this and with some dignity said, 'Sir, I have watched and I have learned these past months. I am capable of far more than breeches roles. Miss Newley has been my inspiration and my model. Please let me show you what I am capable of.'

The next week was one of the most difficult in Eliza's life to date. Richard Cavendish attended every rehearsal, apparently unable to leave the play in the eminently capable hands of the theatre's manager. Cavendish had made it his goal to coach the novice Eliza in playing the pivotal role in his comedy of manner, playbills for which were already starting to appear over the city announcing her name in the role of Lady Heartfort. However, on the Thursday of the final week of rehearsals, no one in the company would have wagered a sixpence that she could bring it off.

'No, Eliza, no!' groaned Cavendish, holding his head in despair. 'You turn stage left, otherwise you will block Jacobs. And your voice in the last speech! It's far too shrill. You sound more like a flower seller than a lady of the *ton*. Good heavens, girl, do you remember nothing from yesterday?' He threw himself back down on a bench in the pit in disgust, running his fingers through his dark hair. Susan, on stage, privately thought he looked even more attractive in this slightly wild state, the anguished author in torment. She knew better than to say so to Eliza though. She would only snap and make pointed comments about his temper and immoderate language.

'Come, let's begin the scene again,' interposed Turnbull in a conciliatory tone. 'Ned, from the top if you please. And smile and leer a bit more at Lady Heartfort. You are supposed to be trying to seduce her.'

So they began again and this time Eliza remembered her position on stage, toned down the flower seller's voice and seemed to satisfy the author who commented, 'Better, Eliza. Much better. Thank you everyone. Tomorrow then. And on time please.'

Eliza, who was playing her breeches role in the farce, was staying on at the theatre. To tell the truth, she was exhausted, living it seemed in a constant state of nervous exhilaration or deep tearful depression. She was trying to cope with the demands of the rehearsals, keeping the script in her head, remembering the direction from her twin taskmasters, Turnbull and Cavendish. There was little comfort at home these days anyway with her mother and brother sniping at her for her "actressy airs" and sister Flora, sullen and resentful when they were alone together.

She missed her father more than ever. Why did people say that loss became easier to bear as time went on? She longed for his affectionate hugs and his teasing. She knew how proud he would be of her for what she achieved so far, and she longed to do honour to his memory on the first night of *The Heiress*. So she sat in the empty dressing room, munching an apple and studying her lines. From the auditorium came muffled sounds of preparation for the evening performance, carpenters banging and shouts of encouragement as one of the stage hands was putting a piece of scenery in place. She looked at Lady Heartfort's speech in Act 4, but the words danced before her and a sudden wave of black despair washed over her. Whatever had possessed her to think she could do this? She pushed aside the script with distaste and got up and began to take off her dress. As she hung it up, she smiled wryly at the repaired hem. Richard Cavendish certainly knew how to wreak havoc in her life one way or another.

She had put on her breeches and tunic and sat before the mirror applying powder in a half-hearted way. Soon the room would be full of women of all ages, chattering, undressing, quarrelling, laughing, drinking (Mr Turnbull forbade it but it went on), crimping and combing. And she would joke and gossip with the best of them, losing herself in the easy camaraderie for a time.

An urgent knock on the door was followed by it opening to reveal Richard Cavendish, his face a little flushed, his eyes bright. At least she was dressed this time, she thought with relief.

25

'Ah, Liza,' his speech was slightly slurred. 'Why are you here so early? Didn't you go home?'

'No sir. I … I stayed,' she replied rather unnecessarily.

'So who are you tonight?' he asked with interest, coming uninvited to the room. 'Stand up, let me guess.'

Although she was soon to stand up in front of a thousand people in her cobalt blue tunic and breeches, she felt awkward and embarrassed standing there with an audience of one. He came across the room and walked slowly around her, his gaze appraising and professional and in no way louche. Then he gave a short bark of laughter and clapped her on the shoulder.

'Don't look so apprehensive Eliza. You make a very handsome young man and I know you will make a very lovely Lady Heartfort.' She lowered her gaze and sat down again in her stool. He pulled out another stool and sat opposite her.

'I know I'm working you very hard at the moment, but we will succeed, you and I.' His voice had lost its slur and was now intense and deep. 'This play means everything to me. And for you it will mean the start of a glorious career, I know it. I have to be hard on you, you do see that.' And to her amazement, he leaned across the space between them and took her hand.

The touch, so unexpected and so tender, was all it took for her raw emotions to come flooding out. For so long she had been deprived of the warmth and affection of her family and was so anxious about her new and very public career that a touch of Richard's hand seemed like an affirmation that she really existed and that she mattered. Dismayed, as he saw the tears fall, the grip of his hand tightened and suddenly he had drawn her into his arms where she stood sobbing into the shoulder of his frock coat that smelt faintly of wine, smoke and sweat. His arms encircled her in a way that made her feel safe and as he held her, he said gently, 'Don't cry, Eliza, please, I didn't mean to upset you.' As his hand stroked her hair, her arms had slid around his neck. Then in a heartbeat he pulled away from her, looked deeply into her eyes and kissed her lightly on the tip of her nose.

'No more tears – you've spoilt your powder,' he joked as he held her at arm's length. 'I'm away to the coffee house and will see you tomorrow,' and he turned on his heel and was gone.

Eliza redoubled her efforts at getting the part as perfect as she could make it and in the few remaining rehearsals, her confidence grew. Since that evening in the dressing room she felt a bond with him, and before she went to sleep at night she would try and conjure up that feeling of the strength of his arms round her, his hands in her hair and the smell and taste of him as he held her close. There had been no kiss, only the playful valedictory peck on the nose, but it had fed a need in her and had put their relationship on a subtle new footing. Gone were the impatient tirades and the sarcastic criticism, replaced by gentle coaxing and teasing.

Susan noticed.

'You seem to be a little more tolerant of our esteemed author now,' she commented as they walked home towards St Giles one afternoon. 'You even have a smile for him I notice. I thought you said he was no wit,' she added slyly as they both stepped aside to avoid a woman lurching towards them, drunk from one of the many gin houses they passed.

Eliza laughed and took her friend's arm. 'I was too harsh on him. He has helped me. He is a kind man deep down and I want the play to succeed on Wednesday.as much as he does.'

'Has he made advances to you?' Susan asked, serious now. 'You don't have to oblige him, even though he is the playwright. Although I must say I would be tempted.'

Eliza giggled. 'No, of course not. He is not interested in the likes of me. I wonder if Miss Newley has been enjoying his attentions while recovering from her accident.'

'That was strange wasn't it – that accident?' said Susan thoughtfully, 'Falling downstairs like that. Are you sure you didn't creep into her house and push her, Eliza?' at which they both laughed. 'He won't be able to resist her forever. And why should he anyway? She is beautiful, sophisticated, the toast of London. And she has a fine house in Gower Street. They are bound to become lovers even if they are not already so,' she concluded in a matter-of-fact way. 'It happens all the time in the theatre. Not yet to me, unfortunately.'

Eliza smiled but felt no pleasure at this neat assumption.

The twenty-sixth of May was the opening night of Richard Cavendish's play, *The Heiress*, a play by an unknown playwright, starring as its female lead a virtually unknown twenty-year old actress. John Turnbull tried to keep up a façade of optimism he did not always feel.

To his cronies at Whites he was in expansive and sanguine mood. 'I tell you, gentlemen, this new playwright of mine is another Congreve, though not as broad, if you understand me. Your wives and daughters need not fear to blush at his wit but only to enjoy the humour of his writing. And, of course, Mr Jacobs is as ever superb as the villain.'

'And your leading lady?' prompted the Duke of Portland who regarded himself as patron of the arts and a man who took a particular interest in the up and coming young actresses at Drury Lane and its rival, Covent Garden.

'Eliza Grahame. As yet untried in a major role but a star of the future, I guarantee,' claimed Turnbull, taking the proffered snuffbox from the Duke. 'Fresh and unspoiled.'

'Hardly the best qualification for one playing a lady of fashion then,' added Allsop, the Whig MP who had joined the discussion.

'… but a consummate actress, therefore able to appear sophisticated and worldly as the part requires,' continued Turnbull with determined good humour. He knew that support from the upper echelons of London society was paramount to the success of his play and was doing his utmost to "puff" the premiere.

'And is she a pretty girl, this Eliza? Of good figure, pleasing to the eye?' The Duke' expression suggested an interest that had little to do with matters theatrical.

'She is most handsome and has a comely figure.' Turnbull could not be blamed for exaggerating Eliza's charms, given the need to make the opening night a success.

Eliza was pretty, intelligent and lively but he felt that her attractiveness lay in her spirit and the warmth she brought to the part. She seemed to have grown into it during the past few weeks, largely due to Richard's tuition. That young man had initially had an abrasive edge and high opinion of himself that had made him difficult to work with, but those aspects of his character seemed to have softened in the past few weeks. Maybe the much-hinted-at affair with Sarah had something to do with that. Turnbull knew that all he had to do was to get the theatregoers of the *beau monde* to come his play. If it were to run for five nights, it would be deemed a modest success; to be damned on the opening night would make it a financial disaster.

Shrugging off these alarming thoughts, Turnbull sipped his claret and changed the subject to politics, though not before he had extracted a promise from his friends that they would attend the opening night.

Mr Turnbull had told Eliza she could use Sarah Newley's dressing room while she was away. The cast was being rested on the afternoon before curtain-up at six o'clock so it was late afternoon when Eliza and Susan made the walk to the theatre through crowded streets which the early summer heat had turned into a miasma of dried horse dung and stinking slops.

'If only our patrons in the boxes could see how people really live here,' remarked Eliza stepping over the flyblown carcase of a dead dog. 'My father always said that a time would come when life would be fairer. It certainly wasn't fair to him,' she remarked bitterly, 'dead at thirty-eight.'

'And you'll be thinking of him tonight I'm sure, Eliza, when you make your bow.' Susan took her friend's arm as they dodged past the doorway of a tavern where the innkeeper was throwing dirty water onto the dusty pavement.

Chapter 4

When Eliza and Susan arrived at Drury Lane, there was no queue forming but that was hardly surprising. That only happened when the play was likely to be a sell-out. Once inside, Eliza went to her new borrowed dressing room where her beautiful dresses hung, the blue for Act 1, the white for Act 3.

On the dressing table stood a vase of pink roses whose perfume filled the air. She gasped in astonishment as she looked more closely at them and the piece of paper propped up against the vase.

TO MY LEADING LADY

BEST WISHES AND GOOD LUCK

Tears pricked her eyelids at this thoughtful gesture. No one had ever given her flowers before; in fact, few people had ever given her much. As she re-read the note, Sukey bustled in with a jug and bowl of water.

'You've seen them then?' she laughed. 'This is just the start for you now, Eliza, or perhaps I should call you Miss Grahame?'

'No, please Sukey, don't. Just call me Eliza.'

'Very well, Eliza it shall be until you tell me otherwise. When you are famous and there are drawings of you in all the print shops and you get invited to Devonshire House, then you'll have to be Miss Grahame. Mr Cavendish brought those not half an hour since.'

Eliza felt herself blush and replaced the note on the table.

'Now, Madam,' continued Sukey, in the exaggeratedly refined accent she imagined was the hallmark of a woman of quality, 'may I assist you in your preparations for the forthcoming performance?'

When the curtain rose on Richard Cavendish's *The Heiress*, the theatre was less than half full, a fact that made Turnbull nervous. This would doubtless improve after the first interval and ticket prices went down. Many of the *beau monde* came to a play halfway through anyway, business or a good dinner having occupied them until then. The design of the set for Lady Heartfort's drawing room, the work of a French scenic designer, drew gasps from the audience, music to the ears of the manager who stood in the wings. Mr Jacobs, always a favourite, had a witty speech to begin the first act, which the audience responded well to. When Eliza stepped on stage there was a ripple of anticipation. Her voice was clear and confident, her manner as the spirited heiress suited the character of Lady Heartfort and the privileged world in which she moved. Annie Grahame, sitting in the gallery, wondered how she did that, how would she know how a lady of quality would behave. Frankly, Annie was transfixed by the sight of her eldest daughter, an ordinary girl, docile, sweet, a product of St Giles not Park Lane, making all the world believe she was Lady Heartfort. When Eliza made that moving speech at the end of the act about marrying for love or not at all, she sniffed just as much as the fat old woman sitting next to her who was wiping her nose on her sleeve.

'That's my daughter, that is. Miss Eliza Grahame. That's *my* girl.'

By the end of the first interval there was a definite buzz in the theatre that had conveyed itself to the actors in the wings and backstage.

The heat of the theatre and the stress of the situation had taken its toll on Eliza's make-up, which Sukey was trying to repair in the dressing room.

'They love you! They truly do!' she exclaimed excitedly as she dabbed on another layer of powder and tried to rearrange the frame of curls at Eliza's forehead. 'And did you see? Miss Newley's here? In the best box, walking with a stick. Mr Cavendish escorted her to her seat just before curtain up. The audience gave her a big cheer which she acknowledged.'

'Oh no, I didn't see her,' Eliza replied with a sinking feeling. 'And Mr Cavendish … did he stay with her during the first half?'

'Oh yes. He was looking very pleased with himself. Five minutes to go! Now let me adjust that dress for you.'

Eliza submitted to Sukey's attentions then went quickly to her position in the wings for her entry. As she walked on stage there was a wave of enthusiastic applause and some more vocal encouragement from the gallery. She glanced at the boxes and noted the beautifully dressed Sarah sitting now with a female companion. Eliza's heart lifted and she sparkled even more brightly, using her wit and charm to wrong foot the dastardly Lord and win the love of Mr Hardy.

As the curtain fell at the end of Act 5, the audience rose from their seats clapping, demanding the return of the cast after they had taken their bows. As Eliza stepped forward yet again, cries of 'Author! Author!' were added to the applause. From the wings came Richard Cavendish, wearing a new black coat, a sky-blue waistcoat and buckled shoes she had not seen before. He stepped forward confidently to the centre of the stage, smiling at her and taking her hand and the hand of Mr Jacobs. They all bowed as did the assembled cast behind them. And finally, as the curtain fell, the wild applause began to subside. Still holding her hand, he pulled her gently to him and briefly kissed her on the cheek.

'Thank you, Eliza. You were wonderful. I will always be grateful to you for this, never forget, whatever else may happen.'

Chapter 5

The experience of that first night changed Eliza's world forever.

She revelled in the power the role gave her, the way she could take the audience along with her, make people laugh, touch their hearts. And she was intoxicated by the applause and the fame that the part brought her almost overnight. Flowers arrived at the stage door, notes and messages, prints appeared of her in the shops showing her in the white dress of the last act, holding out her arms to a cheering crowd with the caption "Eliza wins the hearts of Drury Lane."

The play ran for fourteen nights and every house was a sell-out. But soon the playhouse would close for the summer season and Eliza was contracted to tour the north of England with the company who took themselves, props, costumes, scene painters and musicians to do the northern circuit, staying in lodgings and staging their repertoire. It was a challenging and arduous two months, but it was necessary financially and was invaluable experience for the actors.

After the end of the first week's performances of *The Heiress* at Drury Lane, Richard Cavendish was no longer to be found in the theatre and Eliza saw no more of him. Although preoccupied and enchanted by her new-found celebrity, her flowers and invitations, deep down she felt a sense of disappointment that he was no longer part of the magic of the play.

One night, as the play was nearing the end of its run and they were contemplating the northern tour, she and Susan were walking to the theatre along Catherine Street.

'That man in the pie shop is looking at you,' said Susan. 'He recognises you, I'm sure.'

'It's not always nice to be recognised,' confided Eliza, quickening her pace. 'People aren't always polite. They seem to think they own you. Of course it's different when you're invited into society because people are polite then.'

This statement was based on two brief engagements that Eliza had experienced, one taking tea at Lady Berry's and the other at a small reception at Mrs Russell's house in Grosvenor Square, details of which her mother had made her repeat time and time again – the flowers, the furniture, the ladies' gowns. The dress that Eliza herself wore had been generously provided by her former employer whose reputation had been vastly enhanced by her connection with the leading lady at Drury Lane.

As the girls hastened towards the theatre, Eliza said in a casual tone, 'We do not see anything of Mr Cavendish these days. I suppose his presence in the theatre is no longer necessary.'

'Oh, I did hear tell he's been seen visiting Miss Newley in Gower Street. Mr Turnbull did say that she would be expected to return to us after the summer. Her ankle is quite restored now.'

Eliza strove for a light neutral tone and laughed.

'You always did say, Susan, that he would not be able to resist her for long. And when she comes back, my days as Drury Lane's leading lady will be over.'

Sarah returned in fact the very next week, just before the summer holidays. She had gained a little weight and looked better for it. She also appeared more relaxed and less volatile. Entering the dressing room that Eliza was still using as hers, Sarah said in a haughty tone, 'I shall be requiring the use of my dressing room now, Eliza.' She cast her eyes around at items that lay on the table and the dresses hanging up. She touched the vase of Richard's Cavendish's pink roses and petals scattered over the table. 'These surely need to go.'

'I will take them,' replied Eliza stubbornly,' They have yet some life in them.'

'As you wish.' After a pause she continued, 'I saw you in my part of course, as Lady Heartfort. I thought you gave a very creditable performance. When the new season begins in September, I expect Mr Cavendish – and Mr Turnbull – will want me to resume the role, though I am quite happy for you play the part while we are touring.'

'Thank you, ma'am.'

'It was written with me in mind, you see, Eliza. I was Mr Cavendish's inspiration. He tells me all the time,' and she laughed lightly.

'Indeed, ma'am.'

Sarah's expression had taken on a faraway look and her voice had grown softer at the mention of Cavendish. Eliza too had felt a quickening of the pulse and a warmth in her cheeks that she struggled to master. In a voice that strove to be casual, she replied, 'Mr Cavendish was most pleased with my portrayal of Lady Heartfort. He said that I bought to the role an air of girlish ingenuousness that gave the character depth and complexity.'

Richard Cavendish had, in fact, said no such thing but the critic of *The London Gazette* had written those words and they had pleased Eliza so much that she had learned them by heart. She wanted desperately to continue talking about Cavendish and had bristled at Sarah's proprietorial air that suggested that somehow the playwright was merely a tool to enhance her reputation and status in the profession.

Sarah looked surprised at Eliza's reply and regarded her more closely. With pursed lips she said, 'You can take all your belongings to the ladies' dressing room now. And those flowers if you must.'

Eliza played Lady Heartfort twice in the final week, both times to packed houses. One night as she stood ready to make her entrance after the intermission, Susan whispered to her, 'Mr Cavendish is here, sitting in the pit with some friends. He seems to be a little drunk.'

Oh, how Eliza shone in that final act, and when the curtain fell, the audience simply would not let her go. They longed to remain within her charmed circle, to be part of the wonderful illusion that the play had created and not return to their mundane, sad or difficult lives. Flowers were thrown onstage as she curtsied and bowed and kissed her hands to gallery and pit alike.

When she eventually came offstage, there was a glitter about her and, as she gabbled in the changing room afterwards amid the crying infants and the smell of spirits, two bright spots flamed in her cheeks. Several bouquets had been delivered and four or five notes, one on crested notepaper. She was ripping them open and reading out extracts to the other women who were torn between envy and amusement. Susan was changing into her costume for the farce that was to follow, and the atmosphere was ripe with milk, candle wax and women's bodies. Suddenly above the bawdy female shrieks was heard a loud male voice, a little tipsy and very indignant.

'Why is she no longer in her dressing room? Why is she back here? Good God, Turnbull. After her performance here tonight, we need to treat her like the Duchess of Devonshire herself!' Then, 'Eliza are you dressed? Come out here! I wish to see you.'

There was a chorus of encouragement, suggestive comments and shrieks of pretended outrage at the prospect of Cavendish bursting into this female sanctum.

'Go on, Liza. Don't let him in here – we're not decent!' shrieked Hetty, stuffing her generous bosom into her blouse.

'You! You've never been decent in your life, Hetty Ames!' someone shouted to general merriment from the room. 'Get out there, Liza, let him show his appreciation. You saved his skin. Make sure he pays for it.'

Cheeks still blazing and on a wave of euphoria, Eliza threw open the door and made her exit, almost knocking over Cavendish and Turnbull in the cramped corridor where the playwright was continuing his complaint about Eliza's loss of a dressing room.

'They're herded together like cattle in there, Turnbull, the women. It's no place for ... Liza, excellent performance tonight. I'm so sorry you were asked to move out. Sarah had no right. Tell her, Turnbull. We wouldn't have had this success' (he struggled with the word and had three stabs at it) 'if not for you. We ... I ... the company is fortunate to have you. I want you to know.'

He was a little unsteady on his feet, lurching against Turnbull's massive shoulder. Eliza smiled, amused by this unaccustomed sign of weakness. In her present mood, nothing could touch her. She was invincible, the mistress of her art, and even the officious Sarah Newley and a squabble over a poky dressing room could not spoil her mood.

'Gentlemen, if it means that much to the lady, I surrender it gladly. I am just pleased to have acquitted myself well. And I hope, sir,' looking straight at Cavendish with a challenge in her eyes, 'that you will think of me when next you pen a great role.'

His look was serious now as he said, 'My dear Eliza, believe me, you are in my thoughts more than you can imagine.'

Turnbull shot him a puzzled glance, cleared his throat, then grabbed the playwright's shoulder before saying, 'Eliza, well done again. Get off home now, you are finished for tonight. We shall all meet again after Yorkshire. Come on, Richard. You need some food inside you.'

Chapter 6

But Eliza's triumph was short-lived as Drury Lane closed for the summer, signalling the beginning of the Yorkshire circuit tour. Eliza had never been out of London before in her life, so travelling to Yorkshire felt like going to the other side of the world. The players took whatever means at their disposal to travel north, getting lifts on carts and wagons, even, if they were lucky, the occasional ride in a carriage. The public coach, which took two days and made its bone-rattling way up the Great North Road with two overnight stops in crowded and noisy inns with bug-infested beds and thin walls, was an option but an expensive one, so Eliza and Susan took that only as far as Sawtry, sharing the anxiety of the coach's other occupants, a clergy man and an elderly lady, about the possibility of an attack by highwaymen.

Everyone had to shift for themselves when it came to lodgings too. It was a matter of what you could find close to the theatre and cheap enough not to make too much of a dent in what you earned.

Eliza was being paid more now that she had the lead role in *The Heiress,* but she was honouring her promise to her mother and sending money home to her. Sarah Newley was also part of the company in Yorkshire as the managers in Huddersfield and York knew of her great popularity with audiences, especially in the tragic roles. She would not be expected to play these roles every night but putting her name on a playbill was a manager's guarantee of good box office.

Finally, jolted and sore, Susan and Eliza rode into York in style, sharing a carriage with Mr Jacobs and Sarah Newley. Later that night as they settled to sleep in the lumpy musty bed they were sharing in Mrs Farrell's establishment in Chapel Street, they talked of Sarah Newley who had that day condescendingly offered them a ride in the carriage.

'She still thinks of you as a threat, Eliza. Recall how it was Mr Jacobs who was the one to press us to travel with them. She was not exactly enthusiastic. I wonder if Mr Cavendish is up in Yorkshire already.' Susan thumped her pillow into a more cooperative shape. 'I expect she'll want to keep an eye on him. I know I would if he were my lover.'

Eliza flushed at the thought. She could barely imagine sleeping in a bed with a man, used though she was to sharing a bed with her sister and now with Susan. And as to what would go on in that bed – well, she had heard a lot from her fellow actresses, confidences and laughter exchanged in the dressing room, ribald comment, nudges and winks, but herself had not experienced more than a few kisses and gropes from local boys. She knew many of the women were married, some had lovers, and a few had both. Actresses had the reputation for being immoral. Several well-known actresses at Covent Garden and the Haymarket also had wealthy and important lovers, some of whom were publicly acknowledged and not hidden away like a guilty secret. And it was common knowledge that, not that long ago, King Charles had courted Nell Gwynn. What had Annie said? 'You'll be seen by plenty of men enough, but they are not the kind to go marrying you.' Would that apply to Sarah Newley too?

Unable to sleep with all these unsettling thoughts whirling in her head, Eliza wondered if before long she would succumb to desire and experience how it felt to lie naked with a man in her bed. How strange that in her mind's eye the only man she could picture had grey eyes, dark curly hair and white even teeth.

In York *The Heiress* played to packed houses. The manager of the theatre was Patrick Leary, an Irishman who had run Smock Alley in Dublin. He was a loud swaggering fellow who smacked the women's backsides and openly peered down their bodices.

'Make sure you're never alone with him,' warned Susan, 'they say he's fathered more children in Yorkshire than any other man, half of them on actresses.'

Lecherous he doubtless was, but he knew the theatre and his craft and his audiences too. He managed to promote the plays so successfully that queues formed every night and there was an undignified scramble to get tickets.

All the London players who had not worked in Yorkshire had problems adjusting to playing in this strange building that had a small staff of resident scene painters and shifters, many of whom were openly hostile to them. Eliza and Susan found themselves bewildered by the thick unfamiliar accents that rendered much of what they said unintelligible. There were nights when they returned to their lodgings low in spirits and homesick, longing for St Giles, the street cries, the filth and the clamour of Drury Lane and Covent Garden.

But there were compensations. Playgoers loved Eliza in the role of Lady Heartfort and she was invited to several receptions and soirees, most of which she could not attend because she was working. Men sent flowers and notes, some quite suggestive in tone, but others professing the writer's regard for her. Others praised her beauty and, in the case of Lord Antony Denham, expressed a desire to meet her and convey his admiration in person.

'That's him,' whispered Susan as they both stood in the wings ready to go on in the Playhouse. 'Jenny pointed him out to me. He's

43

in the first box in the left. This is his third time of seeing the play. Handsome, isn't he? About six and twenty I should say. Owns Denham Hall. Family very highly regarded in these parts. He's been invited into the green room afterwards to meet you. You know how managers like to keep the quality happy. I wouldn't say no to him.'

Eliza made her entrance, her cheeks a little pinker than usual. And as the scene progressed, took a covert look at her admirer. He sat alone in the box, the best one in the house, virtually on stage. He wore a small wig, which was not now the fashion in London where younger men were wearing their own hair these days, but Eliza had noted since travelling north that fashions generally had not moved with the same speed here as they had in London. His features were good, his complexion fair and his eyes blue. As he was seated, it was difficult to correctly assess his figure, but his shoulders were broad and his coat expensive and fashionable, even by London standards. He chuckled at one of the witty exchanges between Mr Jacobs and Ned, and the laughter lit up his handsome face.

And that face was just as handsome up close as he raised her hand to his lips with, 'Your servant, ma'am' after the performance was over. Leary had invited him and a few others to join the cast for a glass of wine in the green room, and while some cast members had absented themselves and gone straight back to their lodgings or dropped in at one of the many taverns the town boasted, those who had an interest in pleasing the quality or those too timorous to refuse their manager's invitation stood and made polite small talk.

'I have been entranced by your performance in Mr Cavendish's play,' he said, smiling at her. 'This is the third time I have seen it and I shall come again on Friday evening,' Lord Denham said. Eliza bobbed an awkward curtsy, at a loss for words.

'Your portrayal of Lady Heartfort is remarkable. She must surely be the most captivating witty yet warm and generous woman in the world. No man could see her and not be in love with her. I know I cannot,' he continued. Eliza smiled and moved instinctively closer to him as their tête-à-tête was in danger of being drowned out by a raucous joke being shared by Mr Jacobs and another green room visitor who was slapping the actor on the back and guffawing.

'You are very kind, sir. I am sure that Lady Heartfort would be honoured to have the attention of so devoted an admirer.' And one so handsome and stylishly dressed too, she thought to herself, taking in the fine figure in its tight coat, his strong and capable hands and shapely calves.

'Perhaps, Miss Grahame, you would allow me to invite Lady Heartfort to a reception my sister Belle is holding on Saturday evening. I know,' he added with twinkling eyes, 'that her ladyship has no engagement at the theatre. Perhaps you might care to bring a friend as chaperone?'

'Lady Heartfort would be delighted,' was her instant reply, accompanied by a smile.

'My carriage will call for you at your lodgings in Chapel Street – you see I have taken the liberty of finding out this information,' he smiled, and a dimple appeared in his right cheek that automatically produced a smile in her. 'At seven o'clock then. Until then I bid you adieu until I see you next on stage on Friday evening.'

He took her hand again, kissing it as if paying homage to some scared relic, then turned to Leary who had been watching the exchange with avid interest.

As she and Susan made their way back to Chapel Street, the talk was of what to wear for Saturday night's reception because, needless to say, Susan, had appointed herself as chaperone, even though just a couple of years older than her friend.

'I wonder if Sarah Newley will be present,' speculated Eliza. 'I expect she will have been invited. And who is Lord Denham's sister Belle? A member of the aristocracy too?'

'Doubtless, but also sister of your admirer. Don't go forgetting that. Now we must contrive to get the white dress from wardrobe for you to wear. It's the only garment that will make you look as if you can hold your own amid the gentry. It doesn't matter about me,' she said cheerfully, 'I'm just your chaperone, a supporting role you might say.'

Two shillings and a jug of gin kept Sukey happy, though she warned Eliza there would be the devil to pay if the loan of the dress became common knowledge.

'Be sure you don't become too hot when wearing it now. If you sweat too much, the smell will linger well into next season. Not that anyone else could wear it anyway,' Sukey mused, taking a swig of gin. 'No one's as dainty as you, Liza. Miss Sarah's quite the carthorse compared with you.' The gin was making her a little sentimental as she packed up the dress at the end of the Friday performance of the play.

'Here you are, m'dear. Take care now. And what's more you take care over what can happen to a pretty young girl wearing a dress like this,' she said to Eliza, her eyes moist. 'In a palace or a bawdy house, men are but men and don't you forget it neither,' she said wagging her finger at both girls as they edged closer to the door, anxious to get away and back to Mrs Farrell's for the night.

Eliza and Susan were both dressed and ready by six o'clock that evening. Susan had bound Eliza's hair tightly in curl papers for the entire afternoon and had dressed it beautifully so that it hung in one long curling ringlet over her left shoulder, the style she wore it in *The Heiress*. Eliza now stood before the small foxed mirror in the bedroom, looking at herself critically and fidgeting with the necklace at her throat.

'Glass emeralds! Not what Lady Heartfort would wear of course, but I have to have something at my throat. This neck is very low. At least it seems so in the real world. I hardly notice it on stage.'

'When you are queen of Drury Lane you will have the real thing, dozens of them probably, bought for you by your admirers,' Susan assured her cheerfully as she adjusted the hoops of her petticoat.

'Ah yes, but what shall I be required to do in order to receive these gifts?' asked Eliza whose spirits were unexpectedly declining as the time of their departure approached.

'You will choose from your admirers one you truly love ...'

'And he will make me his mistress.'

'Perhaps – and if that is the case, so be it. If he is kind and generous and loves you, is that so very bad? Girls like us, Eliza, girls from St Giles will be doing very well indeed if we meet a rich protector and can help our families. As long as we can put a bit aside, you know, for ... for ...'

'For when we're old and have lost our looks or have had the pox.' Eliza slumped in a chair, her pretty mouth turned down, a frown upon her face.

'Lord, Eliza, don't crush the skirt so! And try not to be so much in the grumps. What do you expect? Marriage? Don't you go holding out for that now. Men think that if you are prepared to let the world see you on stage, then you belong to them by right. They may love what you do, make them laugh, make them cry, but they wouldn't expect their wives to display themselves for all to see. If you flirt and ensnare men on stage, they think you are a jade. They cannot see the difference between what you are and what you play. Come on now, do not be so serious about life. Remember your *Beggars Opera*. "Youth's a season made for joy"'

Their carriage arrived promptly at seven o'clock, and Eliza and Susan were handed in by a very proper and serious coachman dressed in splendid livery. Despite the warm and balmy evening, Eliza shivered a little in anticipation as the carriage drawn by four matched greys drove off in the direction of Wychwood House.

The house was approached by a sweeping gravel drive that led them past immaculate gardens and up to the front of an imposing grey stone house. Two symmetrical flights of steps led up to an impressive pillared portico. Although the summer evening was still light, burning flambeaux illuminated the front aspect of the house where coaches and servants were milling around as elegant guests dismounted from crested carriages. Eliza glanced apprehensively at Susan, but her friend looked exhilarated and not alarmed as she gathered up her dress up elegantly and stepped down from the carriage as if she did this every day of her life. Encouraged by this show of confidence, Eliza followed suit, putting herself once more in Lady Heartfort's elegant satin shoes.

As soon as they were announced, Antony Denham descended on them as if he had been waiting for just that moment, and took them to meet his sister Arabella, a handsome but superior young woman of about thirty who cast a fleeting but expert eye over their clothes and gave them a cursory and automatic nod of acknowledgement before she left them with a flutter of her fan and a swish of blue brocade. Eliza looked round the beautiful *salon* with its pristine plasterwork and crystal chandeliers. A quartet of musicians was playing on a small dais at one end of the vast room, its sound almost drowned out by the chatter and laughter of Arabella's guests. Expertly, Denham detached Susan from Eliza, leading the chaperone towards a small group of local tradesmen and their wives, afterwards steering Eliza in the direction of two couples to whom she was introduced. She made nervous small talk with them but Eliza felt an overwhelming sense of gratitude when Denham reappeared at her side minutes later, found her a seat and went off to fetch her a glass of wine. By now Susan had been swallowed up by the crowd, but Eliza felt no great concern for her. Her friend was well able to take care of herself, was resourceful and would enjoy this first experience of a gathering of the *ton*. As Eliza's glance took in the assembly, she was suddenly aware of a familiar face. Looking very striking in red lace and silk, her hair an elaborate structure adorned with pearls and ribbons, her lips a slash of carmine, Sarah Newley was engaged in conversation with an elderly well-upholstered dowager who kept tapping her on the hand with her fan to emphasise the point she was making. With a jolt Eliza then saw the figure of Richard Cavendish appear at Sarah's side, perceived the actress's face relax and how she turned her face towards him seeming to bathe in the warmth of his smile. There was no doubt in Eliza's mind that they were lovers and the realisation caused her heart, unaccountably, to feel like a stone within her chest.

Suddenly Denham was at her side, a glass of wine held out to her.

'My dear Miss Grahame, I was set upon by my brother's friends. Do forgive me for abandoning you.' He suddenly looked more closely at her. 'But are you well? You look so pale. Perhaps it is too hot in here. Pray take a sip of wine.'

He sounded so genuinely concerned, so caring, that she smiled and took a sip of the wine.

'It is a little warm. I think I should like some air.'

He took her arm and they walked through the double doors that led out onto the terrace.

Out of the corner of his eye, Richard Cavendish saw them and was unsettled by Denham's proprietorial air, the way he leant over Eliza, the way she looked up into his handsome face and smiled wanly. He was suddenly aware of Sarah's irritated voice.

'I asked you, Richard, if you had called on Lord Fullerton today as you proposed. I am glad to see you back in the real world now,' she added tetchily, 'did you discuss the new play with him?'

As Richard marshalled his thoughts, Sarah gazed across the sea of faces scanning the crowd for people she knew or about whom she might gossip. She made no reference to Eliza and her noble escort, but Richard found himself eyeing the entrance to the terrace to note the reappearance of Eliza and Denham. He was trying to listen to Sarah's running commentary on the latest York gossip, on which she seemed very well informed.

'Of course, Bella's brother – where is he? Lord Denham? I saw him earlier. Wearing a chestnut coloured coat and green waistcoat. Tall. I don't see him now, however.'

'What of him?'

'Well, apparently, he's not as wealthy as he would have us believe. Lost a lot of money at Newmarket recently. And there were some unsound investments. Rumour has it he will have to make an advantageous match to keep his estate.'

She leaned into him confidentially.

'Miss Frobisher, only daughter of James Frobisher of Whitby has a tempting enough fortune apparently. No doubt she'll have him. But she's a dull and prim little thing so I expect he's sowing his wild oats before he saddles himself with her. Not all young men are lucky enough to be paying court to a lady who is as exciting as a mistress and she intends to be as a wife,' and she gave him a practised and seductive look, accompanied by a playful tap on the shoulder with her fan.

Richard smiled mechanically but could not dislodge the image of Antony Denham leaving the room with Eliza on his arm. Sarah's phrase "wild oats" concerned him more than he would have thought possible.

Lord Denham had offered to show Eliza his sister's library after she had cooled off on the terrace and her cheeks had regained some of their colour. Susan was nowhere to be seen in the press and Denham had assured Eliza that it would be the most decorous place imaginable for a young lady to visit in the company of her hostess's brother. Denham had a masterful way with him that she knew her father would have said was the product of wealth and privilege, the right schools, the right clubs, the confidence of land and money. With this mastery came a smiling teasing humour that was very difficult to resist, so she accompanied him to Lady Arabella's library, a long light-filled room situated some distance from the reception rooms looking out onto the colourful shrubbery.

As the heavy oak door closed behind them, the sounds of the house became distant and muffled. Candles had not yet been lit in the sconces and the room was shadowy. Thick Turkey carpet covered the floor making it the most luxurious room Eliza had ever been in. Shelves of leather-bound tomes reached the ceiling and several volumes were open on tables around. Busts of the Roman and Greek philosophers gazed sternly at those who would seek to improve their minds

'My brother-in-law has obviously heeded Arabella's command to leave his books and pay some attention to his guests,' said Denham, looking round the empty room.

'Give him his books and his dogs, his paintings and his horses and John is a happy man,' he chuckled as he picked up a book at random. 'But ask him to give a speech, dance a cottilion or speak to a beautiful woman and he is of no use whatever,' he joked.

'See this, Eliza – I may call you that, mayn't I?' He led her to a table where an atlas lay open. 'Here is his latest acquisition. The latest world map from France.'

Eliza looked at the book, its brightly coloured images meaning nothing to her.

'Have you been in France, my lord?'

Denham laughed loudly then stopped suddenly, realising the innocence of her question.

'Oh yes, Eliza. I have … several times. Paris is very beautiful. Should you like to go there?'

Her face radiated with an innocence and pleasure that touched him greatly.

'Oh, very much, sir. I should like to see Versailles. They say the French court is very fashionable and full of clever women.'

'And so it is. Many clever women and some very beautiful ones too. Though,' he continued, taking one of her hands and pulling her to him, 'not as lovely and talented as you.'

The sudden shriek of a peacock outside in the gardens startled her and she shrank away from him, but her withdrawal only made him take the other hand and pull her closer still. The stillness and muffled silence in the library reminded her of how far she was from the other guests and she felt a pinprick of alarm, although his closeness, the smell of his expensive soap, and the warmth that emanated from his body produced very different responses in her.

'Eliza,' he continued, his voice gentle yet urgent, 'Eliza, you know how much I admire you and want to be your protector.'

She nodded and kept her eyes on the carpet. He let one of her hands drop and brought his hand tenderly to her chin, raising and tilting it so that he looked into her eyes. Running his fingers over her lips, he lowered his head and kissed her lips with such warmth and gentleness, she could do nothing but yield her mouth to his and feel such a wave of desire sweep through her as he clasped her even closer. She abandoned herself entirely to his eager tongue that sought out her mouth.

She was suddenly aware of his fingers kneading at her breasts and the way his mouth had travelled to her throat. He was saying her name in a broken voice, now pushing his hardness against her and edging her backwards against a tall bookcase. Aroused but frightened by the speed at which this was happening, she tried to pull away, which only seemed to fuel his desire and his hand slid inside her bodice searching out her nipples. She heard herself let out an instinctive sigh of pure pleasure but knew she had to stop this madness. Suddenly summoning all her strength, she pushed him from her, catching him off guard so that he stumbled against a table, then, with as much indignation as she could muster, she shouted, 'My lord, please stop. You are treating me in a disrespectful way. I am an honest woman and you must not take such liberties. I considered you a gentleman. I see I have been mistaken,' she concluded, adjusting her bodice and the green glass necklace.

He recovered quickly, a sheepish smile appearing on his handsome face and a look of contrition as he adjusted his cravat.

'Eliza,' he said pleadingly as he reached again for her hand, which, this time, she snatched away. 'I can see I have been far too pressing. This was ungallant of me. I can only plead in mitigation your beauty and the pleasure of being alone with you. Please forgive me.' The speech sounded polished as it tripped off his tongue. He bowed to her, the picture of abject apology.

'Will you please escort me back to the *salon*?'

'Of course – as long as you say you forgive me my forceful overtures. I would rather die than you think ill of me.'

She extended her hand cautiously which he took and raised it to his lips.

'Let us say no more about it, but please promise never to misbehave that way to me,' Eliza said.

'I am not absolutely sure I can make such a promise.'

Flushing slightly but not totally displeased, she said, 'Very well, but let us return.'

For the rest of the evening, he was the perfect gentleman. He introduced Eliza to persons of note, many of whom had seen her in the playhouse as Lady Heartfort and who were thrilled to meet her. He was all courtesy with his easy manners and ready laugh. Eliza noted how women ogled him, some quite blatantly, and several flirted openly with him in a way she thought she would never learn to emulate. One of these women was Sarah who swept up to them with Richard in attendance.

'My lord, please do not think me presumptuous … good evening Eliza, you look very well this evening. That dress seems oddly familiar.' She smiled slyly, then continued to address Denham. 'I know of your interest in the theatre, milord,' at which she glanced pointedly at Eliza before continuing, 'I think you may not have met the author of *The Heiress*, Mr Richard Cavendish.'

Bows were exchanged, Denham's naturally being the less obsequious of the two.

'You are wrong on that count, Miss Newley. I was introduced to Mr Cavendish on the opening night of *The Heiress*. I believe you were indisposed. Mr Cavendish, you will know already how fond I am of your first play,' he said with an ambivalent smile. 'Perhaps you are working on another?'

Sarah Newley interjected quickly. 'Oh yes, my lord. And this one promises to be even more brilliant than the last.' Richard looked embarrassed and unhappy at this interruption, which made Eliza blush on his behalf, while Denham looked disapprovingly at what he obviously considered interference.

'Well, I wish you well with your play. Is the major female role designed as a vehicle for either of these lovely ladies?' he said, looking pointedly at Sarah who was clinging now to Richard's arm.

Sarah simpered, batting her eyelashes as Cavendish continued.

'My heroine is a young woman of sensibility and beauty. She is caught in the toils of the fashionable world and is almost ruined by its hypocrisy but emerges unscathed and wiser. I would ask your lordship to decide which of these two ladies best suits the role.' Cavendish smiled and bowed slightly. Sarah looked discomfited and frowned at her lover.

'But you make it sound a dull and moral piece, Richard. It is full of your usual wit and humour, is it not?'

'Oh, there is satire for sure,' commented Richard, his eyes now fixed on Eliza who felt the situation fast becoming so embarrassing that she burst in with, 'I daresay, Mr Cavendish, that the heroine has a maid so there might be a part for me. Or perhaps she has a confidante to whom she tells all her troubles. As long as she doesn't have to don breeches as part of her disguise, I should be happy to assist.'

There was general laughter which was what Eliza had intended, but Richard shook his head slightly and replied, 'Eliza, do not sell yourself short. You are a fine actress. Have some faith in your abilities.'

Denham bowed to Sarah and Richard to signal the interview was over and clasped Eliza's arm more closely as they moved off. Eliza would have liked to have stayed and talked more about the new play but recognised that now she would rarely see him without his mistress. She had to admit, though, that their relationship puzzled

56

her. What did she always seem more besotted with him than he with her? Perhaps that was the nature of male and female relationships. Although she was short of real life experience in that quarter, she remembered the female roles in the plays she saw and acted in. When it was her turn, would she be a Cleopatra or a Viola and sacrifice all for love or would she expect equal love in return?

Chapter 7

Flowers arrived at the stage door the next day sent by Lord Antony Denham with a note that read:

"For the fairest flower of all, Miss Eliza Grahame. Her servant Antony Denham."

The company was due to move on to Wakefield; Susan had joked that they would feel at home there as the theatre was situated in Wakefield's 'Drury Lane.' Later that week and Eliza found herself wondering if Denham would pursue her with his attentions, but it was over twenty-five miles from York. She didn't know whether she wanted him to or not, being still in the grip of conflicting emotion after the night at Wychwood House.

She and Susan debated this as they lay in bed at Mrs Farrell's. The weather was sultry and the room airless, despite an open window. They lay with the sheet thrown off, Eliza in a chemise and Susan naked. The darkness made it easier to confide in each other and hide any blushes, though those were far more likely to be Eliza's. Susan was at the end of a passionate dalliance with one of the scene shifters, Jed, and had now started speaking with some authority on the subject of men, love and what she called "congress," a great deal of which had been going on with Jed in a field and even in the bowels of the theatre itself where scenery was stored.

'So do you love him then?' asked Eliza after Susan had related a particularly amorous encounter with Jed.

'Well, I don't know if it's what you call love,' she replied thoughtfully. 'I like what we do and how he makes me feel,' she said, stretching languorously like a cat in the sunshine so that Eliza almost expected her to purr. How Eliza envied her friend the ability to behave instinctively and revel in the sheer pleasure of her experience. She recalled the scene in Lady Arabella's library, the scream of the peacock, the dusty leather smell of the books, the exploring expert tongue and fingers of Antony Denham. For those few dangerous moments she had wanted him to touch her and pleasure her in the way Susan had described and, haltingly, she confessed as much to Susan as they lay in bed.

'Oh no, Eliza,' replied Susan, shocked to the core. 'No, let him dangle a bit longer. It's far too soon.'

'But … you didn't let Jed dangle as you call it.'

Her friend giggled. 'No need to. It's just a bit of fun. If you want to get yourself a man who will keep you, you have to be more clever … you know what I mean? They don't want anything that comes too easy. And anyway, you're still a virgin, aren't you? They get very excited about that. It's worth a lot, maidenhead,' she observed thoughtfully. 'I lost mine when I was thirteen so it makes no difference to me. If I get chance to become a rich man's mistress, I certainly won't give in straight away. It's the only power we women have over men after all,' she concluded cheerfully, pulling up her half of the sheet and arranging herself for sleep. 'I'm going to sleep now Liza,' she said and several minutes later she lay quite still, her breathing regular and deep. Eliza remained awake, heard the church bell strike the hour and the mice scuttling behind the skirting boards. She wondered if Sarah Newley lay in the arms of Richard Cavendish and whether he would come with the company to Wakefield and who would star in his new play.

The end of the summer saw the Yorkshire circuit winding down. There had been no further communication from Antony Denham who had not visited the playhouse in Wakefield where she was a huge success in *The Heiress*. There were no more flowers or letters, though she always looked hopefully in the most expensive boxes wherever they played. The weather continued hot and sultry with the occasional thunderstorm clearing the air, only to give way to stifling conditions almost immediately. Eventually, after a sell-out performance of *The Heiress* at which its author was notably absent, the Drury Lane company prepared to make its long and tiring journey home. This time there were fewer rides in carriages as some of the wealthier had already left Yorkshire; Sarah Newley had gone south with her lover who, it was rumoured, had returned to London on 'urgent business.' Eliza was very reluctant to spend any of her hard-earned wages on the public coach, so like many others, she and Susan took whatever lifts they were offered on carts and wagons, as well as walking the hard, dusty roads in the unrelenting heat. Everyone it seemed was weary and jaded. Even the thought of returning home did not raise many spirits, Eliza's included. As Ned was walking with Eliza and Susan late one afternoon, regaling them with a tale of how he was importuned by the landlady at his last night's lodgings, Eliza could not help but smile at the melodramatic way he described his unsuccessful attempt to save his virtue. However, Ned's account failed to raise Susan's drooping spirits and she rounded on him.

'Typical! You men regard us all as fools and easy prey.'

'But Susan, she was very insistent. How could I in the name of good manners disappoint her? It was she who made overtures to me. Coming into my room in her shift with a bottle of grog was a fairly obvious start,' he chuckled. 'Come now, don't take life so seriously. I think we might make Eaton Socon by nightfall. The Swan might be the best place to try for lodgings.'

'And is the landlady there a comely woman?' teased Eliza, 'Beware though, Ned, they say her husband keeps a brace of pistols at hand to protect his property.'

'Honestly, Eliza, life isn't like a play you know. You do talk such nonsense sometimes.' Susan hurried on as a cart had pulled up and was signalling to the walkers that there was room on the back. As Eliza ran over to the cart already weighed down with its cargo of grain and potatoes, Susan panted, 'He said he's just got room for one – me. I will see you further along the road. Eaton Socon perhaps, or further. Ned will keep a watchful eye on you, I'm sure,' she added sharply.

Thoughts of her imminent return kept Eliza occupied as she continued to trudge along. These past two months she had enjoyed a welcome break from George's surliness and truculence and Flora's tight-lipped envy. She had bought her sister some lace in York that she knew would make a pretty trim for her best dress. By extreme economy she had managed to save a guinea to help her mother with household expenses, which should keep her happy. At times her mind strayed back to the library of Lady Arabella's house and the seductive embraces of Lord Antony Denham, though it was now beginning to feel that she had only experienced those things in a dream. Susan was right of course. Life was not a play where all the loose ends are tied up at the end of the last act, where virtue is rewarded and the guilty punished. Richard Cavendish might be able to create the illusion of such a world and convince us for a couple of hours but after the curtain falls, reality reasserts itself.

61

Chapter 8

Eliza's mother seemed to have changed during her absence. There was a bloom about her, a readier smile and a new skirt Eliza hadn't seen before. She did, however, appear to be a little edgy in Eliza's presence and swung between being uncharacteristically affectionate to her to being critical and snappy.

When Eliza had unpacked the contents of her bag in the room she shared with Flora, she produced the piece of lace and shyly gave it to her sister who had been more withdrawn and taciturn than ever since her return. Presents were rare in the Grahame household and there was always an anxious and awkward moment between giver and receiver. To Eliza's surprise however, Flora burst into tears when she opened the gift, wrapped in tissue paper.

'Heavens, Flora, whatever is the matter? Don't you like it?'

Eliza sat on the bed next to her sister who was weeping uncontrollably. 'Are you ill? Why are you crying?'

Flora snivelled, fighting for control over her tears. 'Oh Eliza, I am so happy that you have returned. I have missed you so much. Mama is so changed since … that man has been paying court.' Eliza's eyes widened in disbelief. Her mother! Courted?

'And George,' continued Flora, fresh tears beginning to well in her eyes. 'George has been pressed. And we have not heard of him. They say he was taken in Deptford with some of his drinking companions. He could be in the colonies by now.' Eliza embraced her sobbing sister, though she could not bring herself to summon up Flora's raw emotion at the loss of their brother, away at sea and not sulking and scowling at her and everything she said and did. Pressing, though, was no light matter. Her father had railed against the system of forcing men into naval service.

'It's little better than slavery!' he would claim when he heard of men being taken. 'We are supposedly free men in England. And we have the finest navy in the world, though the conditions in which men serve are vile. We should have laws passed by Parliament to make such atrocities illegal.'

Eliza rocked Flora gently until her sniffs subsided. 'Mother has a beau then?' Eliza questioned. 'Does she plan to marry again?' She tried for a neutral tone. After all, her mother was barely forty, younger than several of England's greatest who were enjoying liaisons with men not their husbands. Except that in the *demi-monde* of the theatre, such goings on seemed more like plots from the pens of Vanbrugh and Congreve than real life. Her mother, with her hands reddened and rough from her work at the Crown, the washing and scrubbing, was a world away from the gilded salons of Grosvenor Square.

'His name is John Harkness,' supplied Flora, sitting up now and wiping her nose on her handkerchief. 'He's a cooper from Seven Dials. Younger than Mama. I don't like him, Eliza. He's got a way of looking at you.' Her voice trailed off then she added, 'He comes here often. And he and Mama drink a lot of gin together. Then he gets very loud. And … I am so glad that you are home now,' she concluded, taking her sister's hand.

'Well, I promise that I'll look after you now, Flora. Go and get your best dress out of the press and let me see how the new lace looks.' Although she was smiling now and her voice was determinedly light, Eliza's heart was heavy with this new family concern. The words that Richard Cavendish had created in his play, and the world of Lady Arabella's ball were as insubstantial as a feather and she would do well to remember that.

Three days later Eliza and Susan were walking to Drury Lane. The Indian summer seemed only a distant memory now. The roads were awash with heavy rain, but it still didn't manage to clean away the putrefying mess that lay in gutters. The stench of ordure and the filthy spray sent up by carts and carriages, the importunate calls of victual sellers and women attempting to sell their bedraggled bunches of flowers brought home to Eliza just how hard she must try to pull herself and Flora out of the world of filth and poverty. She as an actress, albeit a minor one as yet, had the opportunity to do just that; as an attractive young woman, in the public eye, every time she set foot on the stage she would be able to accomplish it with ease.

The night before she had given her mother the guinea she had saved.

'And it's no more than I'm owed, my girl, after all I've done for you,' was her mother's response to the gift, after which she bit the coin to test it, slammed some cooked meat on the table and then disappeared until the early hours of the morning, returning with a drunk and very loud male companion.

Eliza and Flora held each other in their bed afraid to make a noise until the shouting and drunken laughter had subsided. On the verge of sleep finally, Eliza had made a resolution to seek her escape.

This was the decision she was trying to convey to Susan as they stepped their messy way down Bridge Street that morning, the start of the new season, a day to be making resolutions and plans. Susan, however, was not in a receptive mood, cursing at a small boy who came cannoning into them outside the baker's shop.

'Your talk of carriages in the park and assemblies shows you delude yourself, Liza,' exclaimed Susan as they both hurriedly made for the stage door. 'Those things are not for the likes of us.'

'And Mrs Bracegirdle, Kitty Clive, they were not women who rose to fame and fortune by pleasing the audiences?'

'You have acquired dangerous tastes from a little success, Eliza,' remarked Susan brusquely. 'Actresses like us are ten a penny. As soon as our looks go and our youth fades, we turn into our mothers.'

Eliza had never known Susan to be like this before. Normally her roguish optimism knew no bounds. As Eliza followed her through the labyrinthine corridors of the theatre to the green room where they had been asked to assemble, she hoped it would not be long before Susan returned to her normal lively self.

The cramped and winding corridors, however, felt strangely comforting. The smell of candle wax, wood and paint from the stage scenery combined with the close warm scent of humanity was powerfully evocative. None of the other theatres on the northern circuit had smelt quite like this, and Eliza felt her pace quicken with the excitement of the coming season, despite the dampening words of her friend.

The green room was full of members of the company – sceneshifters, musicians as well as actors – and there was no place for Eliza and Susan to sit. There were embraces and greetings, laughter and ribald jests and news was swiftly exchanged: Lucy Silver had had another baby, her fourth, and was unlikely to return. John Bruton, senior carpenter, had been taken by the Runners and was now in Newgate on a charge of receiving stolen goods, awaiting a sentence of transportation. Eagerly Eliza scanned the crowd for

Sarah Newley. Perhaps she had defected to The Garden or The Haymarket. Were she not to appear for the season, Eliza's career would benefit immensely. Then the door opened as Turnbull entered, his face redder than usual. The chatter died as his eyes swept over the company.

'Friends and colleagues,' he began, his voice not its usual commanding, blustering tone but this time more friendly and intimate, 'welcome to you all at the start of a new season which I am sure will be an exciting one. But also a different one.' People exchanged puzzled glances. What had happened?

'During these past few years, friends, my health has been growing troublesome.' There was a sympathetic murmur. Why had no one really known that? It was true that Turnbull's high colour suggested a tendency to apoplexy, but he had lost no days of performances or rehearsals due to sickness.

'My physician has recommended that I spend less time at the theatre and my good wife seems to be in league with him.' He smiled a small wry smile and spread his palms upwards in a gesture that signified he was but putty in the hands of doctors and women.

The expressions on the faces of the assembled company showed apprehension and concern. As a manager, Turnbull was respected and feared but also loved as a strict but fair father. Who could replace him?

'Mr Turnbull, sir, who will take your place?' The deep velvet voice of Mr Jacobs asked the question that was on everyone's lips.

'I have sold my share in the company to Mr Cavendish.'

The shock of the announcement produced a range of reactions: Mr Jacobs's was a sharp intake of breath followed by 'tsk, tsk'. Two fiddle players exchanged a glance that spelt amused resignation; Eliza felt her stomach cave in and the colour mount to her cheeks, then she experienced a surprising thought; where had the money come from? And then smiling determinedly in the face of the shocked response, Turnbull continued. 'So you will have here in this noble theatre not an actor manager like Garrick but a playwright manager, the first Old Drury has known.'

'And when, sir, does our new manager (Mr Jacob gave the word an ironic edge) begin his reign?'

'Ah yes. Well, in fact this very morning,' Turnbull replied, the relief of having conveyed difficult news evident in the tone of his voice. 'He and Miss Newley who is, of course to continue as Drury Lane's *prima donna*, are at present in my office ... or should that be *his* office? Ned, would you go and tell them we are ready for them?'

Discussion broke out as soon as Ned left the room. By now sweat had formed on Turnbull's brow, which he was mopping with a handkerchief. Hetty had buttonholed him and looked to be pleading with him, her hand laid on his sleeve, her eyes wide and intense as he shook his head slowly. Eliza noticed that Susan had managed to get a seat on the end of a bench and was just sitting there, surrounded by chatter, quite indifferent to the buzz of speculation around her. Eliza moved across to her and squeezed in beside her.

'Well, that will be the end of my chance of any big roles now,' she said lightly, trying to laugh off her concern. 'No more Lady Heartfort. Back to the breeches roles for me.'

'You think only of yourself as usual,' replied Susan bitterly, 'only of your career. You're lucky you have one.' Eliza was hurt and astonished. How could her friend be so unjust and so far from her usual self?

'Susan ... I did not ...'

Suddenly the door opened and the heir apparent to Drury Lane stood before the company, Sarah Newley beside him wearing brown silk and a smug expression.

'No decent parts for any one of us women next season then,' grumbled Betty Temple to Eliza. 'She'll get the lot, bedding the manager. That was one thing about old Turnbull. Faithful to his missus. Totally incorruptible. And God knows,' she added drily, 'I tried.'

Richard Cavendish spent the next quarter of an hour trying to be all things to all men and women. Eliza thought to herself, not without a smile, he would make a terrible actor. He was trying much too hard, in turn being ingratiating, friendly, imperious, confident, diffident and inspirational, and failing to convince anyone. He told them they would be working on some new plays, some old favourites too. He would be working them hard but the company would have the best houses Drury Lane had ever known. He begged them for their indulgence and support in his new role and concluded by telling them his new play, *A Treasured Possession* would open before Christmas. His words were met with polite silence and few questions. Eliza watched him closely as he dealt with individual concerns and queries. The cheap imitation Spitalfields silk waistcoat was long gone, replaced by the real thing, striped in red and black, worn under a fine black merino overcoat and over fawn breeches. Soft black leather hessian boots made the overall picture a marked contrast to Mr Turnbull who stood by his side, wig askew as usual, taking a pinch of snuff, his whole costume indicative of past times and past glories. *The Heiress* had had a dramatic effect on Cavendish's fortunes, but Eliza continued to puzzle as to how he could have afforded to buy into the management of the theatre.

There was only one feasible explanation: the financial support of his mistress. That or a remarkable run of luck at the tables.

Cavendish raised his voice above the general chat that had broken out in the green room. 'I shall be pinning up a list of our forthcoming productions together with the castings for each piece. Mr Turnbull did me the honour of collaborating with me in this as his last act before his retirement,' he smiled warmly towards his mentor. 'Rehearsals begin tomorrow morning, first performance of *Much Ado* on Friday.'

At the first rehearsal of *Much Ado,* Mr Cavendish showed his naïveté as a director. Although the cast was used to this production and had played it many times, he began to intervene and change their positions and movements, often confusing them and arriving at situations that they knew instinctively would not work on stage. He was, however, more confident in directing them how to deliver their words, though having to rethink the emphasis of a speech or the previous inflection on words also created bewilderment. Ned was particularly put off in his role as Claudio, complaining to Eliza as she sat doing running repairs on a dress that Maria Webster needed letting out due to another pregnancy.

'I'm not sure I shall be able to work with him, Liza. He wants me to say the words in quite a different way in the wedding scene. I have them deeply engraved in the head the way I used to speak them. Maybe I should look towards another of the theatres. Mr Harries at Covent Garden has asked me several times to join them.'

'I daresay he needs time to adjust to giving direction, Ned. Oh, please don't go to The Garden. I should miss you as a friend. Susan seems to have taken against me for some reason. I do wish I knew why. She doesn't seem to want to talk to me any longer. I can't imagine what I've done to her.'

Much Ado was always a popular play in the repertoire and there was a good house on Friday, the novelty of "under the new management of Mr Richard Cavendish" proclaimed on the playbills no doubt an incentive to the would-be critics and wags in the pit who would be vocal in their quips and comments in welcome of the new manager. Eliza's part as Ursula was minimal, but she had a central breeches role in the afterpiece *Sir Harry Wildair* which she always played with a lightness of touch and charm audiences loved.

The next week Cavendish distributed the parts for *A Treasured Possession* in which Eliza was to play the small yet crucial role of confidante to the heroine, played of course by Sarah Newley, with some twenty lines or so of dialogue. It was a nice little vignette and Eliza was not displeased with the role. Cavendish clearly had strong ideas of exactly how he wanted the part played, and at the second rehearsal exclaimed, 'Eliza, you must sound altogether more knowing, more worldly. Show that by the way you move across the stage towards Sir Archibald. You know exactly what effect you are having on him – not so naïve, so wholesome. Now everyone, once more from the top.'

Confident and relaxed directing his own material, Cavendish carried the cast with him and there was a distinct buzz and energy as the rehearsals progressed. His coat was off, his cravat had become unwound, the dark hair had escaped a little at the sides from its black bow and although he was working them hard, forcing them to repeat over and over again their lines until they got just the nuance he wanted, they were all giving of themselves unstintingly. Eliza was at liberty to observe as much as she had to wait a while until she was needed again, and it struck her how far away he seemed from the brusque and sardonic young man who had stepped on her trailing gown almost a year ago. His voice suddenly broke in on her thoughts.

'Now Act 3. Susan – where's Susan?' he snapped, looking round for her. 'In God's name, Susan! She is holding us up. Eliza, please will you find her.'

Eliza sped back to the dressing room where she found her friend white-faced and smelling of vomit.

'Susan! Mr Cavendish is … what? Are you unwell? What is amiss?'

Susan began to cry softly, wringing her handkerchief in her hand, her eyes downcast, her shoulders slumped as she sat on a bench in front of the looking glass.

Eliza sat beside her and took her hand.

'Eliza, oh Eliza, I am … with child… I have been sick as I have been every morning this week. My parents will disown me. I …'

Susan's tears began to flow faster, her breath coming in huge gulps. Eliza remembered Susan's casual talk of "congress" when they were in York.

'I feel so wretched. My belly will show in a few months. And even now I cannot say that I am puking because I have eaten bad oysters, which is what I said yesterday to my father.'

A banging at the door made both women start. 'Eliza! Susan! You are needed on stage. Mr Cavendish is in a fury. Come quickly!'

'Susan, come, wipe your eyes. We will speak of this tomorrow. Be brave for now. You know I will help as much as I can.'

On their walk to the theatre next morning, Eliza held her friend's arm. She knew there was little she could do to make her feel better, but at least she could show her love and support. Susan's apparent indifference of late had hurt her deeply but now she understood the reasons for it, she could forgive.

'Jed told me all would be well,' sighed Susan as they narrowly avoided a handcart selling cooked meats that was being trundled towards The Piazza with its many coffee houses and taverns. As usual, there were a few prostitutes looking for early trade standing in doorways. One very young girl, thin and bedraggled with a bright red painted mouth, eyed men hopefully as they made their way to The Shakespeare's Head. Susan cast a glance in her direction and pulled her cloak tightly around her. The rain had stopped but deep puddles still stood among the cobbles and had to be negotiated to avoid splashed skirts and wet feet.

'My father will never accept a bastard in the house,' Susan continued. 'He made that clear to Fanny, Maria and me, even before we knew how babies were made. I know that some women – I have heard Hetty speak of it more than once – some women take potions to make them miscarry, herbs and such. Liza, I cannot have a child. My life, my acting would be over. My family would never own me again.'

Eliza put her arm around her friend's shoulders as they reached the stage door. Words seemed inadequate, so she passed Susan a handkerchief as they entered the network of passages, already bustling with whistling, laughter and fiddles sawing out scales and arpeggios. Life had to go on, audiences needed entertaining, and the lives of young women like Susan and Eliza were of little consequence.

In the next few days the girls had little chance to exchange confidences, though Eliza kept a watchful eye on Susan during rehearsals. She did what was asked of her competently but without her customary good humour. She also spent some time deep in conversation with Hetty.

Eliza had learned her twenty lines quickly and easily and was soon word perfect.

'Not only word perfect, but character perfect too, Eliza,' remarked Cavendish, smiling at her as she delivered her speeches with just a touch of the West Country accent she had copied by listening carefully to Henry, one of the leading stage hands.

'You really *are* Miss Primrose. Apparently, fresh and naïve but knowing too. You've got it just right.'

Sarah Newley shot her a less than charitable glance and tapped her foot impatiently waiting for her cue. 'Precious little skill required there. She simply plays what she is,' she muttered to Mr Jacobs.

Eliza heard the comment, though Cavendish had turned away to speak to Ned who was stumbling over his words. She coloured and turned quickly away, all the pleasure she had felt at the playwright's praise erased. Where he was concerned, she still experienced vastly different emotions. She had long since realised that the initial abrasive condescension he had shown to her and others was a mask to hide insecurity and lack of confidence. She could not deny that she desired his approbation, that she found him attractive, clever, witty, exciting to be around; on the other hand, she could not approve nor understand his choice of a mistress. Sarah Newley's ambition made her cold and materialistic. Yet she must have a heart, Eliza reasoned, because it seemed to be exclusively in the possession of Cavendish. Once again, Sarah was gazing at him like a love-sick girl. He, on the other hand, never seemed to be enamoured of her in the same way. Were each of them using the other for their own and very different reasons? Occasionally she found herself thinking of that brief, tender moment when he had held her to comfort her, a moment so different from the heady thrill of Antony Denham's embrace, which had spelt not safety and tenderness but excitement and abandon. Yet for all the urgency of Lord Denham's embraces, and the whispered endearments, she had not seen nor heard from him for almost three months. That surely told her something of the frailty of men.

A week later, the day of the first performance of *A Treasured Possession,* a letter addressed to Eliza was delivered to the stage door by hand addressed to Eliza. It was written on stiff cream paper sealed with a wax crest. Her hands shook as she broke the seal and stood reading it amid the hubbub of the dressing room.

My Dear Eliza,

Please forgive me for my long silence and do not impute it to my having forgotten you since York. How could that be possible since you have imprinted your beautiful person and character so indelibly upon my heart?

My father has been very ill and estate affairs have kept me in the north. He appears to be making a gradual recovery however, and I find I have my time and liberty restored to me. I am to journey to London and plan to see you on stage in Cavendish's new play. I hope you will do me the honour of having supper with me on the night of the opening.

I long to see you again.

Your servant Antony Denham

He was coming tonight then, at last, this very night. So in the middle of all this last-minute panic, the nerves, the tears, the missed cues, the tantrums, she had to be ready to see Lord Denham – Antony – after all this time. And she would have to be ready to have supper with him. She wondered where he would take her. Perhaps to one of those eating houses in Covent Garden's Piazza, maybe one where there were private rooms. Or perhaps he would take her to eat with some of his of his acquaintances.

As she folded up the letter and put it in her pocket, she could hear the ear-splitting hammering of the carpenters as they were finishing off an elaborate backdrop that was to be the centrepiece of Act 4.

Scurrying along the corridor to the dressing rooms, she decided not to tell Susan as yet of the letter. Her friend had been so morose, so withdrawn since her confession. When Eliza had tried to bring up the subject, Susan had snapped at her and told her not to speak of it. again.

The final run-through of the main scenes was, as usual, a subdued and low-key affair. Eliza had noted early on in her career at Drury Lane that actors held back to a certain degree in those final rehearsals so that they had more to give during the actual performance when he or she needed to have reserves to draw upon. So the final rehearsal was a muted affair with Mr Jacobs appearing almost indifferent and detached, as was his way on these occasions. Eliza stood in the wings awaiting her cue, breathing deeply in order to have complete control over her voice. So much had happened already this morning she needed those few moments of calm. As Sarah Newley stood on stage, Eliza mouthed her words silently; she knew the part as thoroughly as thoroughly as she did her own modest role. If Fate decreed another serious accident should befall Drury Lane's *prima donna*, Eliza would be ready to step into the breach again.

But such a crisis did not occur. When the doors opened at five o'clock, the crowds who pushed and elbowed their way to the box office were bigger than they had been for Richard Cavendish's first play. Many were not prepared to gamble and wait for the intermission to pay half-price, though sensible gentlemen had sent their valets or groom to sit in their places until the second half of the performance.

Lord Antony Denham had done no such thing however. His box, right on stage, was occupied by him and him alone as the curtain rose.

Susan had glimpsed him from the wings and imagined she was bringing Eliza news, when she grabbed her in the corridor as they scurried towards the green room.

'He's here, Lord Denham. Eliza, he's here. Box on the stage. He must be here to see you.' Susan's gloom had vanished and the mischievous sparkle had returned to her eyes.

'I know. He left a letter for me, Susan. He wants me to have supper with him afterwards. Oh Susan, I am so … excited. And scared.'

'Now remember, Eliza,' Susan whispered, 'don't be too easily won. I beg you. Be circumspect. Don't –'

'No, Susan. It will not be that. He merely wishes to meet me.'

Susan scoffed. 'Well, he's not going to propose marriage. Don't fool yourself into thinking that. He's going to offer marriage to you. Once you've lost your virginity, you've lost your biggest asset. Don't do what I do – do what I say. Be quick, it's your cue after Ned.' And she kissed Eliza's cheek with tears in her eyes.

The Prologue to Richard Cavendish's second play, *A Treasured Possession,* spoken by Ned in his character of Lord Feckless, was greeted with enthusiastic applause, even from the pit where they accounted themselves arbiters of theatrical taste and were notoriously difficult to please. There was a certain amount of good-natured catcalling from the gods and a light rain of fruit on those below, but the mood of the packed house was expectant and appreciative. Mr Jacobs's first speech as Sir Willoughby Dangle produced thunderous applause and a loud drumming of feet, which he acknowledged in a brief dignified smile. There was a ripple of restrained admiration as Sarah Newley swept on stage in one of the four splendid gowns she was to wear during the production, but Old Drury's response to her was always respectful rather than rapturous, more admiration than affection.

Eliza did not appear until the end of the first act and was gratified by a flutter of recognition and 'ahs' of pleasure from those regulars in the audience who knew her as Lady Heartfort and in many of her breeches roles. She delivered her lines expertly and playfully, casting a languorous glance at Ned whom she was trying to ensnare. Then hiding behind her fan, she allowed her gaze to stray to the box in which Lord Denham sat, all attention, his long legs stretched out before him, a smile playing on his lips. She noted how ladies of fashion in the auditorium blatantly ogled him and, truth to tell, he did look remarkably handsome lounging there, a picture of careless privilege and good breeding, yards away from her gazing at her quite unashamedly. Blushing, she turned aside and made some more stage business out of flirting with her fan at Ned, swishing her skirts playfully and then turning the full beam of her smile on him in a way they had not previously rehearsed. As she made her exit a few minutes later, there was a burst of applause that made her cheeks glow as she hurried back along the corridor to change for the next act. Susan was already pulling on her gown over her stays that were straining over her increased girth. Spots of colour showed on her cheeks as she pulled Eliza to her in agitation.

'Come lace me, Liza, as tight as you may. I will not get into the dress if you do not. God's life,' she continued in a whisper, 'my belly betrays me already.'

'But it will surely harm you if I lace so tight.'

'Do you think I care? Do I want to be brought to bed of a brat? Hetty has given me an infusion of pennyroyal, which she says will be powerful enough taken with twopence of gin. Don't look like that. Make haste. I shall take the potion tomorrow when Mother and Father are in church.'

Further debate was prevented by a quarrel that had flared up between Mary Isaac and Lucy Peters who had dropped grease from some cooked meat down the bodice of Mary's gown. Harsh words were spoken, hair was tugged, but further damage was prevented by the need for most of the women, including Susan and Eliza to get ready for their next entry.

As with his first play, Cavendish was summoned by an ecstatic audience to appear onstage. This time Eliza stood towards the back of the line up and saw, not without a twinge, how the playwright held out his hand to Sarah to step forward to join him and receive the acclaim of the crowd. Glancing towards the box, Eliza noticed Denham on his feet, applauding enthusiastically. As their eyes met, he held up his clapping hands towards her in a gesture that marked her out for his especial praise.

He was waiting for her in the green room where he was mingling with the performers, including a very gushing Sarah Newley and a more guarded Richard Cavendish who accepted his congratulations with a slight bow. Eliza, whose hair had been covered by a wig during the play, had had her own hair dressed quickly by Sukey who had let her borrow a green paduasoy gown with a cream underskirt from wardrobe and had threaded a green ribbon through her hair as a finishing touch. As she entered the green room where the actors were beginning to drift off home, the chatter ceased and several of the actresses racked their brains to think where they had seen that dress before. Denham advanced towards her, bowed deeply, then kissed her hand before saying, 'My dear Eliza' in a tone that left no bystander thinking it was a social nicety. Sarah, with whom he had been speaking previously, looked put out and flounced off to hang on Richard's arm and gaze into his eyes. Heads were turned, eyebrows were raised, comments were passed. Dalliance while on the road in York was one thing but pursuit of the lady to London three months later was a development that needed comment. Indeed, milord must be truly smitten. Such were the thoughts of Sarah Newley as she sipped her wine and watched the younger woman blush and smile at the obvious attention. Sarah had been all too aware of the warmth with which Drury Lane audiences greeted Eliza as well as the encouragement and praise her lover had heaped upon the chit. For Eliza to become Denham's mistress would suit Sarah very well, perhaps removed to a different sphere, giving receptions on the fringes of London society though never the best houses of course, but it was possible to move quite comfortably among the *demi-monde*. Even better, she might be transported to Yorkshire where she would cause Sarah no sleepless nights.

'Well Eliza, are you ready for us to leave?' asked Denham. 'I have ordered a celebration supper for us. Let me help you on with your cloak. My carriage is outside. Let us make our farewells.'

Outside at the stage door, a smart carriage was waiting, the greys pawing at the ground and snorting impatiently. The theatre crowds had thinned out by now but there was still much activity. Laughter, some of it inebriated, hurried assignations being struck, two dandies lurched along, their arms round each other, singing at the tops of their voices and heading towards the Piazza. Denham laid a protective arm around her shoulder and hurried her towards the coach where his man Francis had let down the steps for them. Denham tapped with his cane on the roof of the coach and they set off. Clearly the eating houses of Covent Garden were not their destination.

'Eliza,' he said, taking her hand, 'I wanted you all to myself. I could not endure the thought of dining with others and in a public place where we might be interrupted. I am therefore taking you to my London residence in Hanover Square.'

'And are we to dine there ... alone?'

'Apart from my excellent staff, yes we are. My chef is a Frenchman. You will not eat food that is finér, I assure you.'

Eliza's chief concern was not for the quality of the food but the intimacy of the arrangements. Should she be agreeing to this? She had envisaged a dining room in one of the many restaurants and chophouses in Covent Garden: there were some very classy ones frequented by the quality as well as the seedier establishments whose clientele had much lower standards. But to be taken to his lordship's residence in Hanover Square was another matter. He must have felt her body tense as they sat close together because he said, 'Rest easy, Eliza. I am doing nothing to compromise your honour. You know my high regard for you.' She nodded without speaking as she remembered the images of Lady Arabella's library and the screams of the peacocks.

When Denham handed her down from the carriage after their short journey, she found herself outside a tall elegant townhouse with a porticoed entrance, in an elegant square far from the noise and busyness of Covent Garden. He led her up the steps to a solid front door, which was opened immediately by a young black boy who bowed deferentially to both of them. Another servant dressed in a sober grey livery took her cloak and ushered them into a sitting room where a table set for two was laid. In the light that came from the fire in the grate, the china and glassware glinted and twinkled. The wax candles burning in the wall sconces and candelabra would have surely kept her mother's household in light for a year, Eliza found herself thinking.

'Thank you, Jennings,' said his lordship as chairs were moved out for them to sit, 'you may bring in the food now.' He poured two glasses of wine from the fine glass decanter on the table. 'And when you have done that, you may leave us. I shall ring if I require you further.'

'Very good, my lord.' Jennings bowed and left the room, closing the door gently.

Staring down into her glass, Eliza found that she could think of nothing to say to her host. She was so far removed from her normal surroundings, so overwhelmed by the opulence of the room, shy in the presence of a man she had not seen for three months but who seemed to be wooing her and making her completely tongue-tied. Denham saw all this at a glance and smiled gently at her.

'I have taken you aback I see. I am sorry if you expected there to be other company, but I could not bear to share you with any others. Dear Eliza, all these months …'

There was a discreet tap at the door and Denham, who was refilling his glass, splashed a little wine on the snowy tablecloth. As Eliza watched the red spread, Eliza found herself thinking of Susan.

On his lordship's command to enter, Jennings brought in a tray laden with silver domed dishes, which he set down carefully on the table where his expert eyes took in the growing stain on the table cloth.

'My lord, shall I …'

'No, Jennings there is no need. A slight misjudgement on my part. Thank you.'

'Very well, my lord,' Jennings replied, leaving the room.

For Eliza, there had been no time for much food that day. That was why perhaps she had felt the effects of the wine immediately. Denham was removing covers to reveal dishes of game and pies with shiny pastry, and dishes of vegetables. A jug of delicious sauce gave off such an appetising aroma that Eliza's stomach rumbled in response. She found herself ravenously hungry as she watched Denham put food in her plate. All she had eaten that day was a pie hastily crammed into her mouth after rehearsals. The delicate and mouth-watering food was irresistible, and she applied herself to it enthusiastically.

And oh, how he protested his love for her, how he gazed into her eyes, how he promised undying devotion. He ate little, so ardent were his words. She listened, she ate, she didn't interrupt, gazing down at the diminishing food on the plate. Then he stopped and poured them both more wine. She began to make self-deprecating comments about her unworthiness, to fend off the avowals of love, but her head was swimming with this unaccustomed flattery as well as the wine and wonderful food. She found herself falling back on the words and sentiments of the stage roles she knew, and longed to have Susan by her side with her earthy advice and superior knowledge of how to handle her suitor. What did it mean for him to say he loved her? Did *she* love him? She honestly didn't know. There in the candlelight, in this elegant room that oozed money, rank and style, his handsome face gazing at her. Was it love that she felt?

'Milord, you do me too much honour,' she stuttered and his face showed his impatience at such a stock reply. He rose from the table and came over to where she sat. Lifting her gently to her feet, he folded her in his arms. His lips were sweet with wine, his kiss urgent and his body hard and pressing against hers. The heat of the room, the fuzziness in her head and the primal desire she felt for him almost overwhelmed her. She was aware of his voice, broken with need, pleading with her to be his and felt his fingers tugging insistently at the bodice of her gown.

'Eliza, please, I love you. Come to my chamber with me I beg you. I will die if you do not. Take pity on me,' he murmured into her hair. But even in the throes of her own desire she pulled back, Susan's words running through her head. She could not succumb to this love or lust, however enchanting his words and promises. Suddenly she gave him a slight push, just enough to make him stagger against the table and knock over a wine glass that rolled across the table and fell on the floor, smashing with a high clear sound. The mood was broken. Sanity and clarity returned and she smoothed her ruffled bodice.

'My lord, I am sorry if you misinterpreted my response.' Now he was glaring at her, very much out of countenance at her rebuff, aroused and angry, a dangerous combination she knew in a man.

'I am sorry to have misled you ... if indeed I have. I am,' she continued with difficulty, gulping and struggling for composure, 'I'm an honest woman, not a trollop, though I am an actress,' she added proudly. 'I know many think we have loose morals,' she was moving slowly towards the door. 'I must trouble you for my cloak. I thank you for an excellent supper.' He crossed the room quickly and put his hand on hers as she reached for the door handle.

'Eliza, once more my ardour has put me in danger of losing you. Please sit down. No – don't look like that. I shall sit across from you. Please. Take care of the glass on the floor. I shall ... I shall not touch you. And my carriage shall take you home in ten minutes. You have my word. I beg you for just ten minutes to talk to you. And despite my behaviour, I promise you I am a man of honour.'

He smiled a little uncertainly at her but that was enough. She returned to the table and resumed her seat.

'My father was taken ill shortly after you left York. As his only son I had much to do to organise his affairs. Indeed, it seemed at one time that he would die. My mother was distraught.' Eliza could see the genuine emotion on his face as he relived the terrible events.

'I am so sorry, sir. I ... I too lost my father almost two years ago. It was a terrible blow.'

'We sent for doctors from London. The shock of it all affected us all as a family, Bella, my sister – you met her at Wychwood – she miscarried the child she was expecting.' He tried for a lighter tone. 'And you might ask, what have those events to do with what has happened here tonight? I need to explain my apparent indifference these past months. Eliza, do not flinch. I see fear in your eyes still when all I wish to see is love. I have been clumsy, unthinking. You know that I cannot pay court to you, and that when I marry it must be with position and fortune in mind.'

'Of course.'

'Eliza, I wish to be your protector, your lover. To look after you financially, to make your life as easy and as comfortable as possible. To see that you want for nothing.'

'And ... I would be your mistress?'

'Yes, 'tis no uncommon arrangement as you know in society these days. I could name a dozen titled men who have such arrangements with beautiful women, many of whom are openly acknowledged in the best circles.'

'Yes sir, I too know of many such arrangements,' agreed Eliza quietly, her eyes drawn to the deep red stain on the cloth. There was a silence broken only by the occasional spluttering of the logs on the fire.

'I would have documents drawn up, legal documents where everything was laid out clearly for you to see. A settlement. And a pleasant house of your own, of course.' A wheedling note had crept into his voice. Suddenly Eliza felt very, very tired, drained of all her spirit. The long day of rehearsals, the euphoria and tension of the opening night, the unaccustomed food and wine, the conflicting emotions she felt had all taken their toll on her.

'My lord, I do not know what to say. When your lordship marries – might I ask what arrangement – what would my position be?'

'Such an event is not imminent, Eliza.' The wheedling note had disappeared, and Denham's tone was now guarded.

Eliza rose from the table and spoke neutrally.

'I must consider what you propose.'

'So,' he was on his feet now also, scanning her impassive face for signs of a response. 'I shall detain you no further. I promised ten minutes and no more. I shall have Francis drive you home,' he said, picking up a little silver bell and ringing it. 'May I expect an answer soon?'

She nodded.

Sounds in the hall indicated his summons had been answered. The double doors were opened, and Jennings stood there holding her cloak for all the world as if it were the costliest fabric in London and she, Georgiana, Duchess of Devonshire.

Once outside and climbing into the coach, she commanded 'St Giles,' in an imperious tone. 'Charles Street if you please.'

If it had not been midnight when the coach, emblazoned with Denham's crest put her down in Charles Street, no doubt it would have caused a sensation. But as it was, there were few to hear the clopping of the hooves and to see Eliza dismount on the cobbles. The Saracen's Head was still serving, and raucous singing and cheering could be heard, followed by the sound of breaking glass. A few hopeful prostitutes had positioned themselves in doorways, one many years younger than Eliza with a grubby face and a slash of red for a mouth, hugged her thin shawl around her shoulders. In the shadows, grunting noises indicated that business was being transacted.

Eliza let herself into the house in which a thick darkness smelt of onions and neglect. Struggling to find a candle, Eliza bumped around the room, tripping over items on the floor and sensing even before the flame struggled into life that there would be unwashed dishes and discarded dirty clothing everywhere as well as empty gin bottles. Their home had never been like this before John Harkness had come into her mother's life. She, Eliza herself, was as much to blame for the slow slide into squalor. She and Flora must do more to keep the place clean and tidy. The thought crossed her mind that if she had her own establishment, she would escape the filth and be able to give her mother money. Annie had completely lost interest in keeping house these days and was becoming unrecognisable as the hardworking practical woman who had kept the family together after her husband's death, handling George's outbursts and Flora's moods with equanimity. Her appearance had coarsened of late and she seemed to care for no one and nothing, except the drink and noisy couplings with John that were usually followed by heated arguments. Her pride in Eliza had disappeared and she no longer took up Eliza's offers of complimentary theatre tickets.

'What's the use of plays?' she had remarked sullenly when invited. 'It's all lies what you see on the stage. And you're a fool to go peddling them to stupid folk.'

Tonight the untidy rooms were deserted and Eliza concluded that Flora must be in bed, so, taking the candle stick, she made her way to the bedroom and pushed open the door. As she did so, there was the sound of strangled sobbing and, by the flickering light, Eliza

87

could see the shape of her sister lying on the bed, her body rising and falling as she sobbed.

'Flora, what is it? What is wrong? Are you ill?'

Flora rolled over slowly so that Eliza could see that her face was streaked with blood and her lip swollen. Flora did not speak but the look in her eyes was more eloquent than words.

'Was it … him? Has he done this to you?'

Slowly Flora nodded as her sister pushed the tangled mass of hair out of her eyes, revealing a bleeding ear.

'Why, Flora? Come, please sit up if you can. I need to wash your face and see what the damage is. Where was our mother while he did this to you?'

Eliza's voice was angry now and her hands shook as she lifted the candle to get a closer look at Flora's injuries.

'Did she witness this and stand by?'

Flora shook her head, having now raised herself slowly from the bed, but as she did so, great racking sobs began to convulse her body and she doubled over in pain. With horror Eliza noticed that the neck of Flora's dress, trimmed with the pretty lace she had brought her from York, was ripped and hanging in strips.

'Did he do this?'

Nodding, Flora pulled the torn bodice together making Eliza shriek in terror, 'He has taken you by force? He has raped you? This is monstrous, and it is all my fault. I should have been here.' A fleeting image of Antony Denham fumbling at the neck of her dress flashed across Eliza's mind and she clasped Flora firmly to her.

Flora drew back slightly. 'No, Eliza, no.' She spoke the words as if they were enormous balls of delicate glass that she had to expel from her mouth with the greatest care. 'He did not ... do that. I pushed him and he fell. Then he ran off. Mama was at The Crown.'

Relieved beyond belief, Eliza took her sister's hand and sat down with her on the bed. 'Thank God for that at least. Now I need to look at you.'

Eliza gathered some cloths, a basin of water and some arnica. She bathed Flora's face after tying back her hair and looking carefully to see where the wounds were. Occasionally Flora flinched, but otherwise she was as docile as a hurt animal trusting its owner to tend to its needs. All the while tears streamed down her face, joining the smudges of blood and the bruise already beginning to show.

'Don't let him come for me again, Eliza,' she begged when the process was complete. 'Please. I might not be so lucky next time.'

'There will be no next time,' Eliza answered grimly. 'If you can walk, we are leaving here immediately. I will decide later what to do about him.' Eliza's voice betrayed nothing of the uncertainty that had reduced her insides to jelly. She really had no idea what her next move should be, but she knew that getting away was of paramount importance.

'We will take what we can with us,' she continued, her voice calm and business-like, pulling clothes from the press and stuffing them into the travelling bag she had taken to York. 'I have some money – not much but it will help us.'

'And I have a shilling,' Flora added, raising herself stiffly from the bed in order to help in their flight, 'but we must make haste, Liza. I never want to see that animal again.'

Mrs Wainwright's lodging house in Compass Street was homely, respectable and inexpensive. Eliza knew several members of the Drury Lane company who had used it and who spoke affectionately of the landlady, herself a former actress who had played under Garrick and who, if given half the chance, would regale all her tenants with tales of her glory days playing opposite Macklin in *Love a la Mode*. Although Eliza and Flora had arrived on her doorstep in the early hours of the morning, Mrs Wainwright herself, no stranger to drama domestic as well as theatrical, had appeared at her door, hair in curlpapers but ready to respond to the situation, especially as she recognised Eliza as Lady Heartfort.

'My dear,' she whispered in histrionic tones as she drew Eliza and the still-shocked Flora across the threshold, 'I know only too well that life can produce as many dramas as the stage. I recognise two ladies in distress. Come in. You shall take my large back room on the first floor. Two shillings a week. No, my dear,' she said as she stopped Eliza's hand which was scrabbling in her pocket, 'come on up first and we can see about payment then. This way, my dears.'

The light of Mrs Wainwright's candle revealed a square room, rather gloomy with heavy outmoded furnishings, but it seemed to be clean and the bed, which Eliza tested discreetly, felt comfortable. Both young women looked longingly at it after their ordeal. Mrs Wainwright bustled about lighting another candle on the washstand and opening a large press for them to appreciate its capaciousness, Eliza fumbled in her purse for the rent and their new landlady bade then goodnight. Having kicked off their boots and changed swiftly into their night shifts, the sisters collapsed into bed, kissing each other an exhausted good night, something they had not done since they were little girls.

Eliza woke when the house started to stir into life. The sound of the fire being riddled and footsteps on the stairs, the snatches of whistling and the barking of a dog nudged her into wakefulness. For a blissful split second, she remembered nothing of the extraordinary events of the night before, then her eyes took in the grey and white patterned wallpaper, the unfamiliar table and chairs and the tangle of discarded boots and cloaks on the floor. Flora was still asleep, her bruised swollen lips slightly open, her copper coloured hair streaming over the pillow. She was as yet unaware of how their lives had changed, oblivious to the pain her body would soon be feeling and unconscious of the anguish that her attack had caused. Eliza was sorry to have to wake her, but they both had to step back into the bustle of the real world and its pressing demands of earning a living, though it would be some days before Flora could return to her employment. As Eliza dressed, she instructed her sister to stay where she was in the room, then later unpack their belongings and put them away, but mainly to try to sleep as much as she could.

'But Liza,' objected Flora, raising herself gingerly onto her elbow, 'we have to earn – both of us. How else will we manage?'

'You leave that to me. You must recover properly and then we can discuss what is to be done. I will be back this afternoon with some food. I have a rehearsal soon but tonight I play only a small part in the afterpiece so we will have more time together.' She knew she was forcing the cheeriness into her voice as she might have done if Flora had been a child, but she seemed unable to change the tone, afraid that if she let her sister see her fears that she would dissolve completely into uselessness. Luckily Flora was so relieved at having all responsibility taken from her that she fell into the role readily. 'Now,' Eliza bent to kiss her sister's bruised cheek, 'stay indoors. Don't get drawn into conversation with Mrs Wainwright. I shall return soon.'

Chapter 9

'Note for you, Eliza,' called out Archie at the stage door, putting aside his broom and shambling over to the shelves where he kept the correspondence that made its way through the doors of the theatre – the letters, the bills, occasionally the summonses and the writs to which members of the company were occasionally treated.

He held out the letter with its embossed seal and raised a quizzical eyebrow.

'Milord has become mighty pressing,' he commented with a knowing grin.

She gave him a tight little smile and a curt, 'Thank you, Archie,' and tore at the seal as she scurried to the dressing room. She was late, and Cavendish imposed fines. She had no desire to draw attention to herself at the moment. As she scanned Denham's letter, she almost collided with Cavendish who seemed in a jovial mood and not at all inclined to chide her tardiness.

'Eliza, how are you? Looking a little preoccupied today?' His greeting had forced her to stop and draw level with him.

'The critics have been kind to us. Have you seen the notices? I looked for you last night after the performance.' His eyes had strayed to the letter she was carrying and instinctively she held it more closely to her. 'There was quite a party, though you seem to have left early.' He eyed her quizzically, his expression more puzzled than amused.

'Yes, I am so glad your play was popular.' At that moment the play meant nothing to her. She had no room in her heart or her head for Richard Cavendish and his play. 'I must … I need to …' she murmured, moving away from him.

'Of course.' There was a note of disappointment in his voice that made her anger flare.

'I have much to occupy me at present,' was her parting shot as she strode off, leaving him looking bemused and concerned.

Susan was sitting in the dressing room, her head bowed and Hetty's arm round her shoulder. They looked serious and were speaking in low voices. Susan glanced up as Eliza came in, offering a wan smile and an almost imperceptible shake of her head. Hetty got up and sauntered over to where baby Charlie was starting to cry. With a swift and expert movement, she dropped the bodice of her gown and exposed a generous breast, clamping the howling Charlie onto it. Peace descended, and the other women carried on gossiping. Eliza went over to Susan and took her hand. Susan tried a smile, but her heart wasn't it.

'There is still a child, Eliza. Despite the rue and the hyssop, the vomiting and the retching, there is still a child. Hetty counselled one last try. With borax and zinc.' She paused. 'Not swallowed this time.'

Eliza squeezed her hand. 'If you feel that this is the only way, but please, if you can, wait just a few days.' She folded the letter she carried and thrust it into her pocket. 'Susan, my life too has suffered many changes these past few days. Flora and I have been forced to leave our home in St Giles. We are now lodging in Compass Street. My mother's lover attacked Flora.'

Susan's hand flew to her mouth in horror, suddenly remembering lives other than her own, all thought for herself momentarily forgotten. 'Not raped, Eliza?'

'Mercifully not, but she is shocked and bruised and cut. She swears she will never set foot there again.'

'And, Eliza – your lord? Lord Denham?'

The effort of unburdening herself of the events of the previous night, her thoughts, doubts and fears were all too much for Eliza at that point. She sank down on a stool and began untying her cloak.

'I shall tell you more about it later. I feel so confused at present, pulled in so many different directions. I really need your help. You know I always value your opinion and clear way of looking at things.'

Suddenly she felt tears prickle her eyelids and an overwhelming sense of hopelessness and fatigue.

'Come back to our new lodgings after the rehearsal. We can talk properly then.'

'Five minutes ladies!' came the call from Ned. 'Mr Cavendish is waiting. Act 3 didn't please him last night.'

There was general good-natured grumbling as conversations were cut off and Eliza and Susan joined the others filing out of the dressing room and heading for the stage.

As she sat waiting for her entrance, Eliza took out the note from Denham and smoothed out the stiff cream paper. She had hardly had time to assimilate its contents, distracted as she had been by Richard then Susan. Had she really understood what he was saying?

After the apologies for his uncontrolled behaviour came the reiteration of his passion for her, his desire to be of service to her, to be her protector. He pleaded with her to consider his proposition, to name her own terms. She recalled the elegant room, the deferential servants, and her own feelings of excitement and arousal. Oh, how easy it would be to give in to his requests, to let him take care of her – and of Flora too. Her head began to swim with the enticing prospect in which the brutish John, the ugliness of St Giles and even the demands of Drury Lane receded into a hazy background. Surely a life where she was loved and cherished, valued and desired was not to be casually rejected. Susan had always said that this arrangement was the best that was ever going to be offered her, mistress to a rich and powerful man who was attractive and who doted on her. How could anyone of sense hesitate a moment longer? Act 3 passed in a dream. She spoke her words, though Cavendish frowned and said, 'More convincingly, Eliza if you please. You are not reciting your catechism.' By the end of the rehearsal she had determined to become Lord Denham's mistress.

Chapter 10

In a letter that she redrafted four times, Eliza informed Antony Denham that she would be pleased to meet him soon to discuss his offer. She informed him that she had left the parental home and that she was now lodging in Compass Street with her sister Flora with whom she would continue to live. Then she waited.

That Sunday evening Eliza sat with Susan in Mrs Wainwright's lodging house. Flora, who had seemed to need lots of sleep since her ordeal, was dozing, so their voices were quiet. Susan, acting on Eliza's suggestion, had not administered the borax and zinc remedy advised by Hetty and was in a more philosophical mood about her future.

'Nancy Grey was still working the day before her confinement I remember,' Susan said thoughtfully, 'some of the others too.' She sipped her ale and a shadow of fear passed over her face. 'It's Father, Liza. He will throw me out, I know he will when I can hide it no longer.' She glanced down at her belly, which was as yet no traitor to her condition.

'Well, if it comes to that … and from what you have said, your father is a charitable Christian man,' Eliza continued, trying to convince herself as well as Susan that he would relent and not cast her out, 'he may surprise you by his actions.' Ignoring Susan's derisory 'humph', Eliza continued, 'I may be able to help you soon as I have explained.'

Eliza had told Susan her news as soon as she had arrived when Flora was still awake. Flora had burst into another flood of tears on hearing it, but this time her tears were of relief as Eliza explained that, wherever she was to be accommodated, Flora would be with her and they would both be safe from John.

Susan had perked up by this reminder of help, as well as the ale and the little piece of meat she and the sisters had been cooking on the fire. The smell of the food, the warmth of the fire and the intimacy of the women, united by their recent and different ordeals were producing an uplifting sense of close communion.

'I wonder where he will set you up,' mused Susan. 'Gower Street? Russell Square? Cavendish Place? Or will you insist on St Giles?' she added impishly.

A wave of guilt washed over Eliza as the image of her mother's home crossed her mind. Did Annie even know they had gone? She surely would not know the reason why. Would she care? Was her life to be a slow descent into drunkenness and slovenliness as she had seen happen to others? If she gave her mother money, would it not simply end up hastening her death?

'I hope he does not change his mind,' she added soberly.

There was a silence in which the fire crackled and spluttered and they could hear Flora breathing regularly. Both women pondered on a future that depended on milord's whim. A pretty face at the races, a flirtation at Vauxhall, a rout at Carlton House, any of these could change Antony Denham's plans for the future. All they could do was to sit and await his pleasure.

The room was growing dark. Eliza rose to light candles in the sconces. Susan poured more ale then, as Eliza resumed her seat, she said in a strained voice, 'When I do ... become his mistress, Susan. When we actually have congress. What is it actually like? Does it hurt? Or is it a truly wonderful thing, a union? You see, I do not love him.'

'Really Eliza, it's not necessary,' assured Susan in the peremptory tone of a worldlier being, 'and you may be assured he does know what he will be doing. It will be fine. And he's a handsome proper man too. And there will be fine sheets, a feather bed and good wine and you will feel like Cleopatra, rest assured. Or Lady Heartfort on her wedding night. Just be more careful than I was so that you don't fall for a child – at least not too soon.'

Eliza's face clouded over as she considered that possibility. Nature would take its course, a sentiment often reiterated by her fellow actresses and discussed at length in the dressing room, as well as the means to prevent that happening. These methods were generally considered to be erratic and unreliable. Soon Eliza would have to implement them herself.

It was another three days before Lord Denham made contact. He sent a servant to Compass Street, whose appearance caused Mrs Wainwright to flutter and fuss and fiddle with her wig like a young girl at her first ball. The liveried minion had handed over a letter for Miss Grahame 'with his lordship's compliments,' which Mrs Wainwright assured him would be conveyed to her lodger when she returned from the theatre. Flora had gone back to the laundry sporting a yellowing bruise but now at least she was calmer, though she did confess to Eliza that she dreaded the prospect of bumping into John or their mother.

'What will we do about Mama? What will she think of us leaving like that? Will she know what has driven us from the house?' Eliza sighed as she took off her boots and listened to Flora who was becoming increasingly agitated. It was late, she was exhausted, it had been a poor house, a raucous and unappreciative audience. Some had even booed Mr Jacobs, which was unprecedented. Sarah Newley had fallen into a rage and snapped at Ned; the whole theatre had seemed to resonate with ill-will, conflict and dissatisfaction. But at least she had his Lordship's reply thrust into her hand by Mrs Wainwright who must have been waiting behind the door of her own rooms to deliver it as soon as Eliza crossed the threshold.

'Do not worry so much, Flora,' she said as she broke the seal, her heartbeat accelerating. 'We may be about to have some good news.'

The letter declared in formal tones that he had taken a house for her in Somerset Street. She would have three servants and could take her sister to live with her. He would make her an allowance for living and expenses. There would be a document for her to sign. He ended with a request that she would meet him at the new address at ten o'clock the next morning. He remained, as ever, her affectionate servant Antony Denham.

Flora was overjoyed at the news, her face glowing with a happiness Eliza had not seen in months.

'You'll be a fine lady, Eliza. I can help you choose your dresses, can't I? We won't have to see that man ever again.' Then suddenly struck by the enormity of the changes in their fortune, she gasped, 'And you will have *servants!*'

Eliza said nothing, stretching full length on their bed. So now there really was no turning back. She had made her choice and Flora's future too was bound up in Antony Denham's as was hers. Why then was she not more thrilled to leave behind the shared lodgings, the fusty beds and the prying landladies? While Flora prattled on imagining the life of leisure and luxury – rides in the Park, the season in Bath – Eliza's mind returned to the day she had had in the theatre. And the encounter she had witnessed between Sarah and Richard Cavendish.

She had been returning from wardrobe and had bumped into him and Sarah in the middle of a flaming argument outside the actress's dressing room. Sarah was flushed, her eyes blazing, and she was making little attempt to keep her voice down.

'But why did you not come to me afterwards? I waited for three hours. I was invited to Lady Beresford's but I declined – on your account. Richard, what is amiss? You hardly come near me any longer.' Suddenly she noticed Eliza and stopped abruptly, a look of irritation on her face. Cavendish, who had his back to Eliza, had not noticed her approach and failed to pick up the signal in Sarah's eyes, because he continued, 'You know what we agreed, Sarah. We agreed terms. You drove a hard bargain then and ...'

'Eliza!' intervened Sarah, cutting off any more, 'I see you have collected Ned's jacket,' she continued quite unnecessarily, a forced smile on her face. Eliza nodded, moved away from the warring lovers, and walked towards the men's dressing room, Richard's words swirling in her head. What did they mean? What were Sarah's terms?

Certainly that quarrel seemed to have tainted the atmosphere that evening and the rowdy playgoers didn't help. With an effort she brought herself back to the present and as she prepared for bed, could not help but feel a shiver of anticipation about her visit to her new home in Somerset Street the next day.

Chapter 11

At ten in the morning Eliza was walking from Compass Street towards Russell Square and into another world. Gone was the hustle and bustle of coffee shops, traders' stalls and bakeries, the strident shouts of knife grinders and the push and shove of people going about the daily business of survival, fending for their families, striking the best bargains, keeping their heads above water in a world that threatened to engulf them at any minute if they didn't keep it at bay. As the press of people fell away, the streets grew broader and cleaner, the pavements wide enough for ladies and gentlemen to walk side by side and not get splashed with the mud thrown up by carriage wheels. Here there were more sedan chairs than hackney carriages, she noted, more curricles than handcarts and even the air seemed cleaner and fresher. She passed elegant terraces of houses, their front doors painted black or green or burgundy, their fanlights decorated with filigree patterns of finely wrought metal work. Here there was much that was beautiful as well as practical. There was much that delighted the eye, like iron railings fashioned with the fleur de lys on the spikes, balconies as intricately fashioned as lace work. The whole sweep of these terraces gave a smart uniformity that was elegant, stylish, and as much a contrast to the Rookeries of St Giles as a peacock to a sparrow.

Denham's letter had contained simple directions, which she had committed to memory. Conscious now as to how the pedestrians had thinned away to a few solitary strollers, the scarcity of the shops, apart from an elegant bootmakers and a very superior linen drapers, she wondered how she and Flora would fit into this new neighbourhood. Would they be out of their depth here? An actress and her erstwhile laundress sister rubbing shoulders with professional even perhaps titled people? Then she recalled with a stab of pride that she, Eliza Grahame, *was* a professional person, an actress, as accomplished at her art as any lawyer or doctor and that she could and would change her life and her sister's so that they could live in this lovely district and hold their heads up high.

One final left turn took her into Somerset Street where she saw Denham's curricle waiting outside. He was in the driving seat and the pair of matched greys stood still and submissive, one occasionally snorting and shaking its head skittishly so that the bridle jingled. Seeing her approach Number 17, he sprang from the carriage, a broad smile of relief on this handsome face, raising his hat to her as he led her up the small flight of steps to the front door where he produced some keys with a flourish.

'Miss Grahame, welcome to Number 17, your new home. Please let me show you round.'

Smiling, she followed him into the marble-floored hall that echoed their footsteps. The house appeared to be unoccupied. Denham explained.

'Eliza, I thought it best that you become acquainted with the house first before you meet the small staff I have engaged for you. You can tell me today if the house meets with your approval or if you wish to make some changes.'

'Oh, my lord … it seems so …'

Words failed her as she followed him up the curving staircase that led to the first floor where the main reception rooms were situated.

'Please Eliza, I cannot be "my lord" now that we are to be so close. I must be Antony to you, my dearest,' he said, pushing open the door to the drawing room, his smile showing the satisfaction he felt at her gasp of astonishment.

The high-ceilinged room was elegance itself, from its ornate plasterwork down to its Turkey rugs. Light streamed into the room through tall sash windows and the wallpaper was so new that Eliza could still smell the paste with which it had been applied. Above a white marble fireplace in which a fire burned, a large gilt mirror hung, reflecting the chandelier in the centre of the room.

'I did not know the style you liked so I had them keep it quite simple so that you and your sister, of course, might add some pieces that were to your liking,' Denham realised that the splendour of the room had robbed Eliza of the power of speech. He opened the double doors and said, 'The dining room adjoins as you see.' The pretty room with its warm red walls and stylish furniture could have easily accommodated at least five families from The Rookeries.

'My ... Antony,' she said shyly, turning to him, eyes wide and a smile on her lips, 'this is a truly beautiful house. I cannot quite imagine living here and I cannot think I would change a thing, except ...' she added mischievously, walking round the mahogany dining table, 'Miss Sarah tells me that chinoiserie is all the rage'.

He laughed and the tension between them was broken.

Taking her hand, he said, 'Nothing would please me more than to see you both in residence here.' He raised her hand to his lips. 'Now there is still much to see, but come with me to the next floor where you may view the bedroom I have prepared for you.'

Eliza felt her colour mount and her mouth become dry as they climbed the curving stairs to the next floor where there were four bedrooms in all. In the largest of these a four-poster bed dominated the room, its hangings of blue damask matched by elegant wallcoverings that depicted fabulous birds with golden wings. An elegant washstand, ormolu wardrobe and upholstered chair completed the furniture. Eliza was intrigued by the large wardrobe and opened the door, looking at Denham for an explanation.

'It's an armoire, Eliza, for hanging up your clothes.' Anticipating her reply he continued, 'You may not have enough to merit its size at present but that will change when you are mistress here and you have your own money to spend as you wish.' A little nettled by this, Eliza retorted, 'I already have my own money, Antony. It may not be much, but I earn it. I am no beggar.' She closed the door of the armoire gently and studied the paintings that adorned the walls depicting frolicking semi-clad nymphs in a pastoral setting. Denham noted her frowning at the paintings and was about to speak when she said with clarity and conviction, 'I do not altogether like those pictures, I feel they may not be suitable for my sister. She is young and unused to such – such depictions.'

'They are scenes of classical mythology, Eliza,' replied Denham in an amused tone. 'Here you see Diana and her ladies ...'

'Nonetheless, I do not like them and should like them removed.' It was Lady Heartfort's voice that spoke now, and it brooked no refusal or discussion. Then she added, 'It is a beautiful room. Please show me where Flora will sleep.' She smiled at him and he, nodding acquiescence, led her into the other bedrooms. When she had examined all the bedrooms thoroughly, one in particular she thought would charm Flora with green wallpaper and yet another smaller armoire. They emerged onto the landing and Denham gestured to the final flight of stairs, covered only in simple drugget unlike the carpet of the main floor.

'The staff will, of course, sleep up here. Perhaps you may require more than three servants – another maid maybe to tend to your person?'

'No, no, Antony!' Eliza stopped mid-step, looking at him horrified. 'I intend to train Flora to be my lady's maid, and I have never known what it is to have people do my biding.' Her voice was no longer that of the worldly Lady Heartfort but of Eliza Grahame, actress, late of St Giles, former shop assistant. 'I have much to learn, sir, about the world you have moved me into. My life will change dramatically and I need to become accustomed to those changes gradually.'

Denham nodded slowly and smiled fondly at her.

'We will do whatever you wish, Eliza. I am only too happy that you have consented to receive my protection, to let me look after you – you and Flora. Now let us speak of when you will become mistress of Number 17 as well as mistress of my heart.'

Two weeks later, Eliza and Flora said their goodbyes to Mrs Wainright and brought their modest belongings to Somerset Street where they met their staff, a moment far more nerve-racking for Eliza than any first night at Drury Lane. But for this occasion, she assumed the persona of Lady Heartfort once more, seeking to hide her lack of experience and naïveté behind hauteur and a stern countenance. She explained her tactics to Flora when they were alone in the drawing room away from prying eyes and wagging tongues. Flora had been incandescent with rage at her sister's curt dismissal of Mrs Jenkins from the dining room where, declared the lady of the house, the beef served at dinner had been overcooked.

'Eliza, how could you? The poor woman – it might have been our mother – looked mortified. I thought she might burst into tears. And then you told Wilmot that his shoes were not properly polished! If our father could hear you now. To speak to others in

106

this way!' Flora had been walking around the room angrily, her love of the novelty of her new home quite forgotten in the face of her sister's arrogant behaviour.

'Flora,' replied Eliza gently, 'I only play a part. I do not know quite how to behave now I am mistress here, but my instinct tells me that to be timid and apologetic is not the way. I must appear somewhat harsh and difficult to please. This is what ladies of quality do. Yes, I know,' she added quickly when she saw Flora was about to interject, 'I am not of the *ton,* I never shall be. I'm an actress, part of the *demi-monde.* I'm never going to entertain the Duchess of Devonshire or mingle with the highest in the land, despite Lord Denham's position. But this is our world now and we must obey its rules the best we may.'

'Even if it means being rude to servants?' asked Flora waspishly.

'Being firm, gaining their respect and perhaps a little later appearing more ...'

'Human?'

'Perhaps.'

But dealing with the unaccustomed servants and a mutinous sister were easy matters compared with her heady new role as Antony's Denham's mistress.

In preparation, she had had some intimate discussions with Susan on her role in the bedroom, what she would be required to do and how she might expect to feel. It was almost a week since she and Flora had moved in and her appearance in one of Drury Lane's favourite after pieces, *The Pretty Hoyden,* meant that she was not home until after midnight, tired, still full of the nervous energy that playing the central role in a lively farce involved.

She had dined with Denham at Number 17 before leaving for the theatre but, as he kissed her goodbye before taking his leave, he whispered, 'Tomorrow evening, my love, as you are free from your theatre duties, let us dine later and I will stay the night with you.' He gave her an affectionate and playful glance as he left the room and a mixture of excitement and fear welled up inside her as she imagined lying with him in her splendid bed among the draperies, their naked limbs entwined, his hands caressing her body and experiencing that moment when he entered her for the first time. Susan had said that it hurt but it was more of a pleasure than a pain and her body would desire it more than anything else, so it was not a thing to fear.

'Besides, he will be an experienced lover, you mark my words. Men like him have been bedding servants and whores since they were at school. He has learned as he went along. And that is good because he'll make sure you enjoy it too. Don't look so starchy about it. It's all meant for enjoyment, though make sure you do what I told you afterwards. Don't fall asleep in his arms all romantic like. If you don't do the necessary, you'll be with child within the year.' She looked down at her growing belly that was becoming difficult to disguise even under loose fitting gowns. 'Don't be caught like me,' she added sadly. 'It's only a matter of time before my pa finds out and then I'm out on the streets.'

'You know that I will never let that happen, Susan,' Eliza said, taking her friend's hand in hers. 'You will be welcome at Number 17, you know you will. Please rest assured.'

'But Eliza, surely your sponsor will not expect you to open your door, which is really his door his door, to any waif and stray fallen woman.'

'You are not a fallen woman! Do not say such things.'

'But people who do not know me will say as much. Actresses, harlots, fallen women. It is commonplace to lump us all together, is it not?'

They were sitting in a quiet area off stage while rehearsals for the new production went ahead. Richard Cavendish's voice had an edge to it that Eliza had not heard before today, which might or might not have to do with the way the rehearsal was progressing but which she had heard in his conversations with her over the past few weeks. She had not been allotted a part in *The Recruiting Officer* though she had hoped for the female lead, Melinda, but he had given that to Sarah. Perhaps it was professional jealousy that made Eliza bitter about it, but she preferred to think that her disappointment had more to do with Sarah's unsuitability for the role. Sarah's strength was not in comedy and this was a comic role, which Eliza knew she could bring off really well.

As Susan tried to regain her composure, the two friends sat listening to the increasingly frustrated commands of the manager that culminated in an abrupt silence and then the agitated figure of Sarah, brushing past them, her face set, the lips thin with rage and annoyance.

Susan smiled wryly and raised an eyebrow, giving one final sniff into her handkerchief. 'She's totally miscast in this play. She wants to play it like Lady Macbeth, and it needs the lightness of touch that you, Eliza, would give it. I wonder he cannot see it. He seems much out of humour with you these days.'

'With everyone it would seem.'

'Does he know of your new home?'

Eliza simply nodded.

The rehearsal had resumed, Cavendish's tone now more gentle and conciliatory, though he had not followed his lover to her dressing room to make amends. There was even a tentative ripple of laughter from those on stage, and though she was not involved, Eliza felt her body relax in sympathy with the rest of the company.

'He has said nothing. I expect he has heard the tittle-tattle. Lord Denham's actions seem to be known quite widely when he is in London.'

'And you yourself are not unknown to the print makers and the magazines. Mr Cavendish has doubtless heard the news. Perhaps it will attract more people to the performances – no, don't look so shocked, Eliza. When Kitty Lester's husband was killed in a duel two years since, her performances as Portia were a sell-out. People like to gawp,' she concluded philosophically. 'But when I am brought to bed of my bastard child, there will be no such public interest in the event because I am just another actress being let down by a man. Now,' she continued briskly rising from the stool, 'get yourself back to your beautiful house – and yes, I will come and visit you there this week as you invited. Prepare yourself to be enticing and seductive for your lord and prepare for the delights of Venus that await you later this evening.'

Eliza had dressed with care and ordered supper to be served at nine o'clock that evening. Flora had eaten at the earlier time of six o'clock and would keep to her room that night as the sisters had planned. Antony Denham had gone to Brooks, his club, and returned in good time to eat with Eliza. He had obviously enjoyed a convivial evening and was animated and voluble when he thrust his greatcoat and cane at Wilmot in the hall.

'Madam is in the drawing room, sir,' intoned Wilmot, bowing stiffly.

Standing nervously before a fire that had just been lit, Eliza turned to see her benefactor. He smiled at her, raising her hand to his lips, his eyes sparking with the effects of the wine he had drunk and his anticipation of the pleasure to come. They made rather stilted small talk until supper was announced, after which they moved into the dining room where the red walls and glittering sconces created a perfect atmosphere for their first formal meal together in the house.

Denham was trying to make an extraordinary occasion as normal as possible, having guessed that Eliza felt ill at ease, but she was more than happy to try to learn how to behave and how to converse in circles unlike her previous ones. So when Denham, having commented favourably on the soup they had been served, began to tell Eliza a little about the talk that night at Brooks, about the concern that was widespread about happenings with the revolutionaries in America and the fears that his friends, Whig and Tory alike, had for the way the Revolution might end, he found her an eager listener, anxious to seek information and canvas his opinion on these weighty matters. Her father John had always kept a watchful eye on matters of politics and ideas, and to tell the truth she had missed the conversations they had had when she was quite a young girl where he had found her to be a bright apt pupil, far more so than George. She knew how he had felt about the ideas of Burke and his sympathy for the colonists but assumed that these ideas would perhaps not be popular with Denham's privilege and class. She was surprised to be told that this was not necessarily the case. They both relaxed into a spirited discussion that seemed to chase away her anxieties, and as the meal progressed, she found she could smile and laugh at some of the comments he claimed to have heard put forward earlier that evening by prominent members of Brooks, often in their cups or more interested in what gambling was going on elsewhere in the club.

By the time the pudding had been placed before them, her awkwardness had vanished in the face of a lively tale involving one of England's most prominent peers, a wager of two thousand guineas and a case of mistaken identity at a masquerade.

'I also heard that *The Recruiting Officer* is soon to come to Drury Lane. Am to have the honour of seeing you in one of the female roles, Eliza?'

She tried to keep her voice neutral as she answered, 'No I regret to say. Mr Cavendish has not cast me in either of the main roles. In fact I am not to appear in this new production.'

He paused in the act of pouring wine into his goblet and looked quizzically at her.

'No? Well, the man's a bigger fool than I took him for then. You would do very well for Melinda. Did he give his reasons?'

'No, and he doesn't need to. I am not a leading lady. Sarah Newley will continue to get the best roles for as long as she shares his bed.'

'Ah, now. That reminds me of something I almost forgot,' he said, smiling playfully. 'Please ring, my dear, for the table to be cleared and if you are willing, I should like us to retire.'

Chapter 12

It was three weeks since Eliza had become mistress of Number 17 and she was slowly becoming accustomed to her new role which was more than could be said for her return as the player of breeches roles and little else. *The Recruiting Officer* had had only mixed success: the critics of the pit had been vitriolic in their appraisal of Sarah's performance as Melinda; "woefully leaden" and "totally lacking in spark" reported *The Gentleman's Magazine*. The play had been taken off and there was a hasty return to *Macbeth* and The *Relapse,* neither of which had parts for Eliza. There had been a noticeable drop in audiences over the past month and Richard Cavendish was short-tempered and preoccupied. One night, as Eliza dressed for her performance in the afterpiece *The Pretty Hoyden,* she was surprised to find that Susan had not yet arrived at the theatre. Her concern grew as time went on, and fifteen minutes before the curtain went up on the piece where Susan and she played their parts as two friends, Jemima and Kitty – Kitty had the singing role, which Susan carried off very sweetly and always had much appreciation from the audience – there was no sign of her.

Eliza went in search of Cavendish and found him in his office, his booted feet on the desk and a sheaf of papers in front of him.

'Eliza, what is it now? Can't you see that I am busy?'

'It's Susan, Mr Cavendish. She has not yet arrived. I am afraid …'

He sighed in irritation, reluctantly swung his feet down from the desk and, taking a swig from the glass in front of him, got up from his seat.

'She has become increasingly unreliable of late, your friend Susan,' he said, striding from the room with Eliza following him. 'She must mend her ways, we have no room for slackers here. Who will be able to stand in for her?' They were making their way briskly along the corridor to the ladies' dressing room and Eliza was hurrying to keep up.

'She must have good reason not to be here,' she said, trying to mollify him, all the time her mind working on what might have happened to her friend. Surely she would have been able to get a message to the stage door? Eliza could not bear to dwell on a possible occurrence that would make this impossible. In fear she put her hand on Cavendish's arm. 'Please don't be too harsh on her. Jenny will be able to stand in for her. She is still here. She has done the role before. You could omit the song.'

Cavendish shrugged off her imploring arm.

'I can't have members of the company who are unreliable. We are going through difficult times. The public don't seem to know what they want anymore.' He had come to a halt outside the dressing room and for the first time in minutes was looking at her properly. 'The Garden is outstripping us night after night. Even the Haymarket.'

'Perhaps you need another Richard Cavendish play.' She smiled at him uncertainly, seeing a fleeting spark of the clever playwright and the gifted director.

He frowned, his eyes darkening with what seemed like anger.

'I have as much opportunity and desire to write just now as our colonists have to pay taxes to His Majesty, Eliza. The creative process requires peace of mind, freedom from anxiety as well as inspiring ideas. I fear I shall never have any of those again.' He

114

turned to the door and, with a peremptory knock, pushed it open, shouting, 'Jenny! I need you to go on instead of Susan. No song. Get yourself dressed.'

Lord Denham was out of town for a few days looking over some bloodstock in Newmarket. Eliza had missed his presence in Number 17, particularly the occasions on which he stayed with her. Not only were there the pleasures of the bedroom, where, under his guidance, she was learning not just how to give but also how to receive her pleasures, but also the enjoyment of their tête-à-têtes over supper, his gossip about what was going on in the world, the sporting world in which he was much involved, and the social and political gossip shared with her. A new coffee house had opened, the Whigs were gaining support, the Devonshires had just left for Yorkshire. And Harries, the manager of Covent Garden, was on the lookout for a promising new female talent. That was the news he had given her the night before he set out for Newmarket.

'Perhaps,' she suggested to Flora who was trying very hard to learn how to be a lady's maid, 'I should consider a move in view of what Mr Cavendish had said recently.' There had been no word from Susan, so Eliza had determined to visit her in St Giles and see for herself what was amiss.

'No, Flora, not the silk. I am not going walking in Hyde Park. We are going to St Giles. The dark blue. I'm not trying to attract attention. And we do not want to stand out.'

'What if we ... we see *him*?' gulped Flora, memories of the brutality of her mother's lover returning with a rush of emotion that made her cheeks pale. 'Or Mother?'

'Then we will deal with it as best we can. Everything has moved fast for us since – since that night. We must soon make contact with her – whatever the outcome. She is still our mother and there is reason to fear for her safety. But for today, let Susan be our chief concern. No, no jewellery.'

'But Lord Denham's gift …'

'Flora, you know how interesting a woman wearing jewellery is to our former neighbours in St Giles. The dark pelisse and the blue bonnet. Just so,' she smiled in encouragement as her sister laid out the clothes.

'Will that be all, my lady?' laughed Flora, dropping a mock curtsy to her sister.

'Yes, and please let Mrs Jenkins know we shall be here for supper.'

They travelled by hackney until close by Palmers Yard where Susan lived, then alighted and walked the few teeming streets that were already thronged with people who jostled and pressed them as they walked. Susan's family lived in rooms on the ground floor of a run-down building whose hall stank of decaying vegetables and dogs. Eliza's hand was shaking as she knocked the door. Two grubby urchins sized up the sisters as they stood awaiting a response, then the smaller of the two volunteered, 'They're not in, none of 'em. Who are you? Chapel?'

'Mind your own business, you –' retorted Flora. Her sister shot her a warning glance. This was no way for a lady's maid to speak, even in St Giles.

'Thank you,' she added, smiling at the ragamuffins who then slunk off. As she and Flora turned to go, a voice from inside the room cried, 'Liza, is that you? Oh, Liza come in! The door is unlocked.'

Inside, Susan lay on a bed, one of the two makeshift ones the room contained. The room smelled of old cooking and the musky odour of too many people living there in unwashed clothes. By contrast, Flora and Eliza's old house in the same area had been a clean but shabby place –until, that is, her mother's liaison with John.

Moving closer to her friend, Eliza could see her face bruised. Susan smiled through a split lip.

'Yes, he knows, I could hide it no longer. I have until the end of today to get out.'

Eliza sat on the bed and pushed the tangle of dark hair off Susan's tear- stained face.

'So much for Christian forgiveness then, you said it would be so.' Flora was gazing at Susan with a mixture of horror and sympathy. Instinctively she touched her own cheek, which had healed, though the real wounds within still remained. The move to Somerset Street and the patronage of Eliza's lover had taken her away from real danger, but the violent world of St Giles was brought home forcibly once again by Susan's bruised face and sense of exhausted defeat. Eliza, however, took command of the situation by getting up from the bed and looking round the room for Susan's clothes. She had brought a roomy valise with her, hoping that this was indeed to be a rescue mission.

'Get up, Susan. You will come back to Somerset Street with us. We will take a hackney, so put into the valise what you wish to take. I am sure than in time your parents will feel differently towards you. In the meantime, you will be safe with us. Come on, stir yourself. You do not want to incur your father's wrath by being here

117

when he returns. Flora, help her up. I have a cloak with me that you can throw over what you are wearing now.'

'But Eliza, look at me! How will I face your staff? Mrs Jenkins?'

'Pull the hood far down.' Susan was now out of bed and searching for her shoes. 'Think you are one of those mysterious hooded and masked women who go to routs at The Pantheon and Vauxhall, eager to escape public notice. Perhaps Lady Heartfort herself heading towards an assignation.' Eliza's tone was cheerful, brusque even, trying to lift her friend's spirits and make light of this difficult situation. In truth she had no idea how Antony Denham would feel about her harbouring a pregnant battered actress, an outcast from her parents' home, but she could not see her friend brought this low and not attempt to ease her situation.

The bag had been packed with Susan's meagre possessions, the cloak covered her clothes and the hood disguised the worst of her injuries. Once outside, the three women made their way to the main thoroughfare and Eliza engaged a hackney carriage to take them to Somerset Street.

Dazed and bruised as she was, Susan could not help but admire and be amused by the authoritative tone that Eliza used with her housekeeper. Her chin was held high and her voice and tone could have truly belonged to a woman who had been giving orders since her infancy.

'Miss Turner will be staying with us for a short while, Mrs Jenkins. Please make up the green room for her stay. She will dine with us tonight.'

'Very well, madam.'

'Please see that there is hot water in her room immediately. She has been travelling and I know will want to refresh herself before dinner.'

Susan, entering into the spirit of the thing, drawled from the depths of her hooded cloak, 'Indeed, Eliza. Such dust and discomfort on the road! I declare I am quite shaken about. I should like to have my valise sent up right away.'

And she swept up the stairs as if she had just arrived from Bath instead of St Giles.

Chapter 13

Antony Denham was not wildly enamoured of having Eliza's friend to stay at Somerset Street, but he concealed that fact quite well from her under a cloak of gentlemanly courtesy. He need not see Susan or Flora too often as the house was large, the girls had their evenings at the theatre and Susan was not anxious to make her presence felt, slipping in and out of the house as discreetly as the staff, only she used the front door. Eliza's naïve gratitude for the help she was able to offer to both Flora and Susan gave him some pleasure and increased her dependence on him that was quite gratifying, especially as his visits to Yorkshire and the letters that came from there were of an extremely irritating nature. Marriage seemed to be the common theme, and this was not a subject he wished to address at that time. So Lord Denham dealt with this problem much as he had dealt with most of the problems in his young and privileged life; by ignoring them, going off to Brooks or to Epsom or riding in the park. He was having too much of a good time, able to make love to his pretty, bright and pliant young mistress whose gratitude to him knew no bounds and whom he was teaching the arts of the bedroom with great success and enjoyment. Little wonder then that he tried to ignore his mother's and his sister's letters that reminded him of the need to address the question of his future wife.

A month after Eliza had moved into Somerset Street, he had received a brusque missive form his mother who announced that she could be coming to town the next week and she would be expecting him to have settled the matter of his future.

My Dear Antony,

I received no reply to my letter of last week, which I consider to be most unmannerly and undutiful of you.

Miss Dursfield of Rotherham has been seen at many balls and routs around York this last fortnight and seems particularly fond of the company of Viscount Giles Naughton. Rumour has it that he is on the verge of making an offer, so I am reminding you once again of the need to return to us here as soon as you can and put yourself in her way once again as you did two months ago. I can no longer keep funding your London life as I have been. I understand the need to make a good impression on society in the capital, but your life surely belongs here back in Yorkshire with a wife who also lives here and who brings sufficient income for the wellbeing of your family.

Your sister is in accord with me on this subject, and we both urge you to think of your future as well as the future of your family in settling the matter of your engagement with all haste.

Your loving mother,

Harriet Denham

As if to underline the message of his mother's letter, Denham's tailor and his wine merchant had presented bills to him that very morning as he was drinking his hot chocolate and discussing with his valet the clothes he would be needing for the day. The amounts due on both these bills had made him wince and reminded him uncomfortably of how much he had just paid out to the establishment that had furnished Somerset Street. Recent losses at the tables had made a hole in his ready cash. There might be some sense in his mother's injunction to return to York where at least he would be able to escape his creditors for a while. He should probably offer for the Dursfield girl too. A long engagement would give him time and leave to return to London for a while and enjoy Eliza who might even be happy enough to continue as his mistress after a marriage; there were sufficient numbers of the quality who lived in such a way.

Selecting a pearly grey silk waistcoat instead of a red brocade one for his visit to the theatre later, he finished his chocolate and scribbled a hasty conciliatory note to his mother in which he promised to make a visit to Yorkshire within the next ten days. With a final flourish of his quill, he felt himself liberated to spend his time as he wished in the pursuit of his many pleasures, so he summoned Francis and told him to make sure the curricle was ready for a turn in the park. This is where he would see a number of his acquaintances with whom to exchange news and gossip, not to mention the opportunity of observing the ladies in their most fetching outfits and most flirtatious moods. Duty would loom large in his life soon enough; in the meanwhile, there was a life to be lived and appetites to be satisfied.

Chapter 14

'So Lord Denham is to leave for Yorkshire? You will miss him, I know.'

Susan gave her friend a sidelong glance as they both powdered in front of their mirrors before the performance of *Much Ado*. Once again, for Eliza it was as if her triumph as Lady Heartfort had never been and she was back to playing Margaret, Hero's friend, in *Much Ado*. Mr Cavendish seemed to overlook her entirely for parts of any size, a fact that Antony Denham had taken up with him just a week before in the green room.

The two men had faced up to each other after a performance of *The Soldier's Promise*, and Denham had made his point very clearly.

'Miss Grahame seems to have been overlooked in the casting of most of your recent productions, Cavendish. I feel that her talents are being seriously undervalued.'

'My lord, you are perhaps biased in the matter,' replied Cavendish, smiling slyly and causing Eliza to blush. 'Miss Grahame is an accomplished actress as you say, but at present I feel there is nothing exceptional about her work. She has been of late much preoccupied with changes in her personal life as I'm sure you are aware.'

Denham bridled at the implication and instinctively moved in closer to Cavendish.

'She is a professional, Cavendish, not a green girl from the chorus. You of all people must remember her amazing performance in your own debut play. With the right opportunities, she could rival Sarah Newley who, in fact, seems to be the only actress that your company affords any chances of late. But then,' he added, 'that is perhaps because *you* are biased.'

Fortunately for Eliza, Cavendish was approached at that moment by Sir Tobias Smedley who greeted him in his usual bluff and hearty way, taking him firmly by the elbow off into a corner, leaving Denham to fume and chafe at his failure to make any impact on Cavendish. With a trip to Yorkshire in the offing and very likely an engagement too, Denham was anxious to see his mistress succeed in her chosen profession, to return to the days of her popularity as Lady Heartfort where she had so quickly captivated the hearts of young men like himself. Then there had been some kudos in being her admirer, but lately, frankly, she had returned to relative obscurity and heads did not turn in the same way anymore. In the clubs of St James's, when he made an appearance, men no longer cast him envious glances as the protector of Miss Grahame. He could not help the worrying thought that perhaps he had been over-anxious to set her up as his mistress. True, she was very sweet and was an enthusiastic lover. She had none of the airs and graces that he often saw in the kept mistresses of friends, was quite frugal, never spending all the allowance he gave her for clothes. But she did have Flora and Susan established in the household too which was an extra expense. As he stood, glass in hand, watching her in conversation with Ned and the others in the company, laughing in the most natural and unaffected way, he felt a twinge of conscience as he entertained the thought that were she a more successful and popular actress, he would not need to "protect" her for much longer and that would make his marriage easier to manage, She came towards him and, placing a hand on his arm, smiled at him and said, laughing, 'My lord, you must settle a dispute we have been having here. Which of the royal princesses would you say has the sweetest disposition?'

Gladly abandoning his darker more selfish and mercenary thoughts, he took her arm and advanced upon the group.

It was with some relief that Antony Denham made his way to York a week later, despite the prospect of matrimony, family duties and a mother to whom little was secret. His townhouse in Hanover Square had become a favourite destination for tradesmen and duns whose importunities had disturbed his naturally sanguine temperament. Surely he had not spent quite so much money since coming to London? Was it possible that Somerset Street and its stylish furnishings had set him back so many hundreds?

The Great North Road where there was little prospect of being pursued by so many people lifted his spirits, though he thought with tenderness of his leave taking of Eliza the night before, of her tears and the warmth of her fond embraces. He would, of course, miss her, but how glorious would be the reunion in a few weeks' time.

That week, before his departure, he had made a point of calling at Covent Garden to see an excellent production of *All for Love*. The house was full, the audience appreciative and attentive and the curtain calls seemingly unending; Thomas Harries had invited him into his office for a glass of claret. Harries was in his forties, a thin intelligent man with a sharp nose and quick darting grey eyes that seemed to be able to assess people and situations shrewdly. Since his arrival, he had made some inspired decisions after taking over from Thomas Wilkes weeks before, purging the company of some of its lazier players, including a couple of men past their prime who had been coasting along. Harries's standards were stringent, but morale within the company was by all accounts much improved and the radical weeding out had caused the whole

125

company to raise its game. A season of new productions was under way, including *The London Merchant* that had received ecstatic reviews.

Refilling Denham's glass from the decanter on his desk, Harries offered him his snuffbox, which Denham declined.

'Much obliged, sir.' He sipped his wine and added, 'I thought that Mr Kemp was excellent tonight. He is a very impressive acquisition to the company. Popular with the audience too I see.'

'Yes indeed. I persuaded him over from the Smock Theatre in Dublin. I have plans for him – but I won't reveal those to you, my lord,' he smiled, inhaling the snuff fastidiously and wrinkling his nose. 'I know you too have interests in the theatre. I would not wish Richard Cavendish to steal my thunder.'

Denham let out an exasperated 'Cavendish!' which caused Harries to raise an eyebrow.

'Do you and Mr Cavendish not see eye to eye then? It seems to me that the young man is a better playwright than he is a manager and a businessman. I saw Miss Grahame as Lady Heartfort these six months since. I admired the play hugely and her performance in it. He has not achieved success since, I fear.' He snapped shut the silver snuff box and sipped his claret. 'I have not seen Miss Eliza appear much since then.'

'Which is because he does not cast her,' replied Denham testily, setting down his empty glass. 'She is used in the afterpieces and in the breeches roles. I fear she is the object of Sarah Newley's jealousy. She is Cavendish's mistress, of course.'

Harries nodded gravely: none of this was news to him; the gossip from the close world of London's theatres was often as dramatic as the plays that were staged nightly. Harries knew how

126

the land lay when love, politics and money became entangled with the theatre. It was then that intelligent men whose dispassionate nature allowed them to see more than those who involved themselves more emotionally had advantages: Harries was such a man, an observer, cool and appraising, focused on success, always on the lookout for fresh possibilities. He was already beginning to see such a possibility in the frustrated expression of Lord Denham who was clearly anxious to promote the career of his mistress.

'Miss Grahame might have greater opportunities here, my lord. I do not keep a mistress in my cast. I believe that can compromise artistic judgement,' Harries continued smoothly. 'She would be considered on merit alone.'

'Of which she has a considerable amount,' added Denham warmly, rising from his seat and picking up his hat. 'I am most grateful to you, Mr Harries. I shall convey your comments to Miss Grahame and suggest that she pay you a visit. She would, I'm sure, enjoy seeing *All for Love*. I am myself out of town for a while.'

'My lord,' Harries bowed, but not so low as to seem to be pandering to his aristocratic visitor. As Denham left the room, the manager was already considering the advantages to be derived from having pretty Eliza Grahame in his company, fully supported by her amorous sponsor, not to mention the discomfort of his rival, Richard Cavendish.

Chapter 15

Denham Hall was an imposing residence built in the Palladian style some sixty years previously by the highly successful Sir Tobias Denham who had found favour with Queen Anne and flourished accordingly. Its present owners, Antony Denham's parents, had not found such royal favour and, not having the unlimited capital of their predecessors, had been forced to stint on the upkeep of this very expensive house.

Sir Julius Denham, so close to death only six months previously, had rallied well and was to be seen in the locality riding, shooting and hunting much as before. He was a brusque but affectionate father, a little awkward with his son and daughter, almost as if they were children he didn't quite recognise, but as Antony strode into the drawing room to greet him, he clasped his son firmly round his well-tailored shoulders, pumping his hand warmly.

'Father! You look well, sir, far better than when I saw you last. I am delighted to see you look positively hearty.'

'Yes, yes,' cut in Lady Denham, seated beside the tea tray. 'He is much improved, and I am glad to see you here at last doing your duty. It has surely taken you long enough to come to see us.'

'Mother,' said a subdued Denham, stooping to kiss her cheek. 'I am here now as you see. And I am all duty as ever.' The smile he shot towards his mother did nothing to change her stony expression, so he took a seat opposite her and fondled the ears of his father's favourite springer spaniel. His mother handed him a cup of tea and, without any further preliminaries, launched into her plans.

'Your father and I are giving a supper party on Friday. The Dursfields are invited, of course. You must approach Clarissa then.'

She took a sip of her tea. Father and son exchanged sympathetic glances, recognising an edict that had to be obeyed.

'Just as you say, Mother.'

'And she is a pretty little thing,' added Sir Julius taking a seat by the fire. 'You could do far worse.'

'Of course, the money's trade,' continued Lady Denham, 'that I suppose is inevitable. Woollen mills or some such I believe. Her father will be generous, of that I have no doubt.'

'Wants the association with the title of course.' Sir Julius stretched his legs before the fire. The spaniel lifted its head and wagged its tail automatically then settled to doze comfortably once more. Antony set down his cup as bored acceptance washed over him. This was what had been bound to happen. He really had no choice. He needed to marry to ensure an income, a future position in society, the perpetuation of the title. His parents had all the appearance of wealthy aristocrats, but the carpet was faded, the bedrooms damp and the plasterwork cracking. Marriage was nothing to do with passion and all to do with necessity. Miss Dursfield was pretty enough, had a fine figure, was well-educated but certainly no blue stocking, which was all to the good. She had a pretty laugh, small white teeth and had listened to all his arguments against the Colonists attentively last time they met. She didn't make his heart race as it had done the first time he saw Eliza on stage at Drury Lane, nor had he longed to possess her, but they would suit well, and, thanks to her father's fortune, they could live in style and he need never fear the pursuit of his creditors. Anyway, if he could keep his London house, he could still retain some independence, if only until the children came along.

Bored acceptance turned into philosophical resignation. As his parents talked, Antony looked out of the long windows onto the neat gardens and the manicured topiary. The grand drive was flanked by elms planted fifty years ago. One day this estate would be his and then it would belong to his sons. Any son that might be the offspring of a viscount and an actress would not be able to carry off what was expected of him.

He got up and, smiling broadly at his parents, said, 'I must go and take a stroll before dinner. I have almost forgotten what this place looks like. And that will never do.'

Clarissa's mother Elizabeth was helping her daughter choose a dress for the supper party at Denham Hall. Three rejected dresses had been flung onto the bed already, and Elizabeth was eying up the fourth critically, a yellow brocade robe *al la francaise* worn only once before and not in the company of the Denhams.

'The colour enhances your hair, my love. Perhaps with the topaz set?' Clarissa looked uncertain.

'London, Mama, it was bought in London. Is it not a little too *a la mode* for York?'

'Perhaps, my dear. Everyone is so set in their ways here. It caused quite a stir at Almacks, did it not?' she said, laughing the affectedly brittle laugh that she had acquired after a short season in London and which embarrassed her daughter enormously. She was always trying to be the most fashionable, the most extravagant, the most talked about member of society. Elizabeth, the daughter of an obscure Yorkshire squire, had been overcompensating for her relatively humble roots for a couple of decades by flaunting her husband's considerable wealth and making herself and three daughters leading lights in the field of couture and taste. The fashions of Bond Street, the manners of St James and the pleasures of Vauxhall were all transplanted to Yorkshire, to Thorsby Manor to be exact, the fine country house that Elizabeth had persuaded her husband to buy with the wealth he had made from Yorkshire wool.

If Elizabeth had found a way to ape the fashions of London and try and bring sophistication to Yorkshire, she had failed miserably in gentrifying her husband Harry. His wardrobe might contain the finest Savile Row creations, his horses might be exercised in the gallops at York but he remained a bluff no-nonsense Yorkshire man through and through, impervious to his wife's attempts at making him one of the *ton*.

He did not respond to wifely instructions about how he should speak, eat or drink, and took great delight in lapsing into broad Yorkshire dialect, addressing her affectionately as 'lass' whenever he thought she was forgetting her roots. Therefore, social occasions they attended together became a source of anxiety to Elizabeth, especially when they brought her uncompromising husband into close contact with the upper echelons of the gentry. When her greatest aspiration was to marry her daughters, eldest first, naturally, as well as she possibly could, then this anxiety was such that she was finding it difficult to sleep at nights. As Clarissa wrinkled up her nose at the brocade, she exclaimed tetchily, 'Well, if not that, then which? I cannot imagine a dress that will show you off to greater advantage. There is no time for a new dress to be made, even if you were able to find a material you like.' Close to tears, she exclaimed, 'You really are a most troublesome child!'

'Mama, Mama!' Clarissa's voice was soothing and rational. 'I think this cream will do very well. See? It has been worn only once before.' She pulled it from the armoire and held it up before her, smiling and moving so that the fluid skirt and bodice caught the light. 'It is simple yet elegant, is it not?'

Elizabeth was mollified and returned her daughter's smile.

'Yes, my dear, you are right. Maybe the pearls with it. I am sure that Yorkshire has not witnessed such a gown. And even Antony Denham, straight from London, could not fail to appreciate it stylishness.' Satisfied that the thorny issue of Clarissa's clothes was settled, Elizabeth closed the bedroom door and took a seat at the dressing table, tidying a few stray strands of hair and giving a practised smile at the mirror.

'Come and sit by me here, my dear, and let us plan our strategy for Friday evening. Do not be too cool to him. A man likes a little encouragement.' She gave her daughter a telling smile. 'Come, Clarissa. There is much to be considered.'

Chapter 16

While Clarissa and her mother were plotting and scheming about how they would bring Lord Denham up to the mark, *The Heiress* with Eliza in the role of Lady Heartfort was announced by Cavendish at the morning rehearsal. All the loneliness and uncertainty caused by her lover's departure to Yorkshire evaporated for Eliza with the news that she would be centre stage again, giving form to the playwright's witty and tender dialogue. She recalled the words he had whispered to her as they took their curtain call together on the opening night of the play and the enigmatic way he had looked at her.

As he announced the cast, her face broke into a smile and Susan, who sat beside her, now heavy and slow in the later stages of her pregnancy, took her hand and squeezed it. Eliza's thoughts flitted to the absent Denham who had said he had first fallen in love with her when she played the role in York. How she longed to tell him the news! She would write, but perhaps that was unwise as she had received no word from him since his departure for Yorkshire. Several callers had asked to see him at Somerset Street having failed to find him at Hanover Square. There had been a couple of official documents delivered for which his urgent attention was required. Eliza knew that as an aristocrat there would be dozens of people seeking to make his acquaintance, looking for favours and preferment, and so was not unduly concerned at how his life seemed to be spilling into hers.

Her liaison with him has been gossiped about in the fashionable pages of *Town and Country Magazine* as well as the *London Magazine* in the usual thinly veiled way:

Lord A - D - of Yorkshire has become a patron of the arts, having taken on the protection of Miss E - G - who delighted us last year with her performance of Lady Heartfort in Richard Cavendish's play. It is to be hoped that under his lordship's patronage the lady's stage career will rise to great heights once more, once she abandons the breeches and minor roles in the afterpieces. Has R - C - forgotten her so soon?

The revival of the play clearly proved to Eliza that Richard Cavendish had not forgotten her, and she began to throw herself into rehearsals with great enthusiasm. They were to open in a week's time and Eliza waited anxiously for news from York, hoping her lover would be able to see her on the opening night. But soon she was forced to take notice of news of a more practical nature.

One morning Mrs Jenkins asked leave to speak to her, and Eliza, thinking it to be some query about the evening's meal, stopped in the hall to talk.

'No, no, madam. I mean, could I speak to you in private?' She nodded towards the dining room.

'Oh, yes, of course, Mrs Jenkins. In here perhaps?' Eliza opened the door and asked a very serious-looking housekeeper to take a seat.

'I will stand if you do not mind, madam,' she answered stiffly.

'Very well. As you wish.'

'This is a very delicate matter, madam, about which I would not normally concern you, but with his lordship being away ...'

'Yes, Yorkshire. I expect his return any day soon,' asserted Eliza, using her actress's talent to sound convincing.

'Yes, madam. It's just that I am having difficulty in buying in food for the household because... well, his lordship has not left sufficient funds.' A warm tide of embarrassment and disbelief swept over Eliza and she struggled to retain her equilibrium.

'But surely, Mrs Jenkins, Lord Denham's credit with the shops is good. It is, I know, possible to obtain goods on credit and ...'

Mrs Jenkins's mouth was set in a thin line and she shook her head.

'That is exactly what I have been doing, madam. We have not actually received any money, Mr Wilmot or myself, to pay household bills. It is all credit and now the suppliers, Tollands the wine merchant, say they will not supply us.'

'Then I will pay!' exclaimed Eliza, getting up from her chair. 'His lordship will reimburse me when he returns. He has had much on his mind of late. His estates in Yorkshire need his attention. It is clearly an oversight. How much do we need?'

When she heard the figure, Eliza blenched. She had nowhere near that sum of money herself, even though she had been saving her wages and her allowance from Antony.

She went up to her room and took out a purse containing twenty guineas from a drawer and gave it to Mrs Jenkins, asking her to present it as part payment towards the debt so that they could at least eat until the situation was resolved and Antony back in London.

'And Mrs Jenkins,' she said, pressing the purse into the housekeeper's hand, 'please do not hesitate to economise on provisions while his lordship is out of London. My sister, Miss Turner and I have simple tastes. We are happy with basic

135

wholesome food. As long as it's cooked as beautifully as you always cook it for us, we count ourselves well pleased.' And she shot Mrs Jenkins one of her luminous smiles, causing perceptible softening of the housekeeper's iron features. Later that day Mrs Jenkins would pass on that compliment from Eliza to the rather superior housekeeper at Number 16 Somerset Street who had scathingly dismissed Eliza's household as 'a troupe of painted harlots who were no better than they should be.'

Chapter 17

Harriet Denham had briefed her son thoroughly in preparation for Friday's supper party. He was to ensure that after the meal he buttonholed Harry Dursfield, perhaps suggesting that they smoke a cigar while taking a look at the new ornamental bridge that had been erected in the gardens. Then Antony was to ask for Clarissa's hand, laying emphasis on his own unworthiness but the depth of passion he felt for the lady. It was then to be hoped that Mr Dursfield would shake him firmly by the hand, mentioning the sum that he was to settle on his eldest daughter. Antony would indicate modestly that he would not be averse to a long engagement and the deal would be struck. No, Lady Denham declared firmly, there was absolutely no question that the lady would be reluctant. Far from it. Rumour had it that she was highly enamoured of Antony ('Perhaps that does not speak very highly of her common sense,' commented his mother), and her parents were even more besotted by his title and his home. Even the stories that had filtered through about his life in London had added a certain sheen to his reputation, especially with the daughters.

'She has enough of the silly romantic girl about her still,' declared Lady Denham, working at her embroidery quite savagely the afternoon before the supper party. 'But still, she will have taken advice from that mother of hers and know when she is offered a good thing. She will do well for you, my boy. It's is up to you to manage all aspects of your life accordingly once you are married,' she said, shooting him a significant glance as she neatly snipped off some blue silk and began to rethread her needle. 'As long as you are discreet, all will be well.'

Anthony felt his colour rising in the face of his mother's worldly advice, then found himself wondering whether his own father had been managing all aspects of his life ever since marrying her. He thought back to the long absences from home, the seasons in London, his mother's circle of friends who had little in common with his father. Such things after all were the way of their world.

The supper party was, as Harriet Denham's social occasions always were, a huge success. The guests had been chosen to blend well together into a harmonious small group with sufficient in common, such as background, income, interests, yet sufficient difference to make conversation among themselves piquant and lively. Even Harry Dursfeld's earthy Yorkshireness found an echo in a textile entrepreneur from Halifax with an interest in road building and waterways. The food had been carefully selected; game in season, shellfish, ice cream creations and a range of complementary wines from the Hall's much-depleted cellars.

Clarissa, who had been placed on Antony's right, was an attentive listener, though she had little to venture in the way of her own opinions. She did surprise him, however, at one point during dessert just as he was readying himself to detach her father from the rest of the men who would inevitably be left to drink port once the ladies had withdrawn.

'I hear that you are a lover of the theatre, Lord Denham,' she said, casting him a look that made his cheeks flush.

'I beg your pardon?'

'It must be wonderful to see the new productions at Covent Garden and Drury Lane. I love to go when we are up in London. Last month we were able to see *Twelfth Night* here in York which was very exciting. I do so like Shakespeare's comedies. Do tell me which new writers and plays are to be seen in London at present.'

She was gazing at him with her clear blue eyes, her face so open and without guile that he hastily concluded her question could not have been a trap to elicit a response. He made some bland comment and the moment passed. But it made him think of Eliza amid the rumpled sheets, her hair spread out on the pillow, her mouth an open invitation to desire. How could he possibly give her up? Reaching for his wine glass he gulped its contents greedily in order to erase the image and to focus on the task ahead.

Chapter 18

By the opening night of *The Heiress*, there had been only one hastily scrawled note from Antony Denham sent to the stage door and seized upon hungrily by Eliza.

My Dear Eliza,

Concerns over the estate and my father's poor health weigh heavily on me at present. Life seems to be a never-ending round of meetings, decisions and problems, and I long to return to your loving embrace.

Do not forget your Antony, absent though he may be. You are constantly in my thoughts, and I regret not be able to return to London for several weeks.

Until then, my love, be brave and if you have the opportunity, go and see Mr Harries at The Garden where I am sure he will give you a great welcome.

Yours ever,

Antony

She smiled sadly at the letter, wondering whether she should send a reply to cheer him in his present troubles. He had not heard of her return as Lady Heartfort, but such concerns would pale into insignificance in the face of an ailing father and the onerous duties of the estate. There would be little time for such trivial concerns. Tonight she must give all her attention to the play and prove herself yet again worthy of her role in it and do justice to its creator.

Cavendish had seemed reinvigorated by the recent rehearsals and shown much of the original spirit and *elan* with which he had originally impressed. Sarah Newley had been little in the theatre over the past week. She had no part in this play and had stayed away from all associations with it. Cavendish seemed to be liberated by her absence and on opening night he had rushed through the theatre's narrow twisting passages shouting last minute instructions and words of encouragement, sharing noisy jests with carpenters and stagehands and eventually putting his head round the door of the ladies' changing room where a jug of gin was hastily concealed by a shawl.

'Eliza? Where is Eliza?' he shouted above the din of crying babies and raucous laughter.

'In the privy! She is very anxious!' shouted Sukey.

'And who can blame her?' added Susan, powdering her cheeks. 'This is her first proper part in months,' she added pointedly.

'Ladies! The house is a sell-out. We take no prisoners! Good luck to you all. And tell Eliza too,' he shouted leaving.

'He's a lot nicer when Lady Sarah's not around, isn't he?' mused Sukey, retrieving the gin and pouring a cupful. 'She's no good for him that one. I don't wonder that he doesn't break off with her.'

'No one breaks off with Sarah Newley, Sukey. Haven't you learned anything? He'll be wise never to try,' commented Susan, getting up slowly from the stool. 'God's bones, I swear this baby won't be able to wait much longer. Perhaps this will be the night.' She rubbed her swollen belly. Sukey drank deeply from her gin and adjusted her wig.

'Wait until Act 3, there's a love. We need you in it for the ball.'

'And I'll need the money too,' grimaced Susan. 'Can't be off the stage for too long. Can't expect Eliza to …'

She stopped suddenly as a rather pale Eliza entered the room.

'Come here, whey face. Let's get some colour in those cheeks of yours. I'm sure even Lady Heartfort had to resort to rouge. Mr Cavendish says it's a full house and wishes you good luck.'

Susan was fussing over her friend, adjusting her hair, straightening the flounce of her dress, then planted a light kiss on her cheek. 'I have informed the infant that it is not to be born until after Act 3.'

The curtain went up to a roar of anticipation and expectation from the capacity audience. Those expecting to come into the play halfway through would be sorely disappointed tonight. There was an air of excitement and wonder at the magnificence of the set from those who had never seen the play. Eliza glanced at the boxes. All full. How different from previous weeks – months even. It was in one of those boxes that Antony Denham had sat gazing at her fixedly all those months ago. How her life had changed. Despite herself, she glanced at the occupants of the boxes, hoping that by some miracle he had managed to return to town in time and surprise her. A sweep of her fan brought her into the dialogue that was pouring forth so wittily from the mouths of the others on stage. There was a gratifying burst of applause from the pit at her first witty sally and that encouraged her to smile at Ned and scowl at Mr Jacobs. She felt a surge of joy. Here she was in control, able to do anything. The feeling was like a draught of the finest wine, intoxicating and heady. Anthony Denham's absence, her concern over money, her anxiety over the birth of Susan's baby, were dissipated in the powerful surge of the moment where the laughter, the smell of candle wax, the audible comments from the pit all combined to make her feel that she was truly in her element, more truly herself here than anywhere, more herself when she was being someone else. With a seductive flutter of her eyelashes, she delivered one of Cavendish's cutting lines to her would-be wooer. The spark was kindled, the scene took light and the audience loved it. At the drop of the curtain the audience were on their feet, flowers were thrown on stage and Eliza blew kisses to gallery and boxes alike.

Her heart racing from the euphoria of it all, Eliza sat in the dressing room unable to remove her dress because her hands were shaking uncontrollably. The women not involved in the afterpiece had melted away and those who had parts to play had gone off to wait in the wings. A knock on the door startled her out of her reverie.

'Come in!'

'Where is everyone?'

'In the wings I expect. I'm not involved.'

'No, no, I know.' Cavendish sat on a stool at the dressing mirror and gazed at her reflection without any further words. Her cheeks were flushed, her eyes sparkling, her face incandescent with joy. Awkwardly, she began to remove the fake emeralds from her neck and to tug at the powdered wig.

'I thought you deserved some respite after doing this.' He gestured vaguely towards the seated figure of his creation, Lady Heartfort.

'They loved it, did they not?' she turned towards him and smiled happily.

'Yes, it would seem they did.' His voice sounded deflated, though he forced an unconvincing smile.

Looking down at his hands as she continued dismantling her stage persona, he continued, 'You were even better, you know Eliza, than when we did it first. There we subtleties.' He broke off, trying to pinpoint a moment, a nuance. 'That line with Mr Jacobs in Act 3.'

"I presume you would not have me thrown into the Fleet for the price of a snuff box." She delivered the line in character and he laughed.

'Exactly. The intonation was so perfect. You got the laugh.'

'You wrote the line,' she reminded him.

'Even though the line itself is not funny.'

She smiled, acknowledging the compliment.

There was a silence. They could both hear the orchestra playing the overture for the afterpiece then a burst of laughter.

'You have learned so much Eliza.'

'Even if lately I have had little more to do than show the audience the shape of my calf or sing a pretty song,' she shot back at him but there was no bitterness in her tone.

He had the good grace to look sheepish. 'I know, I'm sorry. And I promise I shall never undervalue you again. In fact, I want you to take the lead in *The Beaux Stratagem*.'

'Melinda?'

'Yes.'

'But that is Miss Newley's part.'

'It did not suit her. I want you to learn the part. It is a fine play and you will carry it off to perfection. And judging from tonight *The Heiress* will run for perhaps another two weeks.'

He got to his feet, seeming to have regained much of his composure and humour in talking about his plans, plans that now featured her.

'I did not see Lord Denham in his usual box tonight, Eliza,' he said in a neutral tone.

'He is not in town. He is in Yorkshire,' she replied with a lightness she did not feel.

'I hope he returns before *The Heiress* has finished its run,' he said, his hand on the door knob.

Eliza had laid the powdered wig aside and was now loosening her own hair, shaking it out into untidy ringlets as she wiped away at the powder on her face.

'I expect his return any day now,' she lied for the second time that week. 'He has much there that commands his attention.'

'I understand that Susan is lodging with you in Somerset Street. Lord Denham is very generous to the friends of his protégée,' he said, smiling at her in a way that made her colour rise. However, she quickly regained her composure.

'Yes, I am fortunate that he has my interests, as well as those of my friends, at heart. Why, only just before his departure to Yorkshire he told me of the interesting discussion he had had with Mr Harries at the Garden.' Eliza had never intended to tell Cavendish of this but his sneering reference to Antony had made her smart, and before she knew it she was continuing. 'He is coming to see me as Lady Heartfort with a view to asking me to join his company.' She had pinned up her hair and turned around on her stool to face Cavendish. If she had stuck a rapier through his heart she could scarcely have made a deadlier impact on the playwright. She almost felt sorry for her treachery when she saw the anguish on his face. He strode over from the door and stood over her, his hands in her shoulders. 'No, Eliza, you do not mean it!' She shrugged off his grasp and got to her feet.

'You must excuse me, Mr Cavendish. I am planning to leave now. Susan has already left, and I do not want her to be alone at home in her present condition. I am sure you understand.' His hand fell uselessly at his side and he looked embarrassed.

'Of course. I'm sorry, Eliza. But please promise me you will not make any rash decisions. We ... I ... need you here. I have promised you better roles and more money. I have been foolish in ignoring your talent, but I did not always act with complete freedom. It is no matter. It will not happen again.'

'I shall make my own decisions after I have spoken to Mr Harries.' She smiled with a veneer of sweet composure she was far from feeling. 'Now I really must go.'

'Of course. Please do not forget what we have accomplished here tonight. There is something akin to magic in it,' he added softly, then turned abruptly and left the room.

Chapter 19

Predictably, Mr Dursfield had given his permission for Antony Denham to marry his eldest daughter without hesitation – or rather with only as much hesitation as was required to puff on one of Lord Denham's fine cigars and get it going nicely. On the pretext of showing the wool magnate the new ornamental bridge over the lake, Antony had escorted him there and, succinctly for a man supposedly besotted with his daughter, asked for her hand in marriage.

Stopping to light the cigar, a far from easy feat in the freshening evening breeze swaying the ornamental grasses surrounding the lake, the wool magnate placed a meaty hand on Antony's finest merino-clad shoulder and wheezed, 'If tha' love the lass, tha' can have her. But only, mind you, milord, if she has a fancy for thee.'

Antony did his best to assure his prospective father-in-law without sounding arrogant that, indeed, the lady did most certainly return his affections.

'Then the pair of you should suit well,' concluded Dursfield, clasping Denham to him in a bear-like embrace in which the cigar almost came to grief.

Denham was embarrassed by this spontaneous response to his offer, and not a little ashamed. He noticed Dursfield's eyes were suspiciously moist as he continued, 'You'll take care of my lass. I love them girls more than my life. And I want them to be happy. There'll be no straying from the straight and narrow.'

A sudden image of Eliza in the bedroom at Number 17 made Denham feel a momentary pang of premature guilt that he fought down, and with mutual assurances of goodwill and happiness, the two men strolled back to the house.

In the wake of the first performance of *The Heiress*, Eliza once again enjoyed the recognition she had received all those months before. Flowers arrived at the theatre, there were invitations to suppers, routs and receptions; several notes expressed the admiration and love of the writers but then degenerated into detailed and graphic accounts of how that love would be expressed were she to grant a private audience.

Eliza tossed one of these into the fire as she sat sipping chocolate with Susan and Flora. Screwing up her face in disgust at what she had read, she pulled her dressing gown closer to her as if to keep predatory hands away from her body.

'It seems as once they know I am the mistress of one man, they consider me as not worthy to be treated with any respect,' she said, idly playing with the sash of her dressing gown.

'You should have kept it to show Lord Denham.' suggested Flora, who was drinking in the drama of her sister's success, the callers, the notes, the bouquets. 'He is, after all, your protector.'

'Although he cannot protect you very effectively from Yorkshire,' added Susan quietly. 'Still no news?'

Eliza shook her head. 'It cannot be long now. He is much occupied with family matters.'

Susan and Flora exchanged a glance but said nothing. Eliza sipped her chocolate and picked up a sheet of cream parchment from the table.

'An evening at Vauxhall,' she said in a defiantly bright voice, 'that might be very agreeable, don't you think? Lady Somers invites us for next Friday.'

A week after the *The Heiress* had begun its run, the enthusiasm for the production was unabated. Every performance was a sell-out. The magazines had reviewed it in glowing terms, the print shops had rescued their unsold prints of Eliza as Lady Heartfort, and the King and Queen had seen it, sitting in the royal box, with two of the princes, mingling with the cast in the green room afterwards. Their majesties had been profuse in their compliments and King George, taking Eliza's hand and raising it to his lips said in his clipped Teutonic style, 'If the aristocracy of our country were populated by ladies as delightful as your Lady Heartfort, the dear Queen might have cause for concern.'

Polite laughter greeted this remark as it was universally known that their majesties enjoyed a most harmonious and loving relationship, and the King was as likely to start a war with Germany as he was to take a mistress.

But by far the most significant moment of the week for Eliza had been when Susan whispered to her in the wings before the final act,

'Eliza, it's Mr Harries – in the pit. See, the green coat, with the lady in black. Go on, show him what the Garden is missing.'

It was no surprise to her that at the end of the performance Richard Cavendish took her aside after the curtain calls.

'Mr Harries has asked to see you.' His expression gave nothing away. Since their conversation he had not put himself in her way. The cast had been rehearsing a new afterpiece in which she was not required to play the breeches role, and she had only a small piece in *A Trip to Scarborough* where she played Amanda. He treated her with a distant professionalism, not seeking her out nor attempting to ingratiate himself with her.

'If you wish, you could make use of my office to speak to Mr Harries – unless he plans to take you to supper.'

'No, no, your office will be more suitable,' she said quickly. 'Thank you,' trying a small noncommittal smile to which he did not respond.

'I shall tell him. Ten minutes for you to change?'

As she entered Cavendish's office, Harries rose from his chair to greet her, took both her hands and shook them warmly.

'My dear Miss Grahame. That was a sterling performance out there. May I congratulate you? I feel you are perfectly suited to the role – and every bit as lovely as your stage persona, if I may say so.'

Blushing prettily, Eliza thanked him and sat down in the chair opposite.

He began pouring wine from the jug on the table into two glasses.

'Cavendish has most thoughtfully provided us with a libation to help us through our talk. May I offer you a glass?'

She wondered at Cavendish's obligingness in the light of their recent talk. Why would he make it so easy to meet his rival and smooth the way for her to accept an offer? The man was an enigma, a mass of contradictions; from his initial rudeness and the damage to her gown to his heartfelt plea of "Don't leave us, Eliza."

She drank the wine which seemed to go to her head, despite the early supper that Mrs Jenkins had provided for her. They spoke of theatre gossip; the Garden's imminent refurbishment, the new lighting that would illuminate the stage with lime lights, the huge success of Mr Forbes's very impressive Hamlet, 'which you might have witnessed last week,' said Harries, smiling smugly and taking out his snuff box.

Eliza felt foolish as she had not been to see this new star, though the talk was of little else.

'I am afraid that my duties here ...' She let the sentence hang. 'What brings you here to speak with me tonight, sir? No more wine, thank you.'

He set the jug on the table, picked a speck of fluff from the sleeve of his coat and, clearing his throat, began.

'I want you to come to Covent Garden, Miss Grahame. I wish it more than anything. I have fine actresses, beautiful actresses, competent actresses – else, why would we sell out most nights?' He smiled wolfishly at her, opening the snuffbox with a delicacy unusual in a man with such large hands. She was about to speak but a glance silenced her. 'I want, Miss Grahame, to put on plays in which there are parts that you will play to perfection, *The Way of the World, All for Love*. We have an extraordinary number of visits from their Majesties, far more than you here at Drury Lane. The princes are growing up, developing their own tastes. Their patronage is assured in the future. Mr Cavendish to whom you are naturally and quite rightly loyal,' he continued, noting the mutinous tilt of Eliza's chin as he outlined the glorious future of Covent Garden. 'Mr Cavendish is a talented even inspired playwright, but –' he said, snapping shut his snuff box, 'he is not an actor and, may I suggest, also not a businessman. I have been both, Miss Grahame, and I can take Covent Garden to the pinnacle of theatrical achievement. And I want you to benefit from that, Miss Grahame – Eliza. May I call you Eliza? I will pay you five guineas a week and let you organise your free time to suit your – personal life. And I guarantee no breeches roles. Naturally you would have your own dressing room.'

The offer was all that any actress in England could ever hope for. She should have smiled beatifically, clasped his hand and thanked him with every fibre of her being. He was offering her more than twice her current salary, a range of exciting roles. But all she could do was to smile pleasantly and say in a neutral tone, 'I thank you for your generous offer, sir. I am flattered by your words and your faith in me. But I must think carefully before taking such a radical step and beg you will give me time for reflection.'

She had risen now from her seat and extended her hand to Harries who took it with a slight raising of the eyebrows.

'Of course, Miss Grahame. I understand. I shall contact you within the week and hope fervently that you will accept my offer.' She bowed her head slightly and swept past him out of the office, her heart pounding and her mind in turmoil.

With still no news from Yorkshire and further appeals to her purse from an embarrassed Mrs Jenkins, Eliza turned to Susan for advice the very next day as they sat over a late Sunday breakfast, just two days after the supper party in Yorkshire where Antony Denham had become engaged,

Free of all theatrical responsibilities, they lingered over breakfast, both in their dressing gowns, Susan's straining over her belly, slippers on their feet. The table was spread with cheese and ham, bread and muffins but while Susan ate heartily, Eliza ate only toast and drank coffee.

'Have that last muffin, Susan,' offered Eliza, holding out the plate. 'Flora had her breakfast earlier, Mrs Jenkins tells me, and I shall not eat it. I wonder where she went. She seems fond of going off on these mysterious errands of late.'

Susan reached for the solitary muffin and licked the melted butter from her fingers.

'Where do you think she is gone? Do you suspect a tryst? Are you worried about her?'

Eliza shook her head, having given the matter a few seconds thought.

'No, I see no signs of a romantic involvement. I think she goes to St Giles and I see no harm in that. She still has friends from that time – before our flight. She will tell me when she is ready. This move may have been better for all of us in some ways, but she must feel isolated. Though she is like a lady's maid to me, she is not actually one so cannot mix with the other servants who live hereabouts.'

'She is, in effect, the mistress's sister,' observed Susan sipping her coffee, 'and as such is neither fish nor flesh.'

'Mm. We must give her position here some thought, and our future here in general,' she began tentatively, aware of the look of concern on Susan's face. 'I need – we need – to consider the future, especially as my lord, it seems, has neglected us.'

Susan eyed her friend with anxiety. 'Are you thinking that your... position here is in some jeopardy? That perhaps Lord Denham is tired of you?'

'What other conclusion can I reach? I know he has weighty family matters in hand, but to receive no word makes me concerned. And then there is the question of money.'

Eliza's loyalty to her lover had caused her to keep back from her friend information about the lack of funds, but now she could not shoulder the burden of this any longer, so she explained matters briefly to her. What Susan heard made her sit up in her chair and frown lines to appear on her usually placid face. Once Eliza had finished, there was a silence during which the clock chimed the hour and each woman experienced feelings of vulnerability and fear. Suddenly the world of St Giles seemed very close at hand once again.

'But I must focus my thoughts on my career,' said Eliza in a deliberately bright and cheerful way. 'I never wished to become a kept woman, an ornament, a thing, I am grateful for his protection, for this house, for his affection (Susan noted she did not use the word *love*), 'but I am an actress in my own right, as are you. I want to be among the greats one day like Kitty Clive, Ann Bracegirdle.'

'Sarah Newley?' inquired Susan mischievously and had the satisfaction of seeing her friend splutter into her coffee cup.

'Heavens, Susan. I would never want my position in the company to be dependent on bedding the manager. And I did use the word "great," you note.'

Both women smiled at the gibe then Susan became serious.

'If you leave to go to the Garden, there will be more money, guaranteed, leading roles. You would leave behind the jealousy of Sarah Newley and the uncertainty of Drury Lane's fortunes. Mr Cavendish's luck has not always been of the best, has it?'

'No,' Eliza sighed. Why could she not simply agree terms with Harries and grasp the opportunity? The fleeting image of Cavendish on stage receiving the applause at the end of the first ever performance of *The Heiress* came into her head, together with his enigmatic words, "Whatever happens, Eliza, remember ...." Was it

154

perverse to feel that to leave him would make her life somehow poorer?

'I shall think further on it,' she said with a note of finality, and picked up the bell to ring for Mrs Jenkins.

'I think perhaps a stroll in the park would be in order for us. We do not need the carriage, do we? We …'

There was a discreet tap on the door and Jessie the maid entered, a note in her hand.

'Madam, for you.'

Eliza seized the note and tore open the seal.

'Thank you.'

'Lord Denham?'

'Yes indeed.' Eliza's eyes were greedily scanning the hasty scrawl. 'Yes, it is from him. He has missed me greatly and will be back in London on Tuesday.' Her face had broken out into a relieved and forgiving smile.

'So you love him then?' prompted Susan, shifting in her chair and stretching her feet before the fire. 'He has left you poorly provided for, with no news of his plans, has not come to see your triumph on the stage, but you are excited at his return. I can only deduce that you love him. Is that not so?'

Eliza could not answer at first for she honestly did not know if her feelings for Antony Denham were love. She knew the desire he aroused in her when they lay together, the pride she felt when she appeared in public with him when he dealt so smoothly and easily with everyone he encountered, from ostlers to marquises. She loved the house in Somerset Street, its gracious rooms, its elegant comfort, she loved being waited on and deferred to, the clothes that had started to fill up the wardrobes. And to be quite honest, she loved the feeling that Susan and Flora were safe with her, safe because of her. If Antony Denham had caused all that to happen, then she must love him. So she smiled brightly at Susan and rose from her seat saying, 'Of course I love him.'

Two days later a lavish bouquet of hothouse blooms was delivered to Somerset Street. It was accompanied by an effusive loving note from the sender who promised to be at the theatre that night for her appearance in *The Heiress*. Eliza was conscious that the next day she had to give Mr Harries his answer and knew that, once she spoke to Antony, his advice would be to seize on Harries's offer and to give up Drury Lane as soon as her contract permitted. But still, as she gazed at the soft petals of the pink roses and drank in the heady scent of the lilies, she felt ill at ease. Hadn't Cavendish promised her better roles? Should she not put her trust in him as he had in her? And there was that promise that Sarah Newley would not monopolise all the best parts.

The day passed slowly for Eliza. There was only one caller, to whom she declared herself "not at home," a pushy young actress from the Haymarket who had been trying to ingratiate herself with Eliza in the hope of recommendations. She and Susan had ridden in the park where some members of the *ton*, Lady Harrington and Sir Digby Carruthers, had openly acknowledged them and some theatregoers engaged them in conversation about the current productions, going off into effusive praise for Richard Cavendish and his skills as a playwright and manager. None of this helped Eliza overcome her feelings of dread and trepidation about the decision she would soon have to make.

Chapter 20

After a sleepless night, Eliza woke thick-headed and low in spirits. She snapped at Flora who was dressing her after they had eaten breakfast.

'Not the grey fichu, silly girl, it does not match the dress at all. What are you thinking? The pink one. I always wear the pink one.'

Sitting before her looking glass, Eliza observed the mutinous jut of Flora's lower lip, the icy look in her sister's eyes and felt guilty at the outburst of which Lady Heartfort would have been proud. She hated the idea that she could become as superficial and self-absorbed as ladies of the *ton*. Relenting, she smiled at Flora, saying, 'I am a little nervous about tonight, Flora. Lord Denham will be in the audience for the last performance of *The Heiress*. I'm sorry to be sharp with you.'

Immediately Flora's features relaxed and she nodded her head, holding up the pink fichu for her sister's approval.

'I understand, Eliza, I think I do anyway. You have many responsibilities. I'm sorry to be a featherbrain at times. Lord Denham will be delighted to see you looking so well, though,' gazing at the reflection of her sister in the glass, 'a little more rouge will enliven your complexion I think.'

As she applied colour to Eliza's cheeks, she asked, 'Have you seen Susan this morning? Did she have breakfast earlier? Is she due at the theatre early?'

With a start Eliza realised she had not seen her friend that morning and hurried upstairs where she found Susan in her room lying in bed looking woebegone, her dark curls slick with perspiration on her forehead. She struggled to sit up and force a smile, but Eliza could see the effort required.

'I do not feel well, Eliza. Please tell Mr Cavendish. I'm sorry but they can easily do without me.'

Eliza smoothed the sheet and pushed back her friend's hair from her pale and sweating face.

'Are you having pains? Is the baby starting? Should we send for the midwife?'

'Too soon, I think.' Susan sank back on the pillows. 'I feel nauseous, lacking in any strength. I can't imagine where I shall find the energy required to deliver a child.' She laughed shakily but her fears were very apparent.

Bending over to kiss her friend's forehead, Eliza said, 'Be sure to ask for anything you need. I shall tell Mrs Jenkins to call in on you and Flora will be here as well. I must leave shortly for the theatre. I'm sure that soon you feel well enough to be bossing us around as usual.'

Susan gave her a wan smile in return and had closed her eyes before Eliza had left the room.

A queue was forming outside Drury Lane Theatre as it had for the past ten nights. When Eliza alighted from the hackney that had taken her there, a ragged cheer went up and she smiled shyly in acknowledgement before slipping through the stage door along the twisting low-ceilinged corridor until she came to Richard Cavendish's office. Her knock produced no response, so she knocked again then pushed open the door to see him sitting at his desk, writing with total concentration, lost to her presence. His desk was covered in sheets of paper scrawled over in his bold and impatient handwriting. Some sheets had escaped onto the floor and as she approached the desk, Eliza collected them up. His first glance betrayed his impatience at the interruption, but his look softened as she held out the wayward papers.

'You are writing … I mean really writing again?' she said with genuine delight as she smiled at him. 'A new play?'

'Yes, Eliza. You see me in the throes of creation,' he replied with irony, looking down at his untidy appearance, unbuttoned coat, grubby shirt escaping from his breeches. He grimaced at his ink-stained fingers and threw down his pen, stretching back in his chair, arms akimbo, hair escaping from a loose ribbon at the neck. 'I seem to forget all else. Sit down.'

'I don't have time, sir. I come to tell you that Susan is unwell and cannot appear tonight.'

He pursed his lips. 'Is she in labour?'

'No, not yet. But she is quite poorly and cannot leave her bed. She must conserve her energy for the birth I think.'

'Well, it is a small matter to cut her part in Act 3. It will not be noticed. Inform the others please, Eliza. And please tell me Eliza,' he said, rising from his chair and stretching his limbs lazily, 'please tell me you have given no more thought to Mr Harries from the Garden.' He looked down at the desk between them littered with the pages of his play. 'Eliza, this is a play in which you will triumph. I am writing it with no one but you in mind,' he added with an intensity that caused Eliza's colour to fly to her cheeks and her heart to hammer in her chest. Shaking her head in bewilderment, she struggled to speak.

'Please, please, I beg of you, do not give me anything else to think about – tonight of all nights. I cannot bear it.' She broke off and turned to the door, fumbling with the knob in her haste. Denham, Susan, Cavendish, even Flora, they were all relying on her to do what was right for them, to make them happy. How could she know what was best for her and would make her happy?

As soon as Lady Heartfort swept on stage in Act 1, she saw her lover lounging in his favourite stage-side box. One glance from her took in his grey velvet coat, his hair arranged so carefully to look so artlessly casual, and the sparkle of diamonds from his cravat pin and buttons. He was not alone. Two young bucks shared his box, along with a young woman in her twenties, dressed expensively, and sitting closely with one of Denham's companions whose arm she kept touching in an intimate gesture.

Eliza noted how Denham's smile widened at her opening lines and how he visibly sat up more attentively to give her his full attention. The woman in his right raised her quizzing glass and passed a comment to her companion.

The house was packed, the atmosphere febrile and unpredictable. The audience laughed at things they had never considered amusing before and were silent when they were normally expected to laugh. In Act 1 Ned needed prompting twice, then fluffed his line. The audience in the gallery drummed their feet and hooted in derision. Mr Jacobs's supreme professionalism held it all together, but by the time the interval came, Eliza had the feeling that she was on a runaway horse that was taking her into dangerous territory. She desperately wanted to feel the reins firmly in her hands again and exert some control.

As Eliza was powdering her face at the interval in an attempt to lessen the glow, Flora burst into the dressing room, her face tense, her eyes wild.

'Eliza, it's Susan. She is in labour and in such distress.'

The older women looked at one another knowingly, remembering their experiences of childbirth.

'The midwife says the child is the wrong way up.'

Nell nodded in sympathy. 'My second was a breech birth.' Someone else nodded sadly, remembering a similar unsuccessful delivery. Eliza gulped and tried to sound strong and purposeful.

'The midwife will do whatever is best for Susan. Go back there now. I shall come as quickly as I can when the play is over. Her friends can do nothing for her here, but tell her to be strong. Now go back quickly. She will want you there.'

The bell had rung for the end of the interval and there was a flurry of activity in the dressing room as costumes were adjusted and hair smoothed. As the curtain was raised for Act 3, Eliza's cheeks were burning and her breathing difficult to master. The audience were rowdier, though not ill-humoured. She saw to her surprise that Lord Denham was not in his box and neither was the young lady of his party. She also noticed with a sinking heart that Thomas Harries was sitting in the pit. It had been exactly seven days since he had made her his offer and he would be hoping for an answer. How could she think with all this turmoil in her head and her heart? What if Susan died? Complications in childbed often resulted in the death of a perfectly healthy young woman.

Further thought was impossible as she became Lady Heartfort again, for probably the final time. Dressed in the beautiful white gown, the glass emeralds she had sported in Wychwood House at

Lady Arabella's at her throat, she quipped, flirted, intrigued and danced her way through the ballroom scene, and when the denouement came, the audience were almost at fever pitch and stamped, applauded and demanded a dozen curtain calls.

By this time Antony Denham had returned to his box, though the young lady had not. Cavendish was demanded on stage. Thankfully he had changed his clothes and tidied himself up. He gave a short rather stilted speech, smiled nicely, made a great deal of Eliza and Ned who tried to look modest and unassuming but were really on fire with the triumph of success on a difficult and emotionally charged evening.

Finally the audience let them go and Eliza hurried off to meet Antony in the green room. A quick glance round the chatting players and visiting VIPs revealed that, at least for now, Thomas Harries was not present. Richard Cavendish was surrounded by a group of fops who were laughing uncontrollably and tapping him with their quizzing glasses. Even at a cursory glance, Eliza, could tell how annoyed he was by the fake bonhomie. Sarah Newley had appeared at his side and was flirting heavily with Sir Rufus Erskine whose chins wobbled tremulously at her witticisms and who was edging her ever more closely into a corner where he could drool over her, Antony was with his young buck friends and, on seeing Eliza, greeted her with a kiss in both cheeks, holding her at arm's length as if to commit her face to memory.

'My dear Eliza. It has seemed so long like since I saw you. I have missed you so much.' He let his hands fall and turned to his friends.

'Miss Eliza Grahame, gentlemen. This, my dear Eliza, is the Honourable Toby Shevington, and this rascal whose praise of your performance, my love, would have made your lovely ears burn, is

162

Giles Lucas.' The gentlemen, whose pink cheeks and sparkling eyes indicated an evening of steady drinking, bowed low to Eliza. Lord Lucas took her hand and kissed her fingers and, as Eliza smiled at him, she glimpsed in his features her brother George, pressganged some years ago and from whom she had never heard. With a jolt she realised how little thought she and Flora had given him since then. They did not know whether he was alive or dead, fighting in the Colonies, being worked to death on a ship of the line or rotting in a jail on the other side of the world. In another life he could have been the drunken young man opposite her, spoiled and bored, to whom the world offered endless possibilities and promise. She drew Antony aside.

'Antony, I must return to Somerset Street at once. Susan is in labour. She needs my support.' She didn't add that she was desperate to avoid coming face to face with Thomas Harries who was looking at her from across the room as if she were his next port of call.

A flicker of annoyance passed over Antony Denham's handsome countenance, but he replied smoothly,' Of course, my dear. I understand. My carriage will take us there immediately and once you are satisfied that Susan is well and comfortable, we can renew our acquaintance.' The amorous look he gave her brought a flush to her cheeks and a shy smile to her lips, despite the anxiety she was feeling about Susan. Taking her arm, he led her out of the theatre and into Catherine Street where coachmen and linkboys lounged and smoked while waiting to conduct stragglers home. Horses jingled their harnesses and stamped their hooves, snorting impatiently. Only a few yards away the Ladies of Covent Garden stood in doorways or more brazenly paraded in their cheap finery on the look-out for customers.

Lord Denham's man Francis saw his employer approach and broke off his conversation with another coachman, moving quickly to unfold the mounting steps for his passengers.

'Your lordship. Madam,' he touched his hat obsequiously, but Denham was in no mood to dwell on niceties; he hastily handed Eliza into the carriage, climbing in after her, almost tripping himself up in the hoops of her gown and cursing softly as he took his seat close beside her.

'Somerset Street. And make it quick.'

Wilmot, whose imperturbable professional expression seemed in Eliza's eyes to have slipped, let them in. Maybe he was discomfited by the household of hysterical females as he certainly registered some relief on seeing Antony Denham again. From upstairs came the thin piercing cry of a baby and Eliza's face broke into a relieved smile as she took off her cloak hastily in the hall and made for the stairs.

'Oh, Wilmot, please show Lord Denham into the sitting room and bring up a bottle of the claret. And something to eat.' Eliza ordered, then she was running upstairs to Susan's room.

Denham turned to the butler who was helping him with his coat and said, with ill-concealed irritation, 'Two bottles, Wilmot, if you please. Is there a fire in the drawing room? Something to eat too.'

'Of course, my lord. I shall have Mrs Jenkins put a tray together for you, though she is rather occupied with the young lady's confinement and the birth.'

Denham mounted the stairs heavily. The evening was not turning out at all as he had envisaged, and even the large win he had had at the tables earlier on now seemed to have lost its shine.

164

The baby, a girl, was quiet now, plugged to Susan's breast and feeding hungrily. Hester Markham, the midwife, a lumbering woman with a lazy eye, was gathering up linen and bowls. The air was ripe with the smells of blood, milk and birth, hot with the fire crackling in the grate. Eliza was feeling faint from the atmosphere and somehow shy in the presence of the exhausted Susan whose eyes were fixed on the baby at her breast. Eliza came up to her and planted a kiss on top of Susan's unbound and damp hair.

'Susan, I am so happy it is over.'

'I fear it had only just begun, Liza,' replied her friend wryly, touching the soft fringe of hair that framed the baby's face. 'But yes, she is here. And I am still alive. It was the hardest thing I have ever done.' She shifted uncomfortably in the stained and rumpled bedclothes. 'How does anybody ever want to have another?' she asked smiling ruefully. That remark made Eliza feel that she had her friend back mow, battered, bruised, more philosophical, but essentially she was the same Susan and they would all survive.

'What will you call her?'

'Elizabeth – Betty for short. For my mother. Though I doubt she will ever see her.'

The heat in the room, its ferrous smell of blood and birth was making Eliza queasy, but she perched on the side of the bed and watched the baby's tiny mouth sucking rhythmically, its eyes closed, its little fist clenched in an attitude of determination, determination to hang on to life whatever the odds.

'I had hoped it would be a boy, Eliza.'

'Oh, Susan, but – look at her. She's perfect.'

165

'Fewer problems with boys, I think. Being born a girl brings with it all kinds of problems it seems to me. And how can I protect her from those, Liza? I cannot protect myself. If it had not been for you, I don't know what would have happened to me.' Suddenly Susan's control broke and tears flooded her eyes, dripping down onto her feeding daughter.

Eliza put her arms gently round Susan's shoulders, saying, 'No, no. don't say that. You still have me. I'll see to it that nothing bad happens to you – or to Betty.'

The midwife heaved herself out of the comfortable chair where she was enjoying a glass of brandy.

'I think, madam, that mother needs to rest now. I will take baby after she has fed and let her sleep. She had a very difficult time, madam,' the midwife confided in low tones to Eliza who could only guess at the story behind those words. Feeling an outsider in this close world of maternity, Eliza made for the door, promising to see her friend in the morning.

By the time Eliza had joined Lord Denham in the drawing room, most of the two bottles of claret had been drunk and his lordship was not in the sunniest of moods. Full of petulance and self-righteous indignation, he turned to Eliza as soon she was settled by the fire.

'You know full well I had hoped to have you to myself tonight, Liza,' he slurred.

'And so you shall, Antony. I was anxious for Susan earlier.'

'Now you are assured that the slut is happily settled with her bastard, you will find time for me.' This barb, delivered with a sneer, shocked Eliza to the core; she had never heard him speak in this way before, and of her friend too.

'Antony! You know full well she is no slut. She is an honest girl who was … well, imprudent, unlucky. She has had no other lover since Jed. Any woman could find herself in that situation.' Her cheeks burned as she thought of the relief she felt every month when her courses began. Is this how Antony would see her if she became pregnant?

Denham had made his way unsteadily to where she sat. Taking her hand, he hauled her to her feet and pulled her to him roughly, breathing heavily, the fumes rank with the wine he had been drinking all night.

'Let's go to bed, my love. I want to show you how much I've missed you,' and he took her hand and put it on the hardness in his breeches.

She shrank a little and turned her head to escape his vinous breath.

'Come on, Eliza, you are not usually so coy. Don't tease.' He became insistent, groaning into her hair, licking her neck, his hand moving to her breasts where he rubbed her nipples hard. Suddenly there was a cry like a caterwauling tomcat that split the silence of the house and made him recoil in shock.

'In the name of God! What is that?' He broke from her, frustrated in drunk confusion.

'It's the baby, Susan's baby, Betty,' she replied, relieved that he had stopped manhandling her and even amused that he did not recognise the thin piercing cry of a newborn.

'So I am disturbed in my own house – even here – by the wailing of the brat. Am I to have no return on my investment then?' He had caught her once again by the sleeve of her gown and, in pulling at her again spitefully, the fabric ripped, and Eliza fell against the arm of the sofa. His eyes were blazing as he lurched towards the door, spitting out the words, 'Is this the Foundling Hospital, Eliza? Did I agree to take in fallen women and their bastards as well as that sister of yours when I set you up here? And what do I get for my generosity? Noise, trouble, and you as cold as stone. Just remember what you are doing here, Eliza!' Flinging the words at her, he fumbled for the door handle. 'But don't trouble yourself, my dear. I can get what I want right now easily from the ladies of Covent Garden. They'll be more than willing. And will not cost me half as much as you.' He opened the door clumsily and stormed out into the hall, calling on Francis to bring round the carriage as he was going out.

It was two days before Denham returned to Somerset Street, two days in which the sleep of Susan, Eliza, Flora and, to a lesser extent, the staff of the house, had been disturbed by baby Betty. They, after all, worked harder than their mistress who had been used to sleeping late after a performance. Those two days saw rehearsals begin for *The Beaux Stratagem* and the absence of Sarah Newley, whose role as Melinda, Eliza was trying to commit to memory. Cavendish had given Eliza's part in the afterpiece to a newcomer, Sadie Morris, a buxom, knowing beauty of seventeen who clearly relished the breeches role.

The manager himself was short-tempered at rehearsals and, noting his ink-stained fingers and general air of distraction, Eliza surmised he was still writing. She had had no further communication from Thomas Harries but was determined to visit him at the Garden before the week was out to give him her answer.

Thursday was an evening off for Eliza, which she felt she needed badly in order to rest, to marshal her thoughts, to ponder on Antony's behaviour and what it meant for her future. She had been stung and hurt deeply by his words, though she questioned whether she was being naïve. After all, their relationship was a practical even commercial one. True, he had dressed it up as being her protector, loving her madly, but she was just a kept woman, a mistress, a courtesan.

She was deluding herself with ideas of love and romance. He didn't love her; he desired her, he liked her high-profile career when it reflected on him as her keeper, but that surely wasn't love, otherwise he couldn't have spoken to her like that on the night he left. And although she had agreed with Susan that she surely must love him, that was just a glib reply. She felt about him much as he did about her; sexual attraction, desire, pleasure in his company, most of the time anyway. But was that love? It wasn't the love of Cleopatra for Antony, of Beatrice for Benedict, a love that raises the lovers beyond physical passion, money, self-interest. That she hadn't experienced. Maybe it didn't exist beyond the pages of books. Maybe all that ordinary human beings could do was just settle for what came closest.

These thoughts were racing through Eliza's head as she strolled back from the theatre that afternoon after the morning rehearsal. Spring was well established now and the wide streets and pleasant squares of this new part of London made a pleasant setting for these philosophical thoughts.

Antony had sent her an apologetic note following his sudden departure from Somerset Street, promising to be with her in the next few days, a promise that made her uneasy. She was becoming increasingly concerned by the visits from his creditors and knew she had to press him on financial matters. She had been drawing on her own reserves for Susan's confinement, paying for the midwife and little Betty's basic needs. That was how it should be, but she certainly couldn't support the feeding and maintenance of the house on her actress's wages, even if Richard Cavendish was to increase them.

She was beginning to admit to herself that she was becoming a little frightened of his lordship and saw the theatre as a safer less stressful place to be.

Chapter 21

Sarah Newley had been very annoyed at the huge success of the revival of *The Heiress*. True, it had been a triumph for her lover and once again had brought his name to the public's attention, swelling the coffers of Drury Lane in a gratifying way at a time when the Garden was reaping the benefits of a refurbishment with new lighting and seating, but nevertheless, to Sarah, Eliza's triumph had rankled like a suppurating boil. And to be perfectly honest, Sarah was becoming a little tired of her playwright lover. She had pursued him relentlessly since his first day at Drury Lane. She had needed a challenge; her previous lover, Viscount Winthrop had been such a sop, so besotted with her, so over-accommodating and such a disappointment in the bedroom where his puny efforts to keep her satisfied were frankly derisory.

Despite his generosity, she had been in the process of breaking with him when Richard Cavendish had first appeared, apparently quite indifferent at first to her charms. But the viscount had been generous enough to sign over the house in Gower Street to her, so the way was clear to her to charm Richard in the fashion she had charmed many men before him. He was, however, persistently indifferent to her which piqued her interest and she had to apply herself to the conquest. Matters were suddenly made a great deal easier for her when she had the good fortune to discover some information about his family that she was able to use as a lever and which worked on him like a charm. However, she knew that this power she exerted over him had little to do with Venus. At the outset of their affair, she was prepared to delude herself he was her lover because he could not resist her, but even as he made love to her and brought her to new heights of desire and pleasure, she knew for him it was because of the hold she had over him and nothing to do with love. Sometimes when they were out in society together, she caught a glazed and distant look in his eyes, a cool antipathy, even a sense of being captured like a songbird in a cage. Well, she was sick of it. A very influential baronet had started paying her attention; a case of emeralds had recently been delivered to Gower Street, with a note desiring a private supper with her. She longed for an ardent new lover, extravagant presents, adulation. Richard Cavendish would never be rich, though he might one day be famous and was certainly putting all his efforts into the play he was currently writing which had been making him far too busy to visit her in Gower Street. They met at rehearsals where the euphoria of the recent *Heiress* production was beginning to wane and Richard was seemingly just going through the motions of planning the programme of productions and rehearsals, his mind clearly elsewhere on this new play. Without much thought to Sarah it seemed. He was wheeling out that old favourite *A Trip to Scarborough* which admittedly always sold seats but required very little from the players, most of whom could have played it in their sleep.

Before Sarah left for the theatre that morning, she opened the case of emeralds. The necklace made of graduated stones of breath-taking clarity and a green as dense as a forest, winked up at her from their velvety bed. The jeweller's embossed gold address announced a Bond Street location, which brought a smile to her lips. She shut the case with a soft but decisive snap. Time to move on.

When Sarah arrived at the theatre, she made straight for the manager's office. Richard was sitting at his desk writing, looking dishevelled and tired. He glanced up at her as she swept in without knocking, gave her a brief smile then stabbed his pen viciously into the inkwell and was ready to resume writing. Then a tap at the door made him reply with a curt 'Come in,' as Eliza entered. Immediately, as Sarah removed a glove, she noted Richard's face brighten, the lines around his eyes relax a fraction and she registered him put down his pen and turn towards Eliza. This was the cue Sarah had been waiting for.

'Oh, Eliza,' she drawled, pulling off her second glove with great precision before Eliza could address Richard, 'I understand congratulations are in order.'

Eliza looked at her in puzzlement.

'Well, at least probably not for you,' she continued, taking a chair opposite Richard and smoothing out her skirt with studied care.

'Congratulations to Lord Denham, I mean. On his engagement to Miss Clarissa Dursfield.' She had delivered the announcement with her innate sense of theatrical timing, and saw the colour drain from Eliza's cheeks. Sarah sensed Richard's body stiffen and his expression harden.

'Oh, did you not know, Eliza? I am so sorry to have surprised you like this.' Her solicitous smile belied the venom in her heart, which both Richard and Eliza knew. Eliza rallied. She beamed an almost convincing smile and stepped towards the door, her errand in the room apparently forgotten.

'Oh yes, of course His Lordship has informed me. I wish him and the lady well,' then she was gone, brushing past Sarah. Cavendish sprang up from his desk and turned on his mistress with hatred in his eyes as his chair clattered onto the floor.

'That was a vile thing to do, Sarah. Vile and cruel. Is it true?' he asked, moving menacingly towards her. 'If it is, he is an even more abject human being than I took him for.'

'Quite true. But before you leave to comfort the distraught Eliza, I must tell you, Richard,' she continued, squaring up to him and looking at him hard, 'I wish to release you from your recently reluctant association with me.' She was gratified to see the shock and surprise on Richard's face but noted also the faint signs of relief.

'But you and I had an arrangement, Sarah ...'

'Yes. We had an arrangement, I know. I no longer find this arrangement convenient to me. We are no longer lovers, Richard. In truth, you were often a reluctant lover. Perhaps that could be the title of a future play,' she quipped, moving away from him now and walking distractedly round the small cluttered office with its stacks of scripts, shelves of books, shabby mismatched furniture and its air of cheerful neglect.

Sarah continued. 'The bargain was, as I'm sure you will recall, that I could keep to myself certain facts I knew, provided that you gave me your undivided attention and preference for the major roles in the plays performed here. Am I correct?'

She stopped her circuit of the room and turned to face him.

'You know you are,' he replied tersely. 'So?'

'So, I am going to suggest a slight adjustment to our bargain. There will no longer be an ... intimate connection between us. I am not accustomed to having to persuade men into my bed and do not take kindly to it.' He was looking at her now, unsmiling and tight-lipped. 'But what I require of you is that you give me the leading role in this new play of yours. This the price of my silence on that ... little matter to which I alluded. Do we have a bargain?'

He stepped towards her, eyes ablaze and jaw clenched. Hurriedly she moved backwards, the sneer fading from her face. She looked at him in some alarm, his face just inches from hers, grey eyes blazing.

'You harpy! You vicious creature not worthy of the name of woman. Do your worst. You have kept me in thrall this past year. I have despised myself for ever agreeing to the bargain. I did it only for my family as you know. Now, I no longer care. No,' he continued, stabbing a grubby finger towards her and seeing her flinch, 'you will not have a starring role in my play. Eliza Grahame is to have that role which she will carry off to perfection. You will play the roles I assign you and I will never be held to ransom again by you, either in my theatre or in your bed. You are excused rehearsal for today,' he concluded, spitting out the words before storming from the room, leaving her frozen in disbelief.

Chapter 22

A week and a day after the birth of baby Betty, Eliza knew she had to go to Convent Garden with her answer for Thomas Harries.

Last night's performance of *The Beaux Stratagem* had been a modest success. The house had been well-behaved, appreciative, though the audience could not be described as rapturous. She had seen little of Cavendish, only heard him shout impatiently through his office door. 'Go away, I'm busy,' when Ned had knocked on it. It would be best if she gave her answer to Harries and then tell Cavendish as quickly as possible. It was an interview she dreaded. But she had made her decision.

Antony Denham had left for Yorkshire again, his departure announced in a hastily-scrawled note delivered to Somerset Street, along with a thick envelope containing a wad of banknotes and a bank draft for Eliza. He also sent his instructions to settle bills. His note to Eliza included assurances that he would be soon back in London when he could free himself from his obligations in Yorkshire. Now that Eliza knew categorically what those obligations were, she realised she had to break with him as soon as possible, however difficult that would be. She had no intention of staying on as his mistress after he had married Miss Dursfield. There were plenty of women who could happily shut their eyes to a similar situation, but she was not one of them. That was why she was making that difficult journey to see Thomas Harries at Covent Garden where she could earn five guineas a week, leaving behind the enigmatic Richard Cavendish to finish his play and continue his volatile affair with Sarah Newley who would surely land the starring role in the new play if it ever materialised.

Last to leave the dressing room, she tied her cloak, delaying her errand. All the other women had scurried off as soon as they had leave to go. They all had places to be, children to feed, husbands and lovers to cook for, friends to meet for a glass of spirits or a stroll in the park. The weather was pleasantly warm now, the trees in leaf, so you could stroll in Hyde Park, watch the members of the quality promenading or driving in their carriages and curricles, displaying their latest acquisitions in horse flesh or fine clothes. It cost nothing to look after all. Cutting the ties with Antony Denham would mean that she would be forever an observer of such scenes instead of a participant, but were those things so important to her? After all, her feelings for the man had soured since the night of Betty's birth where she had briefly glimpsed a cruel and vicious streak in his nature. She would not sacrifice her self-esteem for such a man.

She could prevaricate no longer. She left the dressing room and plunged into the warren of corridors that would take her out to the stage door and the real world outside. Except, that since she had made this place her home two years ago, it had often been her real world. Maybe Cavendish would want her to work her notice, perhaps playing Melinda for as long as they could still sell seats. There was no shortage of young hopefuls who would be pleased to flirt their way into his good books to take over the parts she had played. The next time Cavendish reprised *The Heiress,* no doubt there would be another Lady Heartfort and for that she felt a pang of emotion.

Outside the manager's office, she saw Richard in conversation with Ned. She smiled at both of them and, as she made to pass, Richard stopped what he had been saying and said, 'Eliza, could I have a word with you before you leave? It won't take a minute.' He laid his hand gently on Ned's shoulder in dismissal and ushered her into the office. Closing the door, he made no offer of a seat, just strode to his desk and picked up a sheaf of handwritten pages, much blotted and bearing evidence to crossings out. Holding them towards her and unable to keep the note of triumph out of his voice, he declared, 'Here it is, Eliza. This is it. The new play. It's finished. It will be your play. We will start rehearsals next week.' The joy and excitement in his voice made her heart sink and she could not meet his gaze.

'Sir ... I am not able ... I cannot be in your play. I am on my way to see Mr Harries at Covent Garden. I am accepting his offer.'

Disbelief instantly became anger as he threw the proffered pages onto his desk. Stepping towards her, he took her shoulders none too gently, making her flinch slightly. Looking hard into her eyes, he spat out, 'Eliza! No, how could you? I told you things would be different. I thought all this discontent was in the past and that you understood. The play is written for you to take the leading role. It is *your* part. Why now?'

She shrugged off his hold on her and said, 'I need to think of my future, especially now. Harries has offered me a higher salary, guaranteed me good roles, benefits. I cannot ...'

'You have a wealthy protector who has set you up in a fine house. You surely –'

'Do you imagine that I will continue in that arrangement when Lord Denham marries?' She flung the words at him, her eyes blazing, cheeks pink. 'Do you not know me better than that?'

He was shocked at her outburst and stepped back in the face of such passion.

'Well, I ...'

'Clearly not. I will not be the kept woman of a married man. Do you think I have so little respect for the institution of marriage,

178

so little self-regard? Or do you assume,' she continued, rounding on him, 'that once a women has lost her virtue there is nothing she would not stoop to? Well, I, sir, am not such a women. I must move from Somerset Street, find cheaper lodgings for myself and Flora, Susan and her baby. I need to provide for them.' Suddenly the realisation of the enormity of this task seemed to deprive her of her fire and energy. She said quietly, 'I must go to Mr Harries and give him my decision.'

He was staring at her with an expression she could not fathom, but it caused her to lower her eyes. His anger had passed, though he was not apologetic. There was perhaps relief, respect too, in his eyes and something else that made her drop her gaze and feel a glow inside. He reached gently for her hands and held them both within his. Smiling wryly and shaking his head, he said, 'Eliza, oh Eliza, is that your only reason for wanting to leave? I will match it, Eliza, the money that Harries has offered you, I'll double it,' he continued wildly, 'if it takes that to make you stay with me ... with us here. Be in this play of mine, Liza. It is my best yet. Help me make Drury Lane the best theatre in London. You will have no rivals, Liza. You *have* no rival.' He had drawn her closer to him, and she noticed his grubby shirtfront and stained stock. But his grey eyes shone with emotion and energy, and she felt again the bond between them and the desire to be drawn in once again to his charmed circle.

His fingers, now interlaced with hers, were warm and strong. She didn't want to break the spell, but glanced up at him shyly saying, 'Miss Newley?'

'Is merely another member of this company now, Eliza. Though I suspect that will not long continue. We are no longer lovers,' he said, his voice steady. 'That arrangement came about because I was weak and allowed myself to be. I regret it bitterly. I put family matters before my own better judgement. I had no emotional attachment to her.'

Eliza remembered in a flash how he had been with Sarah in public – embarrassed, reluctant, undemonstrative – and still did not fully understand what he was saying, but gave herself over to a profound sense of relief. She wanted more than anything for him to pull her towards him, to feel the warmth of his breath on her face, but he released her hands, took a step back from her and said, in a different tone altogether, 'I want more than anything for you to stay with us here, Eliza, but I do understand how a move to Covent Garden might be what you need. I will respect your decision and ask only that you honour your agreement with us to play in *The Beaux Stratagem* for the next two weeks.

Here she had lost him again. The formality was back in his voice and he had moved to his desk where he was idly picking up random items – a penknife, a quill, an empty glass. Looking down for a moment to the pages that littered his desk, he said, 'It seems to me that men have all too obviously used you to their own advantage of late. I do not wish to be another of them. You must decide. You are your own woman.'

Taking her cue from him, she said in a strong voice, 'Yes I am, Mr Cavendish. And you have helped me achieve that. And so I shall go now to Covent Garden to see Mr Harries and thank him for his generous offer,' she moved purposefully towards the door, adding, 'and tell him that I shall be staying here in Drury Lane.' The smile they shared as she stood at the door, her fingers on the handle, seemed to bring a burst of sunshine to the untidy subterranean office, and after, as she strolled down Catherine Street heading for the Garden, she turned her face towards the afternoon sun and felt a lightness in her step she had not felt for months.

Chapter 23

The house that Eliza found for them was in George Street, away from the leafy squares and elegant facades of Somerset Street, but it was in a decent neighbourhood, a clean and respectable dwelling whose rent was reasonable, and within easy walking distance from the theatre. Susan was returning to work, Flora's intention being to look after baby Betty and take in sewing work. There was a girl who lived close by who would help out with the heavy work in the house.

Eliza would write to Antony Denham after delivering the news to Harries that she would be staying at Drury Lane, which he received tight-lipped and unsmiling.

'You have kept me waiting an unconscionable time, Miss Grahame, to be delivering such disappointing news.' Eliza flushed but held his stern gaze and said with composure, 'It was a very difficult decision to make, Mr Harries. I can assure you I gave it lengthy consideration. But I feel that my loyalties lie with Mr Cavendish, and I feel I should stay in Drury Lane,' she said with an upward tilt of her chin, noting his barely concealed contempt.

'As you wish, Madam.' He bowed stiffly, leading her to the door of his office, as neat and ordered as Cavendish's was chaotic and cluttered.

'Good day, Miss Grahame. And I trust you will not regret your decision.'

Eliza's letter to her former lover took her a long time to compose. She sat at the writing desk in the smart sitting room at Somerset Street that she was soon to leave. The vases and pictures that Denham had selected for their love nest would doubtless soon be packed up when the house was re-let. She had already told the staff that she was soon to be moving out, but they were employed by

Denham and she had no obligations to them, financial or otherwise. Mrs Jenkins seemed surprised, however, that money had been found to pay off the household debts and she must have thought that matters would resume as before. Eliza was diplomatic in what she told the house keeper, but noted Mrs Jenkins's expression of concern when she heard the news.

'So madam, you, Miss Flora, Miss Susan and the baby? All of you leaving? Next Friday you say. I very much regret to hear it. And is Lord Denham to return to London soon?'

'I do not know Lord Denham's plans,' Eliza said stiffly. 'I simply wish to inform you of our intentions. We are to move out and we shall need some help packing our belongings.'

'Very good madam.'

'There is little we shall be taking beyond our own possessions. All remains here for Lord Denham to remove as he wishes. I imagine the house will be let to new tenants.' She gazed round the room with its silk curtains, upholstered chairs, side tables, sparkling chandeliers and dazzling mirrors. George Street was furnished simply, the furniture functional, the rugs thin, the china plain and heavy. But she would take nothing from this fine house, her home for the past months.

'Thank you, Mrs Jenkins. I have letters to write now. As this is a theatre night for Miss Susan and me, we will take an early dinner.'

'Very well madam. And if I may say, I shall be very sorry to see all of you leave. I have been happy to work for you. I wish you well in your new accommodation.'

Eliza was touched and smiled sadly at her housekeeper whose normally austere features had softened. 'I suppose I must become accustomed to being simply 'miss' now, not 'madam,' she added as Mrs Jenkins turned to leave.

Once she had begun, however, the letter was not too difficult to write. The words came easily and from the heart, though she tried to keep the note of accusation out of her tone. She had heard of his plans to marry. She no longer wanted to be within his protection, she wished him well in his future life and thanked him for his generosity to her, remaining his affectionate Eliza.

She sealed the letter, and, with a sense of relief, went to her room to prepare for the morning's rehearsal.

When Eliza and Susan reached the theatre, the dressing room was buzzing with the latest news: Sarah Newley had left Drury Lane and had been taken on by Mr Harries of the Garden for a reputed five guineas a week. Eliza glanced at Susan who raised her eyebrows and said, 'Good riddance I say. Who needs Miss Faceache anyway? I have returned to you and the world has yet to see *my* Lady Macbeth. "Out, out, damned spot!"' she declaimed in a melodramatic way, rubbing her hands and rolling her eyes. General laughter greeted this unkind but eerily accurate impersonation of Miss Newley at her most histrionic. As the laughter subsided, there was a sharp rap at the door and a brusque, 'Are you decent ladies?' and Richard Cavendish poked his head around the door.

'Good morning, ladies. Eliza, can I see you please? Ten minutes for places in Act 2, please ladies.'

Eliza followed him up the corridor, so low in places he had to remember to duck his head for safety. His stride was impatient and urgent. Over his shoulder he flung the words, 'You've heard of course? Miss Newley?'

'Gone to the Garden they said. Is it true?'

183

Arriving at his office, he flung open the door and turned on his heel to face her. 'Eliza. it is ready. The script – the play. Here.' He handed her the pages with a trembling hand.

'Take it. You are to play Araminta who is the main female lead. It … well, you will see that it takes some risks, is a little saucy in places. But I hope you will agree that it is essentially a funny play.'

Eliza was quickly scanning the closely written pages as he spoke, warming to his subject.

'There have been too many of those heavily moralistic plays these past few years, full of worthy and solemn ideas but not much humour.'

'The public tends to like them, though,' she ventured delicately.

'Well, we didn't offer them anything else, did we?'

'Except *The Heiress*, of course.'

He smiled and the connection between them warmed her heart.

'Just so. And now, the company will begin with rehearsals starting tomorrow. Ned will play opposite you with Joshua Taylor playing Viscount Reason. Mr Jacobs, of course, will be his inimitable self as Lord Restless.'

There was the sound of laughter and shrill voices outside in the corridor.

'We'd better make a start on today's business,' he said hurriedly, and Eliza went towards the door with the script, turning back briefly to him as she said, 'It's true then, she is gone? Sarah Newley?' He had not confirmed that news in the excitement of giving her his script.

'Indeed. And you must take her dressing room. You are our *prima donna* now, Eliza.' The look he gave her made her bones melt as if she were on the verge of something so exciting she could barely breathe.

'Come, Eliza,' then he was following her to the door, his hands protectively on her shoulder, 'let us get the bread and butter business done today, then prepare to take the world of London's theatres by storm.'

That evening Eliza was Melinda in *The Beaux Stratagem*, on Wednesday and Saturday she played Rosalind in *As You Like It*; in the morning she was rehearsing Cavendish's play that required her to be on stage in almost every scene. Never had her ability to learn a script quickly been so necessary, a script full of witty dialogue that would need all her skill to deliver to do it justice.

Fortunately, Flora had started to blossom as a skilled manager of their domestic *ménage*; not only did she cope admirably with baby Betty when Susan was busy at the theatre, but she became a thrifty shopper and general housekeeper. She had Nancy to help out in the house as unskilled maid of all work, but apart from one day when none of them had clean petticoats, the butter had run away in the hot weather and next door's cat had sneaked in and carried off the fish for that evening's supper, Flora coped very well indeed, and all four females in the house lived comfortably in a well-run establishment.

'Of course I don't need to be your lady's maid any longer, Liza, do I?' Flora said rather sadly one morning as she made the breakfast coffee, 'seeing as you need never to get all dressed up for society as you used to for dinners, functions and supper parties. Not since Lord Denham.'

'No, that's not necessary any longer, is it?' replied Eliza, buttering some bread. 'I seem only to go to the theatre and come home afterwards these days. It's very hard work at the moment. No time for anything else.'

'All that will change after the premiere. You mark my words.' Susan had entered the room, baby guzzling at her breast. 'Thanks. Flora,' she said as a cup of coffee materialised in front of her. 'I need something to wake me up. This one was very restless in the night.' Eliza and her sister exchanged wry glances; they both knew all too well how restless Betty had been. The walls in the house were paper-thin.

'Once this new play is out, you'll once again be the toast of the town, just like after *The Heiress*. Then Flora, you'll be back to getting her ready, dressing her hair, accompanying her shopping.'

'I don't need clothes,' said Eliza stiffly, gathering used crockery from the table, 'I still have all those clothes Lord Denham bought for me. I just can't bring myself to wear them.'

This time it was Flora and Susan who exchanged knowing looks; neither of them would have had Eliza's scruples.

'That's foolish, Eliza,' said Susan sternly, applying the baby, who snuffled and blinked her eyes, to her other breast.

'They are beautiful clothes, Liza. They fit only you and were chosen by you. It is a waste not to wear them and enjoy them. Forget they were gifts from Lord Denham.'

'You earned them, Liza,' added Flora, a comment that made the plates and cups in Eliza's hands rattle as she swung round to face her sister, eyes blazing with anger.

'No, no … I did not mean that in any way,' Flora stuttered, seeing the rage and hurt in Eliza's eyes. 'I only meant to speak plainly. I do not judge you. It is the way of the world and it is a bargain you and he made. Marriage is much the same it seems to me,' she added with all the sagacity of her eighteen years, checking in the cupboard for a jar of preserves to put on the table in front of Susan.

Although hurt by her sister's remarks, Eliza could see the sense in what she was saying. She was so much worldlier now, not a green girl full of thoughts of love and romance. Most of the time anyway.

'Forgive me, Flora. My head is full of words. I am not thinking straight. Of course, you are both right. The next time I am invited into society,' she continued with a forced laugh, 'I shall wear one of Lord Denham's gifts, I promise you.'

For all the actors in the company, Richard Cavendish's new play, *A Sweet Revenge,* meant a break with tradition, or at least the tradition of the last twenty years. It was Mr Jacobs, the oldest player among them, who tried to quell the fears of the youngsters like Ned.

'But this play is in the tradition of the great Restoration playwrights,' Jacobs declared impatiently as they gathered for a lunchtime glass of ale at The Shakespeare's Head. 'The play is humorous, witty, clever, the situation amusing so this is genuine comedy. Plays have been moving away from real comedy these past years, in my opinion.'

'But where's the moral, Mr Jacobs, the lesson, in this play? How will people improve themselves by watching it?'

'Yes, I don't understand that either, Mr Jacobs,' chipped in James, looking at Mr Jacobs who was universally regarded as the fount of all theatrical knowledge. He sighed impatiently and sipped his ale before saying, 'Gentlemen, gentlemen, does there need to be a moral or a lesson? Or at least a very heavy handed one? The play makes us laugh. In laughing at the silly behaviour of Lord Restless and his foibles, we learn not to aspire to be like him. Then Ned, your character, Bloodless, he is a hypocrite, yes? All agreed? Well, we laugh at him because he professes one thing yet behaves quite differently.'

'Yes, yes, especially with Miss Faithful.' There were nods of agreement and the suspicion of pink cheeks from Ned who was pursuing Letty Winstone who played Miss Faithful.

'The play shows us how hypocrites take in the unwary, how they pretend to be so full of virtue, yet they are deceivers. We learn from that, but in doing so, we are made to laugh because Mr Cavendish has made him a figure of fun. Moral lessons can be taught through laughter and mockery much more than through sermons and dull plays about hard work and fine words, lads. Now who's for another? All this preaching has left me with a thirst.'

The actresses also took some convincing. They muttered among themselves, Susan reported to Eliza who, elevated to her new status in the company, had her own dressing room.

'They seem just a bit ... unsettled because it's new and very funny. And they get some very witty lines too. They're not all that used to having the heroine having the witty lines. That is usually a man's role.'

188

Eliza sighed, saying, 'Have they forgotten Beatrice in *Much Ado,* or Millament in *The Way of the World*?'

'Well no, perhaps. But the usual plays we've been doing, the women are there to look at, to fall in love with or just to be good and virtuous. Am I right? Not Lady Heartfort, of course,' she added hurriedly, seeing Eliza's mutinous look, 'and certainly not your Araminta who turns the tables on the men.'

'And makes the audience laugh while doing so,' came the smart rejoinder.

Susan laughed but said, 'But this play, well, it could be seen as a risk Mr Cavendish is taking. Do you not allow me that?'

They were close to home now, an hour or so's respite before they needed to return for the evening performance.

'It is a risk, I agree, a departure from the usual. I am sure that the audience will be thrilled by it, Susan. Richard – Mr Cavendish – is an accomplished playwright. We should have every faith in him and his play. Now, I wonder what Flora has got us to eat.'

Chapter 24

It was nearing the end of the season. Richard Cavendish spent several sleepless nights wondering whether he should have kept his latest play for the start of the new season. Soon the company would tour the Yorkshire circuit and there had even been an approach from Smock Alley in Dublin. Was he allowing his judgement to be affected by a selfish desire to break the mould, to make a name for himself, to topple Harries from his pedestal at Covent Garden? For there was no doubt at the moment Harries was perched firmly on that pedestal. Rave notices and reviews appeared for his newest production of *The Merchant of Venice*, and Sarah Newley's debut in *Macbeth* received rapturous reviews from Mr Steele at *The Gazette* who was, admittedly, a crony of Harries, who wrote: "Now Miss Newley is able to show the full scope of her serious dramatic talents instead of merely being allowed to posture and simper in the forgettable productions recently staged at Drury Lane."

Richard was stung by these words, biased though he knew they were. But he pondered deeply on the timing of the premiere of *A Sweet Revenge*. Was it the right time? Had he honed the piece to perfection? Were the company ready for it?

To canvas opinion – and for other reasons he hardly admitted to himself –he asked Eliza if she would stay on after her performance in *As You Like It* and come to his office.

The afterpiece, *She Plays to Win*, was in performance as she made her way from the dressing room along the corridor. She heard a sudden burst of laughter coming from the auditorium that indicated the play was going well. She wondered why Richard wanted to see her and why he could not have spoken to her at rehearsal or during the evening.

The office looked a little tidier than usual, the desk more ordered and on it stood a silver tray with an opened bottle of wine and two goblets. He came out from behind the desk, greeted her and turned to pour out wine then motioned her to a comfortable chair near the unlit fireplace.

'Would you like a glass of wine, Eliza? Thank you for staying on like this I won't keep you long. I know you must be tired.'

'Thank you, yes.' She took the goblet from him and settled in the chair, rearranging her dress, waiting for him to join her in the seat opposite.

'A good house tonight, was it not? Very little room for the latecomers after the intermission, I'm happy to say. Most ticket sales at the full price is always good for the finances which is what we want.'

Eliza sensed he was not at ease with this emphasis on the managerial aspect of the theatre, so she simply nodded and sipped her wine, adding, 'It's always good to fill as many seats as possible. And the play is a favourite with the audience. A good safe play.'

'Which cannot be said of *A Sweet Revenge* and its premiere next week, can it Eliza?' he smiled conspiratorially at her and she returned the smile with a slight shake of her head.

'Not at all, Mr Cavendish.'

'And that is why I asked you to stay, Eliza. I need to know how the company views my play, how they feel about this new departure. Do I have their support? I know I have yours, but do they have your faith in me?'

His gaze was so earnest, his whole body leaning in towards her as if willing her to say what he wanted to hear.

'Some are sceptical, it is true. They all think the play is humorous, fresh, lively, a few feel it is too different from our usual comedies to appeal generally to the audience.' She noted the look of concern on his handsome face and continued quickly, 'though surprisingly, your greatest admirer is Mr Jacobs.'

Cavendish's face relaxed into a mile and he chuckled.

'Stephen! The oldest member of the company, revered and well on in years even when Garrick ruled here, Eliza. But perhaps not so surprising. He has played Congreve, Wycherley, all the great Restoration playwrights as a young man.'

'All of them much too strong for the tastes of our audience now, I think.'

'Yes. Times and tastes have changed I know. But Jacobs is on my side, you say?'

'Yes, and working hard to convert some of the others too, so I hear from Ned.'

He sighed and picked up his glass, took a gulp of wine and relaxed back in his chair, one leg crossed over the other.

'And you, Eliza? You were excellent today in rehearsal, especially in the final scene. How are you feeling about our premiere? Will we take London by storm or have we a monstrous flop on our hands? Have I indulged my ego and risked the future of the whole company? What of our future, Eliza?'

'No one can know for sure,' she replied, her voice low and steady. His words had thrilled her with their ambiguity. Both she and Richard were recuperating from stormy relationships, anxious to recover their equilibrium. They were together in this risky venture that could, if it went wrong, potentially damage both their careers irretrievably. But as they looked at each other, what was unspoken and as yet unacknowledged lay between them, and Eliza knew that she would hazard all to be in it with him.

He drained his glass and rose from his chair to refill it, offering to do the same for Eliza who declined. She got up to leave, saying she should get back to Flora who had been with the baby all day.

Setting down his replenished glass on the tray, he said, 'Then I shall come with you, to escort you home. I know you have left Somerset Street. Is it all definitely over between you and Lord Denham?'

'Yes, certainly.' She was putting on her bonnet ready to leave. 'There really is no need for you to accompany me to George Street. It is only a very short walk and it is not even really dark yet. I am used to the streets and feel quite safe.'

'Nevertheless,' he added smiling, 'I cannot risk the safety of my leading lady out there among the revellers and ruffians.'

He bent to blow out a branch of candles on his desk that had been burning there almost all day, for, despite the lightness of the early summer evening, the rooms in the theatre building were subterranean and always gloomy without artificial light.

'Come Liza,' he said in a cheery voice at the door, 'let me take you home.'

And Eliza thought she had never heard such comforting words.

If a chaotic dress rehearsal makes for a hugely successful premiere, then Richard Cavendish's play, *A Sweet Revenge*, was guaranteed to be a runaway success. Samuel Ford, the usual prompt, had broken his ankle and had been replaced at short notice by Edward Mullins whose reading speed was so slow he was woefully inadequate for the job. Cues were missed, prompts delayed, props went missing, and Joshua Gibbons, playing Lord Swiftly, appeared at rehearsal drunk and distraught after hearing that his mistress had left him for a captain in the Dragoons. Two of the ladies' dresses had been made up with the wrong measurements, and the scenery for Act 2, a secluded spot in Vauxhall Gardens, was, as yet, no more than an idea in Jim the carpenter's head.

Richard was trying hard not to fall apart completely. Wild-eyed and hoarse with shouting at the motley crew before him, he took them through their paces, reducing Nancy, one of the company's newcomers to tears on one occasion. Even Eliza came in for his wrath when she fluffed one of his wittiest lines.

At last they were through it, Nancy had been comforted, three carpenters were working on creating the bosky grove required, and the cast returned to the dressing rooms to lick their wounds and grumble. Eliza couldn't help but feel the play and its first performance were doomed. For the first time in weeks, her heart was heavy.

When Eliza and Susan returned home, low in spirits, despite Eliza's attempt to rally her friend, Flora put a crested letter in her sister's hand, and pointed to a huge vase of hothouse flowers that stood on the dining table.

'We didn't have anything big enough to put them in,' said Flora, 'I had to go next door and ask Mrs Goode to lend me the vase.'

The letter was from Antony Denham, regretful in tone, begging her to reconsider her break from him, hoping he might see her again ('and get into your bed too, I warrant,' said Susan drily).

He wished her every success on her opening night, which, he wrote, he would not miss for the world.

This news turned Eliza's stomach to water. Her anxiety about the play's debut, her fears of what failure might mean to the company and its manager were all intensified by this news that Denham would be there in the theatre and was desirous of rekindling their affair.

She had flopped down in a chair, the letter open in her lap, her face white and drawn. The cloyingly overpowering scent of roses and lilies sickened her and she lashed out at Flora who had just handed a grizzling baby to Susan.

'Why did you put them in water, in a vase? I don't want them in the house, Flora!'

'But Liza, they are so beautiful, so costly. It would be a crime not to put them on display. What was I to do?'

'I want nothing more to do with that man. I have tried to cut him out of our lives. I do not want him or his flowers!'

In tears she got up from her chair, knocking it over in her haste, and ran upstairs, leaving Flora and Susan to look at each other in dismay.

Chapter 25

The playbills had been produced, the tickets printed, the opening night puffed and previewed in the coffee houses and clubs of St James as well as the drinking dens of Whitechapel. Playgoers at either end of the spectrum kept their ears open for theatre gossip, which was vivid and varied and of greater interest to London's inhabitants than exchanges in Parliament and news from the benighted colonies. The open rivalry between Drury Lane and Covent Garden was a rich seam to be mined over a glass of claret or a pint of porter: who had the better repertoire, whose ladies were easier on the eye and which establishment made the most money.

Tickets sold out, queues formed and theatregoers from pit and gallery anticipated a lively and exhilarating new play by a talented playwright who had already proved himself a master of comedy in *The Heiress* and *A Treasured Possession*. And Miss Grahame too. What a talent she had, how charming, how witty! And what a close relationship they seemed to share, playwright/manager and lovely leading lady. That relationship was so very close, the gossips said, though of course everyone knew of his previous high-profile mistress and her titled protector. And so it ignited the spark of gossip, fed by the newspaper and magazines, the chance remarks, kindled to a blaze of speculation that could only be extinguished by seeing the new play and observing for oneself.

There had been a brief technical rehearsal at which Richard had appeared calm but pale and slightly detached as if merely going through the motions. There were mercifully few hitches, his comments to the players were kind and positive. The previous night Eliza had slept little but was trying to clear her mind of all but the words and actions required of her. Author and leading lady said little to each other beyond the strictly professional. What lay between

196

them emotionally seemed now too vast, too important; what was expected of them professionally was the ultimate priority just now.

Susan and Eliza had the afternoon free before the performance. Flora prepared them an early meal. She too was invited to the play and Mrs Goode had been only too pleased to be asked to babysit. She adored baby Betty. Unaccustomed to a free evening, even if it was merely to go to the theatre, Flora was excited and talkative. As they ate, Flora chattered throughout the meal, oblivious of her sister's preoccupied silence.

'Will their Majesties be there, do you think? Or the Duchess of Devonshire? I am so glad I do not have to sit in the gallery as we used to, do you remember Eliza? When you had to bribe me with ribbon and comfits to go with you? I do like plays more now, I assure you, and with you and Susan on that stage, it will be so exciting. And I shall see Mr Cavendish that you speak so much. He will be in the manager's box, and I imagine come up on stage at the end of the play.' And so she rattled on as Susan looked at her friend with concern as she sat throughout in frozen silence.

The walk to the theatre passed in the smallest of small talk: was Hetty Ames pregnant again, would the carpenters finish the last piece of scenery, would Letty's dress be ready? After pushing through the crowd at the stage door who were hoping to get tickets, they parted company. In her dressing room, Sukey was bustling around shaking out the folds of the blue dress Eliza was to wear in the first act. She was chattering with excitement and the twin patches of pink on her cheeks and her volubility suggested she had taken more than a nip of gin. She sat Eliza down and prepared her hair neatly so that the elaborate wig she was to wear would sit comfortably – and safely on her head. Many a dramatic or romantic moment on stage had been spoiled by a slipping wig or a shifting peruke.

'Now, those sparkling drops,' Sukey fussed, looking round the very small room that Sarah Newley had always guarded so jealously, 'where are they?'

'Top of the shelf here,' indicated Eliza, sitting before the mirror, taking in her reflection and trying out a smile and some facial expressions for size. She felt she was just beginning to come back to life after the difficult twenty-four hours that had passed; the shock of Denham's letter and its contents, the chaotic dress rehearsal, the anxiety of the occasion and what it meant to her. All this had shocked her system, almost shut it down to the extent she was hardly able to feel and function normally. Now, as Sukey primped and tweaked her hair, applied her makeup, fastened on her jewellery, she felt herself coming to life, unfurling into Araminta, a character on whom the success of the play rested. In the mirror she saw herself smile, not a stage smile this time but a real one, from the heart.

She turned to Sukey.

'It will be a good house. Sold out. You have done a wonderful job here. I feel every bit the fiery Araminta. Wish me luck,' and she beamed at her with eyes moist with emotion.

Eliza and the whole company at Drury Lane never needed that good luck as much as they did on the night that *A Sweet Revenge* by Richard Cavendish was first performed. The theatre was full, the pit, the province of the would-be critic, the aficionados of the theatre, the arbiters of taste, seemed to be heaving with the well-lubricated and vocal. Almost immediately in the first scene, the heckling began.

And it was directed at Mr Jacobs, moreover, in his stage persona as Lord Restless, a politician and uncle of Araminta. Some young dandy in the pit asked him his position on the war and that gave rise to several witty comments from elsewhere in the house, a lot of laughter, some booing and jeers, all of which seemed to annoy those trying to watch the play in the gallery where several loud-voiced men shouted at the heckler to shut up. Items were thrown down into the pit, a rain of half-eaten food fell on some of those ladies seated beneath who shrieked and screamed about damage to their gowns and their hair.

Actors continued bravely in voices raised above the hubbub, but they were obviously unnerved and Letty and Ned both dried, looking frantically towards the wings for a prompt from Edwin who was slow to respond. This resulted in howls of derision from the pit.

Cavendish, watching from the manager's box, was rigid with anger and frustration, willing on the performers, relieved to see Eliza taking command of her role with a strengthened voice and some obvious playing to the audience to get them on side. Richard saw the purpose of her approach and mentally applauded it, especially as it brought a loud roar of approving laughter from the pit. But despite her best efforts, and all those on stage, as well as the sheer quality of the dialogue and stage business, the first act was going under, swamped by drunken barracking from a small but extremely vocal section of the audience, determined to sabotage the performance.

He had heard, though never seen for himself, of such instances of deliberate destruction. They occurred as the direct opposite of the so-called 'claque' which happened in France where playwright and actors paid for audience members to clap and laugh in the right places in order to boost the popularity of a play. Perhaps it was a horrible coincidence to have so many unruly loud playgoers in the theatre tonight, but somehow he doubted it. The whole thing reeked of a conspiracy, a conspiracy to disrupt and undermine the premiere of his play. Little wonder that the face that swam before his eyes was that of Sarah Newley with its calculating eyes, its curling lip as she promised him that he would regret giving a starring role to Eliza. Could she stoop as low as this? To organise this mayhem on the opening night which would damn his play forever? She certainly had powerful friends in many influential walks of life as well as motives for wanting to see him and Eliza fail. And every disaster at Drury Lane meant triumph at the Garden. Would a woman, prepared to disclose to the public gaze the alleged cowardice of his father years before, have any qualms about organising a disturbance in a theatre? He thought not.

The last scene in Act 1, involving a duel that goes comically wrong between Lord Wiseacre and Tom Bentley, was disastrous: it was virtually impossible to hear the dialogue. Those in the audience who wanted to hear – the majority in fact – tried shouting down the jeers and taunts of the noisy group in the pit and the noise made by both camps escalated. Rattled and nervous, Ned dropped his sword which produced guffaws of laughter and shouts of derision from the pit. A shrill female voice bellowed, 'Let them be heard!' from one of the boxes, but this humane appeal only produced offensive jokes from those supposedly well-bred and well-educated young ruffians in the pit.

The curtain fell for the intermission and the auditorium became a mass of bodies as some tried to escape in disgust and others clustered around the troublemakers offering support and encouragement.

Offstage the players were shaken and fragile. Every one of them had known lively nights, difficult audiences, disinhibited behaviour, but even Mr Jacobs had never seen a house quite like this one, and from the safety of the green room where they had gathered, pronounced that it surely was a conspiracy to sabotage the play.

Richard had instructed the constables, who were regular fixtures in the theatre to preserve order, to go into the auditorium and take away the most vocal trouble makers, or at least to warn them that they would end up in nearby Bow Street if they continued their disruption. He came into the green room, his hair disordered, his face tight with anger and fear.

'Mr Cavendish, sir, it is truly dangerous out there,' sobbed Nancy Price who had hardly dared to move on stage so frightened was she by the aggression shown towards the players. Clasping his arm, she sobbed, 'I cannot go back on, I cannot,' at which Ned put a comforting arm round her shoulders.

A babble of voices agreed with her, but these did not include Eliza's who took Cavendish's arm and led him aside.

'What are we to do? It is as Mr Jacobs said, surely. Sarah Newley is the root cause.'

'I must speak to them, the audience, Eliza. I shall not let Act 2 begin until I have appealed for calm, but I will not be forced by these tactics to take the play off. I will speak to them.'

He looked at her, jaw set firm, grim determination on every feature. 'I will not be beaten. Don't be afraid. We will see this through.'

Thinking quickly, Eliza said, 'Might I not do it? Speak to them? Plead for a proper hearing? Perhaps they will listen to me?'

He thought of the way she had weathered the storm in Act 1 and, as the bell rang for the end of the intermission, he made a decision.

'We will go on stage together Eliza. I shall stand at your side and if you are prepared to speak to the audience as you say, I shall support you. The moment there is any sign of danger, harm or any offence directed at you, I shall escort you from the stage and I will end the performance. We will be in this, as in all things, together.'

She nodded, swallowing hard as he stepped over to the group of actors to explain the plan. She took a deep breath to calm herself and made her way, her heart almost threatening to jump out of her chest, to the wings where Richard joined her.

The curtain was raised on an auditorium much less populated. Several of the boxes were empty now, though the numbers in the pit had grown and it was mainly these who raised an ironic cheer as the figures of Eliza and Richard were revealed in front of the set.

Eliza stepped forward, smiling bravely. She held out a hand with a graceful gesture as if to calm an unruly but much-loved child, the smile never leaving her lips.

'Ladies and gentlemen,' she began, 'or so I believe you to be, though your behaviour has not always indicated so.' Someone began a response to this gentle reprimand, but he was hushed by his neighbours. 'Now I know that you have all come out for an evening of entertainment, laughter and conviviality.' A loud belch greeted this statement, but Eliza smiled indulgently. 'Exactly, sir, but you have done yourselves no service because you are missing one of the – nay – *the* wittiest comedy at present running in London. And I think Mr Harries at the Garden will be forced to admit that by the end of the week.' There was a wave of good-natured laughter then, and she smiled in response to it. 'But you lost so much of our wonderful first act, the handiwork of our playwright and manager, Mr Richard Cavendish here beside me.'

She shot him a radiant smile and gestured toward him. 'He has worked long and hard to write this piece for us, and we have practised and rehearsed for your delight. I beg you, ladies and gentlemen, lovers of the English theatre which is the best in the world, you must acknowledge,' she continued, smiling to a burst of ragged applause and calls of "hear hear." 'We want nothing more than to let you enjoy our play. Please allow us to do our jobs and entertain you,' She extended her arm to left and right, to boxes and pit and high up to the gallery where she blew kisses and received a loud roar of approval, many people drumming their heels on the floor to show their support. She turned then to Richard and he smiled at her in gratitude and affection. A lone female voice shouted out, 'Give 'er a chance. I've paid me money, I want to see this play!' and there was a chorus of agreement from the gallery.

'Thank you, madam,' Eliza replied. 'Ladies and gentlemen,' she continued, well into her stride now, 'we are Englishmen good and true, are we not? We value our freedom, our principles and our honour, do we not?' There was a loud and positive response to this from the pit. 'We are not French' (boos from many quarters and groans of contempt), 'or errant colonists' (more boos and hisses). 'We value fair play,' she continued, though her voice was losing its power now. Noting this with some alarm, Richard glanced anxiously at her then moved closer to her, and taking her hand, interposed with, 'so show us your very Englishness here tonight, theatre lovers, treat us fairly, and let my lovely leading lady save her voice so that she can entertain you with my witty dialogue. Let her and the other members of the cast make you laugh and give you your money's worth.'

There was a huge cheer from the body of the auditorium, a few grudging volleys of applause from the pit, and Richard and Eliza, hand in hand, left the stage, to be replaced by the actors who were to play in the first scene of Act 2. They entered on a wave of good-natured clapping and within a couple of minutes most people had settled as the players delivered their lines. Four minutes later Eliza herself entered as Araminta and the audience clapped and cheered, threatening more disruption of a different kind, but after briefly acknowledging their support, she slipped easily into role, playing one suitor off against another, deceiving her elderly deaf aunt and sharing saucy confidences with her maid, played by Susan.

In the wings Richard Cavendish stood and watched her, marvelling at her skill, her natural charm, her sheer perfection. And as he stood and marvelled, taking a quick glance at the now complaisant and attentive audience, he noted an elegant lounging figure in one of the best boxes who had surely not been there at the beginning of the play.

Antony Denham, as smart and well-turned out as a gentleman of the *ton* could be, was gazing rapt at Eliza, accompanied by two young bucks. His expression suggested that once more he was under her spell. A fiancée in Yorkshire would never stop Denham, Cavendish knew, and his former feelings of triumph and elation over the resumption of his play were fast ebbing away. Would Eliza hold her nerve and cut her ties with Denham forever, or would she be drawn back into his world of privilege, rank and easy pleasure?

When the final curtain fell, the applause was deafening, the atmosphere full of good humour. True, some of the nastier elements in the audience had been already persuaded to leave by the constables, Ferrier and Lovatt, rather than be escorted off the premises, but otherwise the audience had responded well to Eliza's pleas and enjoyed what they had seen.

The buzz in the auditorium was mirrored by the excitement in the green room where, Richard noted, Denham and his friends were greeting the players with easy familiarity. Eliza had acknowledged Denham briefly and politely but had moved on quickly to greet Mr Turnbull who embraced her affectionately. Richard had been doing the rounds of patrons and journalists and had just been buttonholed by *The Gazette's* theatre critic, Sam Willoughby.

'Broken the mould, without doubt,' commented Willoughby, a thin streak of a man in an unfashionable wig who inhaled deeply on the snuff on the back of his hand. He put down his glass and consulted his notebook. 'And the way Miss Grahame turned things around for you, Cavendish. Almost like a drama in its own right, what?'

'She is a remarkable woman,' agreed Richard, following her with his eyes as she shook hands with the great and the good who had been invited to this little party. She was smiling a lot but did not took totally relaxed, perhaps because of the presence of Denham across the room. The three young men were well in their cups and flirting outrageously with Letty and Susan.

Richard suddenly felt overwhelmingly tired and disinclined to be patted on the back and lionised. The strain of the past few weeks, the hectic schedule of rehearsals, the break with Sarah and its fallout had all taken their toll on him, even before the near disaster of that evening. He excused himself to Willoughby, drained his glass and wondered how soon he could decently leave, but Eliza then came across to him and said in a confidential tone, 'I really should go home now, Mr Cavendish. I do not want any further dealings with

Lord Denham and his friends.' Here she glanced across at him and his cronies who were laughing loudly and slapping each other on the back, 'I am very tired, as I'm sure you are.'

'Mm, I am, certainly, Liza.' He scanned the knots of chatting well-wishers and the cast, and, making a snap decision, said, 'I am leaving too. And I will walk you back to George Street in the fresh evening air, and we will leave all these good people to do what they have to do. We are not, after all, indispensable. Come, let's be discreet. They will not know we're gone. It is a good party and has a life of its own. Look, Susan is enjoying herself with Mr Mountfort, a good friend of the theatre, patron and lover of the arts – and pretty women. He looks quite taken with Susan, but let us leave them to it.'

A sudden burst of raucous laughter and the tinkle of broken glass came from Lord Denham's group, causing Eliza to touch Richard's sleeve lightly and say, 'I need ten minutes to change. I'll be at the stage door straight after.'

The night air was cool on their faces as they walked. He had given her his arm for security, necessary when dodging the more inebriated of the roisterers they passed on their way back to George Street. Neither felt the need for conversation; too much had happened that night that was momentous and words could hardly express that.

Turning into George Street, Richard stopped and looked at her, a serious expression on his face.

'Eliza, soon you will hear discreditable things about my family – my father in particular.' She frowned, puzzled by his words and releasing her hold on his arm.

'I want you above all other to know that what will be said is simply not the truth, and that my father, God rest his soul, never did a dishonourable act in his life. But certain scandalmongers feed on these false accounts of events – events on another continent are difficult to verify. They will try to blacken his name, and mine too. Rest assured, Eliza, that the truth will out eventually. In the meantime, do not believe all that you hear.'

'Sarah Newley?' Eliza ventured.

'Yes, it is her malice that has prompted this, as well as tonight's near riot. But we may still overcome her rancour. Do you believe it, Eliza?'

He tilted her chin up with his forefinger so that he was looking deep into her eyes, then he bent his head and kissed her gently on her waiting lips.

Slipping an arm round her waist, he drew her to him and immediately her reaction was to reach up to his neck, her mouth open to receive his kiss. Eventually she pulled away from him, saying, her voice quivering slightly, 'I am almost home now, Richard. Mrs Goode has left a candle in the window – she is minding Betty. I will see you tomorrow when the notices and reviews will appear and will tell us how we did. As for that other matter, the lies of Sarah Newley, we will survive them, shall we not? Together?'

He pulled her once again into his arms before saying, 'Together, what can you and I not achieve, Eliza?' before releasing her to take the short walk home to her door. Once he had seen her go inside, he turned on his heel, making his way back to his lodgings in York Street, feeling that Sarah Newley, public opinion, and the press might make a mighty assault on him, but he had never felt happier in his life.

Chapter 26

In her elegant Gower Street drawing room next morning, the *prima donna* of Covent Garden had been studying the reviews of *A Sweet Revenge*. She had, of course, received a report late the night before from one aspiring social climber and toady who was in her pay, Marcus Rowlands, who had led what he termed the 'riot' at Drury Lane that night. At eleven o'clock, the self-styled ringleader had been ushered into her presence and had given her a highly fanciful account of the mayhem and chaos that he and his cronies had caused in the theatre.

'Hardly a riot from what I hear,' she snapped, her cheeks flushed, eyes blazing. 'It was more a falling out at the tea table as my footman termed it.' Sarah had sent Noakes, her footman, to the play to spy on proceedings and report back. Noakes had declared he had seen more dangerous insurrections at The Shakespeare's Head over a spilt pint of ale.

'You allowed yourselves to be talked down by that silly chit of a girl,' Sarah sneered. When he opened his mouth to protest, she held up her hand imperiously, saying, 'Do not deny it. You and those others are nothing but fools. I shall not be paying you or them the balance of your fee. The play continued and according to the papers, was a huge success. Now leave me!' Rowlands's face was thunderous, but Sarah had rung for her footman who appeared immediately to show him out, as well as Mrs Rutherford, her doughty housekeeper, who had the appearance and spirit of a prize fighter. Nothing would be served by arguing with her and risking the indignity of a forcible ejection. But there were other ways of getting even with madam, thought Rowlands as he made his way, lips set in a thin line, out into the street.

Now, with the newspapers spread before her, Sarah turned to the reviews and some highly colourful accounts of the night's proceedings. And they were not good. Well, they were in fact very good, though not for her.

"Triumph of Reason over Barbarism," proclaimed *The Chronicle*. "Cavendish's play will change comedy for ever."

"The Comic muse returns to our theatres," declared *The London Magazine*. "Eliza Begs for Justice," was *The Spectator's* headline. And the reviews of the play were no less glowing. "Will this be the longest run of any comedy in the history of the theatre?" asked Mr Spiers of *The Theatrical Chronicle*.

She thrust the papers aside and rang her little silver bell irritably.

'Bring the carriage round, Noakes. I am going to the offices of *The Gazette* in half an hour.'

Chapter 27

There was an air of anti-climax at Drury Lane next morning. Some of the cast had overindulged in the drinks the management had provided and there were a few thick heads and queasy stomachs to contend with. Richard had arrived at eight o'clock that morning and gone straight into the auditorium to the pit where the cleaners were sweeping up the mess left from the night before – bottles, screwed up playbills, orange peel and apple cores. The rank smell of spilt wine emanated from the puddles on the floor among the benches.

'Make sure all this is in good order for tonight, Archie,' Richard instructed.

'I always does, sir,' he replied, 'but it's worse than usual. Animals they was last night, sir. Miss Grahame done well.'

'She certainly did,' agreed Richard smiling at the recollection. 'She was Boadicea, Queen Elizabeth, Nell Gwynn, all in one.'

Archie rested on his broom a moment, then said, 'His lordship Lord Denham, he've left a note and flowers for her this morning. His footman called round early. Perhaps he'll make a lady of her, you never know.'

Richard's bubble of euphoria was pricked by this news, but then he remembered Eliza's kiss and said dismissively, 'I'd be surprised to see that.'

Over breakfast that morning Flora had enthused about the previous night's performance.

'I had such an exciting night, Eliza. You, and Susan too, you were wonderful. That speech you gave. So clever. The man next to me,' she said looking coy, 'he said to me he had never heard anything like it.' Susan, noting her animated response and the pink in her cheeks, said, 'Was he a handsome fellow, this man?'

Flora passed coffee to Susan who was nursing the baby. 'He was, in fact. He walked me to our door afterwards and asked permission to call on me.' Eliza smiled at her sister, pleased that the terrible experience with John had not left her with a fear and mistrust of men. Her sister was positively glowing and looking exceedingly pretty this morning. Eliza continued looking at a slightly hung-over Susan feeding the baby, 'And you were not alone in receiving male attention last night, Flora. Susan here,' she nodded across at her, 'Susan was fighting off admirers … successfully, I hope?' she continued, looking archly at her friend.

'Of course,' said Susan, 'but Mr Mountfort was very attentive as you say, and I expect to see him again quite soon.'

'Well, then all three ladies of the house had their wooers last night,' Flora quipped, collecting plates from the table, 'though Eliza seems not to have given any encouragement to Lord Denham. Did you? He was looking at you like a love-struck ninny.'

Eliza got up quickly from the table, her used crockery in her hands, and made for the sink.

'Indeed not. I have told you already, I want nothing more to do with him. We manage perfectly well without him. Mr Cavendish,' she continued, hoping her voice did not betray her, 'Mr Cavendish will be paying me more now, and we can easily live on what we all earn.'

'I didn't see much of you in the green room party last night,' Susan said in a neutral voice. 'Nor, I come to think of it, did I see Mr Cavendish. There were people looking for him – and you too. Quite a coincidence,' she twinkled.

'He walked me home. It was very noisy in the streets outside, more so than usual,' Eliza said, seeing Susan raise her eyebrows.

'How kind of him,' Susan drawled. Betty had fallen asleep on her breast. She removed her gently and laid her down in the Moses basket they kept in the room for her naps. Susan shrugged her ample bosom back into her dressing gown, adding, 'Still, I suppose it was the least he could do for you as you had saved his play – our play, our company – from the worst disaster that must have befallen us. A new play damned on its first night. I hope he showed his gratitude fully,' she teased, at which Eliza spluttered, 'Susan, what are you suggesting? We have a professional relationship, you know that.' Then she added, smiling coyly at her friend, 'at least that is the case at the moment.'

'I knew it!' Susan exploded. 'There has always been something there between you, I've always known that. Even when he was Sarah's lover. And I'm sure she sensed it too. Which was why she hated you so much. So tell me how... '

'A kiss. Just a kiss, though a very lovely kiss. And some words.'

'Of esteem? Desire? Love?'

'No, not exactly.'

'But I see from your eyes that you wish ...'

'More than anything. But there are problems. No, I cannot say more.' Eliza's voice trailed off and her sister went over to her and took her in her arms, her eyes moist.

'Eliza, you will overcome them, I am sure. Love always triumphs.'

'On the stage anyway,' added Susan, 'though real life is another matter. Come Eliza, we must get ready for the theatre. I shall be discreet, don't worry. I shall say nothing to the others and certainly not to Mr Cavendish, you can rely on me. Flora, Betty will, I hope, stay asleep until I get home for her next feed.'

Before the morning rehearsal, Mr Cavendish, looking unusually chipper and relaxed in front of the company more than a little worse for wear after the green room party, gave them all a summary of what the reviews and notices had said. There was much light-hearted banter as people recalled the outrages of Act 1, but then the manager became more serious in tone.

'You all know how close we came to having our play damned by that mob in the pit. You will know how disastrous that would have been for us all.' Mr Jacobs was nodding solemnly. It had happened in Garrick's time: an unwise choice of play by the great actor/manager had meant that its rival Covent Garden had cashed in on the blunder.

'If it had not been for Eliza here,' he gestured towards her, smiling, 'we should not be celebrating these impressive reviews today.' There was a heartfelt murmur of assent and affection for her that made her blush and look down at her shoes.

'Now, there were errors made last night,' he said in a brisk business-like manner, 'so I need to have a run-through, and I promise you, I shall take no prisoners.'

'As usual,' muttered Ned, but with respectful affection.

'Places please for curtain up Act 1. We will have to be speedy and thorough because Signior Vitelli and the orchestra need to practise the music for the afterpiece at one o'clock. Places please everyone.'

Mr Steele at *The Gazette* could hardly believe his luck. Not only had his newspaper printed a full report of the opening night of *A Sweet Revenge* plus reviews, but now, after this quite unexpected and exclusive meeting with Miss Newley, the recent darling of Covent Garden, it also had a revelation, an exclusive one at that, about the playwright's family, featuring a tale of cowardly behaviour by General Cavendish in the face of the rebels in the colonies. He glanced down at the notes he had been taking as Miss Newley poured forth her story and knew that his skill as a journalist would enable him to write a scoop that would shock the nation, have possible repercussions in Parliament itself and take the theatre world by storm.

Of course, he thought, sipping his glass of wine to aid his mental processes, the lady was doubtless biased and had her own agenda. She had pleaded that she was a patriot and felt it her duty to report the perfidy of one of England's most respected military men. The fact that General Cavendish had been dead for more than a year and the incident itself had occurred two years ago and that he could not personally be called to account now made her determination to rake up these charges seem all the more malicious to Steele. That and the fact that Steele knew she and Cavendish had been lovers was also a factor. To most people who had observed them, including himself, it had always seemed a one-sided affair. It was significant that she had broken away from Drury Lane recently. Artistic differences, or the usurpation of her role as *prima donna* by the courageous and spirited Eliza Grahame. Miss Newley had given him the source of her story; General Rupert Allingham, serving in

The Buffs at the time of the incident, then merely a major. The story went that Cavendish, commanding The Buffs at the time, had refused to engage with the rebels at Trenton despite advice and the fact that the British outnumbered the rebels by three to one. Instead, he ordered a retreat, against the strong recommendation of his subordinates who foresaw a British victory. During the retreat, however, his soldiers had been ambushed as they left the area, resulting in huge fatalities. When the incident had been reported, there had been a cover-up, Allingham claimed, and General Cavendish escaped censure.

Allingham had told Sarah the story after a night of passion with her, but she had never acted upon the disclosure or sought to reveal it while she was trying to ensnare Richard Cavendish. Now she clearly cared nothing for the good name of the Cavendishes and wanted revenge. Mr Steele thought briefly of the General's family but it was only a fleeting thought: the family name would be sullied, meaning all would suffer: the playwright son, the widow, the two unmarried daughters. Reputations would be trampled into the dust he knew, but it would make a damned fine story.

Steele put down his glass and took a pinch of snuff from the silver box on his desk, then he picked up his pen, dipped it into the inkwell and began to write. The words flowed easily from practice and skill. At one point he paused and asked himself what was to be achieved by such revelations now, years after the event, with the perpetrator dead. And was Sarah's story true? Still, he was a journalist and had never let the truth get in the way of a good story. And this one, hard on the heels of the young man's triumph, would make the very best of stories.

The audience on the second night of *A Sweet Revenge* behaved in an exemplary way. True, the pit was as noisy and boisterous as ever, the benches filled with those who thought themselves the intelligentsia, the discerning critics among the audience, but they soon settled, and as the curtain rose to reveal Eliza sitting in a well-appointed drawing room that contained, rather promisingly, a screen, there was a huge roar of approval from everywhere in the house, high and low alike. Eliza acknowledged her reception with a smile, then slipped into character immediately.

The rest of the play did not go without a hitch however; Ned's lace cuff caught in Letty's wig as he bent to embrace her and the whole structure looked doomed to fall onto her face, but with an expert flick of his wrist, Ned freed himself and the moment passed. Nor did the veteran Mr Jacobs escape unscathed. Letty, playing opposite him, skipped two pages of dialogue and Mr Jacobs was required to extemporise which he did so convincingly that no one in the audience knew, although the others on stage spent a few tense minutes before Letty returned to the words the playwright had written. The screen, a flimsy piece of stage furniture hastily constructed, wobbled in places as characters used it to hide behind, and Richard, looking at the play from the manager's box, made a mental note to have it rebuilt more substantially.

But all in all, everything went well. The reception the cast received at the final curtain was ecstatic and the author was urged up on stage to take his bow. As he took Eliza and Ned's hands, stepping forward to receive the audience's acclaim, he glanced at her and saw her face alight with happiness. With a jolt he imagined how that expression would change when Sarah Newley's revenge had reached its climax.

After the curtain had fallen, Cavendish was not to be seen. The door to his office was firmly shut as Eliza and Susan made their way out of the stage door where well-wishers had gathered to ask for autographs and to give flowers to the principals. Eliza was always gracious to her supporters and did and said what was required of her before she and Susan could manage to get away, but she did feel very tired and deflated. No word from Richard. It was as if the intimacy of the previous night had never happened.

Eventually she and Susan were away, arm in arm, heading back to the house, giving a wide berth to a group of noisy revellers just leaving The Shakespeare's Head. One young buck detached himself from the group and lurched towards them, clearly under the impression they were ladies of the town. It had happened before and would doubtless happen again. Sometimes when the girls had to walk home alone, they would hire a linkboy at a farthing a time to lead them safely home with a torch of flaming pitch, and deter overtures from men seeking female company. Covent Garden, despite its much-improved roads and double-branched streetlights, could be a dangerous place, especially after dark, but it had a colour and vibrancy that Eliza liked. Having grown up in St Giles, she could handle most situations and was not too precious to feel she was somehow superior to the world she now inhabited. Somerset Street was all very pleasant and safe, a pleasant stage set, but she somehow always felt she was an interloper, a fraud, living as she did safely cushioned from the real world. And her own neighbourhood, just a short step from the Piazza, was respectable and quiet enough. As she lay in bed later, her mind racing with the events of the past couple of days, Eliza felt depressed and ill at ease. Why had Richard not been on hand to speak to her at the end of the performance? What had he meant when he had talked about matters coming to light and events not being what they seemed? She slept little, and when the fingers of the early sun poked through her thin curtains and Betty's hungry wail intruded on her muddled thoughts, she sighed and turned over in bed, not relishing the day ahead.

Later that day, a little rested and restored in spirits, Eliza and Susan, walked to the theatre. Even after the triumph of a new play, ecstatic notices and widespread acclaim, there was still the everyday business of rehearsals and learning of lines, costume fittings and preparations for new pieces. The public demanded a relentless supply of fresh entertainment; if they didn't get it from Drury Lane, it was just a short stroll to Mr Harries's Garden. Neither theatre could afford to sit back and rest on its laurels.

It was early afternoon now, the day was hot and the area around the Piazza was busy, noisy and full of the smells of food and the remains of the detritus from the market earlier that morning. Cabbage leaves and horse dung, flowers wilting in the heat, fresh bread and pungent cooked meats all combined to give the place its distinctive atmosphere, as did the smells of beer and strong spirits emanating from the many taverns and chophouses whose windows and doors were open in the heat of the afternoon.

As they walked to the theatre, Susan and Eliza chatted.

'Do you ever wonder, Susan, how our mothers are getting on?'

'Yes, every day. When I look at little Betty and think that her grandmother will never see her or hold her.' Eliza squeezed her friend's arm. 'I wish there was some way my parents could forgive me for my sin,' Susan said sadly, 'but I know they will never be able to. And you, Liza, you would stand more of a chance with your mother surely.'

'I don't think she will ever forgive me for leaving with Flora. And she will still be living with that odious man who attacked Flora. We can never see him again. Flora is recovering well. But I often think of her, and George too, gone for a soldier or a sailor. Dead maybe, in the colonies. If he lives, I expect he still hates me … if he thinks of me at all, that is.'

In silence they reached the theatre, each woman thinking of the family she had abandoned, or which had abandoned her. Unusually, there was a crowd of people round the stage door and Archie the doorman was looking angry as he pushed back a large group of men who seemed set on storming the stage door.

'Stand aside now! You blood suckers!' he bawled, the veins on his forehead standing out on his ruddy face. As Eliza and Susan approached, their expressions concerned and confused, a strident voice called from the crowd, 'Miss Grahame! What can you tell us about the news about Richard Cavendish? How does it affect your association with him? Did you know of his family history?'

Other voices soon joined in, each more insistent than the last. Eliza didn't understand the import of these questions but did remember Richard's cryptic comments on the night of the premiere. Richard's name was the common factor in all of the questions being hurled at her. Someone bolder than the others had pushed his way towards her and stood before her, so close she could see the pimples on his chin and his crooked front teeth.

'Miss Grahame, will you continue to work with a man whose father was a coward, a traitor even?'

Archie reached his massive arms out, as strong and gnarled as tree trunks, and grabbed the pimply man by the shoulders, pushing him roughly back into the crowd of fellow journalists with an almighty roar.

'Damn your eyes, the lot of you, blood sucking wretches! Let the ladies be – and Mr Cavendish too. Come away ladies,' he continued, ushering them inside the stage door to safety, slamming the door behind them and locking it from the inside.

'Archie! What! Why … what has happened?'

Eliza's heart was thumping in her chest and she could barely breathe.

'Go in, Miss. He will tell you. It is merely tittle-tattle. There is no truth in it I am sure. Bet your life that trollop Newley is at the bottom of it. Go on down to the green room. He's got 'em all in there.'

Both women scurried down the passageway to the green room where Richard, looking pale and tense, sat in front of a semi-circle of chairs, at a small table on which lay a copy of *The Gazette*. Eliza and Susan took seats near the back where people were looking at each other with puzzlement on their faces. Richard glanced their way, his expression serious and intense. Rising to his feet, he began.

'We are all here now, so I just wanted to inform you about a recent development that may affect every one of us.' He picked up the copy of *The Gazette* and said, 'This paper has published some damning accusations about my late father, a distinguished general during the war in the colonies.' A wave of shock passed through the cast. Glances were exchanged. Susan searched Eliza's face for signs of emotion, but she sat, impassive, despite the seriousness of Richard's announcement. So this is what he had been alluding to on opening night. And was this also the work of Sarah Newley? Somehow she felt it was.

Richard continued, 'I shall of course be fighting to clear my father's name,' at which there was a murmur of assent, 'but it will be difficult after these years. In the meantime, I am asking for your support, friends. There will be scandal, scurrilous rumour, but rest assured, I will continue here with you, doing what we do best.'

A voice, Mr Jacobs's, deeply sonorous, spoke out.

'It seems to me, sir, that your success has prompted these scandalous revelations. May I remind you of your own words in *The Heiress*?

"There is no passion so rooted in the human heart as envy." Lord Hardcastle says that and you wrote it in *The Heiress*. Next month there will be other targets, other scandals. We know you and we will not judge.' He turned towards the others. 'I speak for us all, I think, when I say we will continue as usual. As Hamlet says, "The play's the thing."'

A muted cheer rose from the actors and Richard bowed his head to conceal his emotion.

'Thank you all. Now,' he said in a different tone entirely, 'to work. Let us take our places on stage. You were too slow in Act 2, prompter. Let's to it and make tonight's performance the best yet. Miss Grahame, a word please.'

As the actors dispersed, some to take up positions on stage, others to the dressing rooms or to wait in the wings, Eliza went to where Richard was picking up his newspaper from the table. The room was empty now and a stagehand strolled in and began moving chairs.

'One moment please,' called Richard, 'Thomas, isn't it? Do that later, please!'

Thomas grunted in assent and the door was closed.

Richard took her hand and pulled her towards him.

'Now you know what I inferred the other night, Eliza. Now you see the damage that she has done. How can you bear to be associated with me?'

'It is she then who did this to you? She knew the accusations against your father?'

'She had heard them from a former lover. He was about to make it public and – well, she persuaded him not to. It was cowardly of me to involve her. I should have taken on the fight to clear my father's name myself. My mother and sisters will be devastated. I must go and see them in Hampshire.'

She squeezed the hand that she still held.

'Eliza, my love … if I have any right to call you that.'

She nodded and smiled. 'I can think of no words I would rather hear, Richard. And I say them back to you.'

As he bent to kiss her, the door was flung open and Archie entered, red-faced and sweating.

'Beg pardon, Sir, Miss, but that crowd is getting pretty nasty outside the stage door. When you leave, go out by the back entrance – down the tunnel. Should we send for the Runners, Mr Cavendish, to get them away?'

'Yes, after the rehearsal, Archie,' replied Richard, his voice and demeanour calm and controlled. 'We still have work to do here. We will not be browbeaten by the gentlemen of the press – or anyone else in fact. Will we, Eliza?' He smiled at her, took her hand and together they left the green room and headed for the stage.

223

Chapter 28

When Richard was in Hampshire trying to console his mother and sisters, Eliza and Mr Jacobs shared his managerial duties between them. Fortunately, Friday's house, though at capacity, was good humoured and supportive. Saturday night's play was *The Beaux Stratagem* and an afterpiece, *The Lord's Lady* became very rowdy, the men in the pit growing very excited as it featured Betsy Lowther in her breeches role, which she played with maximum suggestiveness. Eliza thought that Richard needed to take her to task about the lewd winks and posturings she affected. That might sell seats, but that sort of behaviour would do nothing for the reputation of serious actresses, confirming as it did the idea that all women on stage were easy game.

Eliza stayed on in the theatre until the entire evening's entertainment was over and, exhausted, summoned a linkboy who was one of a crowd of them lounging underneath the portico. He seized a torch, took her money and together they set off. At least tomorrow is Sunday, thought Eliza with relief. She would rest and try to give some more thought to how she might find out about her mother. She would need to venture into St Giles to find out what had happened to her. Richard's obvious concern for his own mother had touched a raw nerve, especially after her conversation with Susan. She needed to know Annie was safe and well. If she was still with the hateful John, that was her choice, and Eliza could never approve, but she did not want her mother on her conscience and needed to know more.

'Looks like you got a visitor, Miss,' said the linkboy, raising the flaming torch to illuminate the elegant coach outside her door. With horror, Eliza noted the Denham arms on the side of it and fled to her

224

door that was opened immediately by a distraught Flora. Baby Betty's thin wail could be heard coming from upstairs.

'Lord Denham is in the sitting room, Eliza – he insisted. I am so sorry. I could not reason with him.' Tears stood in her sister's eyes but the combination of the physically strong male presence of Denham and his innate sense of privilege and rank had completely overpowered her. Eliza took her arm gently. 'Flora, of course you had to. Don't upset yourself. I shall go to him. All will be well.' She said with a distinct sense that it would not.

Antony Denham had been sprawling beside the unlit fireplace looking bored. He got to his feet as soon as Eliza entered the room and made her a polite bow. If he had been drinking, it was not to excess, and he looked calm and in control, not threatening in any way.

'I wanted to pay my respects and offer you my congratulations,' he began, 'and as you did not reply to my notes, I had to take it upon myself to see you here,' he continued, unable to keep the note of disdain from his voice as he glanced round the plain and modest room.

'At Drury Lane your doorman seems to have taken against my servants and won't let me have access to you at the theatre,' he continued accusingly, 'no matter how well I bribe him.' He attempted a smile, to which Eliza made no response.

'My lord, I think we have said everything to each other that we can,' Eliza began, trying to control her voice. They were both standing in front of the fireplace and she made no move to ask him to be seated or to offer him refreshment. There would be no chink in her armour and she wished this unwanted interview to be over as soon as possible.

'I read about the latest misfortune to overtake Cavendish,' he said, taking out an enamelled snuff box from his coat and proceeding to place a pinch of the back of his hand which he inhaled, wrinkling his nose.

'So, dishonour, loss of reputation, will doubtless follow,' he continued, snapping the lid of the snuffbox shut. 'Unless his father's name is cleared,' he drawled. 'I might be able to help a little with that, friends in high places, don't you know,' he continued looking fondly at her. 'I would do that for him, you know, Eliza. Not exactly for him but for you.'

'But how might that be possible?'

He tapped the side of his nose conspiratorially. 'No need to know the details, dear Eliza, but it can be done. I am not without influence,' he said smugly. 'A full refutation of all those charges made against him, in the House no less, public apology, the General exonerated, the Cavendish name restored, major publicity for him, the theatre, and you of course.'

'And your price, my lord?' Her voice had a steely ring to it as she stepped away from him and turned her head, apparently to examine a cheap print of a vase of flowers that hung on the wall.

'Just one night … one last night with you, so that we can say our farewells properly.' His tone was wheedling. 'We parted in such an unsatisfactory way. I behaved badly, I know I did. But just one night, in the Hanover Square house, my London home. I would make no further claims on you. I accept your reasons for terminating our arrangement. I understand – I admire your scruples about my marriage. But Eliza, I need to be with you, to make love to you one final time. And as recompense

I will do whatever is in my power to save Cavendish's reputation. I have always suspected that you also feel for him. I know he loves you Eliza. I saw it in his eyes as he watched you speak on opening night. He will have you forever, Liza, but I ask only for one night in your arms.'

Ten minutes later Denham left George Street. He was polite to Flora who showed him out as he handed her a guinea.

'For Miss Turner's baby. I was discourteous to her about the child when last I saw her in Somerset Street. Please give her my apologies and this coin to buy a toy for the little one.'

He climbed into his coach, shouting to Francis, 'My club!' as he did so. As the horses' harnesses jingled into action, the thoroughbreds heading for St James and milord's club, curtains twitched in George Street. The arrival of a smart coach with an aristocratic crest would be food for gossip the next day. With luck, Mrs Goode would get the story behind it from Flora.

In the meantime, Antony Denham sat back in his seat, his expression impassive.

He had had his answer.

Chapter 29

The following Sunday, Eliza had a day free from the theatre. Richard was still in Hampshire. He had sent a brief note to her that said that his mother had taken to her bed, inconsolable at the news *The Gazette* had printed. Maria and Lucinda, his sisters, were tearful and confused and he was duty bound to stay at least until Wednesday. He concluded with 'All my love, Richard,' which touched her heart but also added to the whirling, conflicting thoughts and emotions which threatened to overwhelm her at times.

On the Sunday morning she had told Susan and Flora that she was going to spend the day and possibly the night too at Mrs Wainwright's at Compass Street, the house where she and Flora had lodged temporarily when they had fled from St Giles.

Flora looked puzzled at the news and at the carpetbag her sister had brought downstairs with her. Eliza was putting a jar of preserves and some eggs carefully into the bag as well as a couple of apples.

Flora who had been cutting bread, stopped in the act and looked puzzled.

'But why are you going there? We have not seen her for months.'

'She is ill and alone. She needs someone to help with … things. Food and the like. She has the dropsy and can no longer get around as she used to. It is sad to see her, Flora. And she was kind to us.'

'But why you? She has lodgers, family too I'm sure. You need to rest today. You will be ill if you do not look after yourself properly. With all the responsibilities, you have taken on, you …'

'Really Flora, you can be so selfish sometimes,' replied Eliza impatiently, taking another apple from the bowl to add to her bag. 'Think of other people for a change. The elderly need our help when they become frail and weak. It's our duty to help them.'

Flora had never seen this side of her sister before and speculated on how Eliza knew so much about Mrs Wainwright's state of health and decline in fortune, but the set of Eliza's jaw and her determined expression did not encourage further questions, so she placed the bread on the table, simply saying, 'Do have something to eat before you leave. And give her my best wishes.'

Antony Denham took a more than usually acute interest in the supper he ordered from his housekeeper and cook on Sunday evening. He wanted it to be a stark contrast for Eliza from the plain fare of George Street and the hastily consumed pasties, apples, and slices of cooked meat that the theatre staff seemed to exist on during their working day. So he bespoke mushroom broth, mullet, venison and syllabub to tempt Eliza's appetite. From the cellar he ordered Chateau d'Yquem and Tokay, though he knew that Eliza would drink only moderately. He told himself sternly that he would be careful not to overindulge, not wanting his prowess in the bedroom to be compromised in any way.

He chose his clothes carefully, only disagreeing with his valet on one item, the burgundy silk waistcoat favoured by his valet being replaced by the lilac shot silk, a favourite of his.

He spent the morning driving his new curricle round Hyde Park where, quite by chance, he met the Hon. Titus Saville with whom he had a discussion about the Cavendish affair. Briefly Denham outlined his interest in the matter, naming no names of course. The Hon Titus confirmed that a much more favourable slant on the General's behaviour at Trenton could be put forward, to Parliament and public alike – if one knew who to approach. Denham came away from this tête-à-tête much encouraged and after coffee at Whites, he returned to Hanover Square a happy man. At five-thirty he would send Francis with the coach to a venue Eliza had suggested, and after the tantalising food and drink, the luxurious ambiance, his protestations of desire and devotion, he would achieve his heart's desire, at least for one night, although he also knew that many ladies of his acquaintance, from the ladies of Covent Garden to the boudoirs of Knightsbridge, found him irresistible. Eliza had done so once. Who was to say she would not again?

Chapter 30

On Wednesday Richard Cavendish was back in his office at Drury Lane. The place looked tidier, he thought, far too tidy for him to find the notes he had made on Act 3, so he grumbled under his breath and cursed as he tried to locate them. Wine bottles had been cleared away, quills arranged neatly in a pot and a couple of wigs that had lain around in the office since Turnbull's time were absent. A bust of Shakespeare, formerly used as a paper weight, now looking pristine, revived, refreshed, dusted, was placed, for inspiration perhaps, to the left of his blotter with its clean surface, free of doodles and jottings. This was surely Eliza's doing. The thought made him smile and long to see her. Which he did at around eleven o'clock when she and Susan appeared for rehearsal.

She and Ned were on stage practising an exchange from the beginning of Act 3 that involved her slipping behind the screen, recently rebuilt and now more sturdy. They were going over their lines and then broke into uncontrollable laughter when Eliza moved too quickly, catching the hem of her gown in the screen. Richard strode across the stage to where they stood, still laughing and said, 'Eliza! You began without me.'

She turned sharply on hearing her name and colour flooded her cheeks, her eyes sparkling.

'Mr Cavendish! It is good to see you back, sir,' she added coquettishly. Ned looked from one to the other and could see immediately what the whole company had been predicting since the premiere of *A Sweet Revenge*.

'I am happy to be back among you ... all of you,' he replied. 'Now let's do that bit again, shall we? Without the giggles.'

Henson's Chop House on the Piazza was one of the more salubrious eating places in the area, Marcus Rowlands concluded, which was why he had chosen it for his rendezvous with Mr Steele who would doubtless pay the bill as well as a handsome remuneration for the information he was about to impart.

The aromas rising from the plates of food being served to customers around him were making his stomach growl in protest; it was an expensive business, rubbing shoulders with the *ton* especially when your circumstances were as straitened as his. The *ton* spent money endlessly on trifles like snuff, ruffles, tiepins, bottles of champagne and seal rings. Then more ambitiously on racehorses, curricles, Purdey pistols and breeches from Jermyn Street. Not to mention wagers on cards, billiards, money that slipped through their highborn fingers without a thought. That easy contempt for money was, in Marcus's eyes, completely enviable and it was that he aspired to. But to make your way in the world, without their advantages of birth and fortune, was exceedingly difficult: you had to have the readies, the blunt, the chinks to ease your passage. Which was why he was sitting here in Henson's chophouse, with a titbit as juicy as one of Tobias Henson's steaks that sizzled on platters around him.

Trying to subdue his hunger pangs, he sipped his drink slowly, not wanting to meet the cost of another. Better wait for the journalist who could easily afford it. He glanced down at his hands, noticing how frayed the cuffs of his shirt were, pulling his jacket sleeves down to disguise them. He would need to trim the cuffs before he went to The Pantheon later. Or maybe Steele's generosity might run to a new shirt.

Suddenly the man himself appeared at Marcus's side, a tankard of ale in each hand,

232

'Here you are. I've ordered dishes of lamb chops and potatoes, if that meets with your approval.' He offered Marcus a thin smile and set down the tankards on the table, fussing with the tails of his coat as he lowered himself into the seat opposite.

'Now, what do you have for me?' He took a sip of his ale and rummaged in his pocket for notebook and pencil. 'Some information concerning a well-known actress, you say. I trust it is more than just the usual indiscretion or some inappropriate romantic liaison? Tell me what you know.

Chapter 31

Drury Lane was winding down at the end of a busy season. Only two weeks remained before a large part of the company would travel north to the Yorkshire circuit, as Eliza had done during her first year. Richard had rented a large house in York for her, Susan, Flora and baby Betty, while he would put up at The Lion whenever he was in York. London and Hampshire would occupy a lot of his time this summer. His family needed his support, and he would try and come up with a plan to pursue the matter of the charges that had been made against his father in the American War.

He and Eliza talked over the prospects for the summer one night as they sat side by side on the worn sofa at George Street. The rest of the house was quiet, Susan was upstairs with the baby, Flora out on some unexplained mission.

'I shall think of you constantly, Eliza,' he said, squeezing her hand as she sat with her head on his shoulder, his voice sad at the prospect of being away from her for days or even weeks at a time.

'Not so much that it interferes with your writing, I hope, Richard,' she replied, mock serious. 'How else can you write us another successful play if you are languishing and sighing because you miss me.' She smiled up at him, 'and you will need to show your sisters and your mother the sights of London when they come up from Hampshire.' She had hoped that Richard would have introduced her to his mother by now, but there had been no mention of a meeting, which worried her. In fact, although she and Richard had confessed their love for each other and were basking in the glow of their mutual affection and attraction, Richard had said nothing about their future. The Drury Lane company, a worldly bunch used to the complete spectrum of relationships on stage and off, might well be assuming that Richard now shared Eliza's bed, but that was not however the case, at least at the present time. Much as the lovers wanted to consummate their passion, Eliza held back, although she could not guarantee for how long. Richard had not spoken specifically of marriage, which was what Eliza longed for. Was she to assume that he did mean to offer marriage? In the world of the theatre, such assumptions need not be made, though in the real world, if she were a virgin, it would be generally assumed that marriage would be the natural progression. Richard, of course, knew her history and was under no illusion about her past; maybe her affair with Denham made her just a romantic diversion for Richard, a temporary amusement for him, and he would do what many men did and marry a woman with some money, from a good family, to be the mother of his children. Perhaps she was destined always to be a mistress and never a wife. If that really was the case, Eliza reasoned, in her darker moments, then perhaps she ought to enter fully into her role as Richard's mistress and at least enjoy it.

There were to be two more performances of *A Sweet Revenge* before the theatre closed and the journey north began. Eliza was to travel by coach with Susan and Betty. There would be frequent stops *en route*, changes of horses, lumpy beds, poor meals, but at least the actual journey would be more comfortable than Eliza's first. And her status now had changed, her position on the playbills much more prominent, her wages more substantial and her reputation more established.

Some of these thoughts were flitting through her mind as she sat with Richard on the sofa, his arm around her shoulder, candles flickering in the wall sconces, their light casting a warm glow over the shabby room.

It had been a long day in the theatre and a difficult one. There was a sense of transition, uncertainty, as members of the cast said goodbye to one another for the summer, maybe forever. Times were uncertain in the theatre. People came and went, formed new friendships and alliances. No one could really anticipate who would be back in September or who the public would want to see.

'One more performance, Eliza,' sighed Richard, breaking the comfortable silence and smoothing the fringe of brown curls that lay on her forehead, in a gentle rhythmic way that was almost sending her to sleep. 'Then you will take Yorkshire by storm.'

'I hope I do not see Lord Denham while we are there – at least not when I am on my own, without you. I really do not want to see him again. Perhaps though, it will be inevitable.'

Richard could feel her body tense under the weight of his arm. She sat up straight and lifted troubled eyes to him. He frowned, puzzled by her obvious discomfort.

'But you did not part on bad terms, my love, did you, after the green room party? There was no falling out, no argument. And you haven't seen him since, have you?'

Eliza remembered the planned rendezvous, the venue she had chosen, the look of triumph in Denham's eyes when she had agreed to it. How angry he will have been when she did not keep that appointment, how dented his pride, how determined to have his revenge on her he would be now. And how adamant he would be to offer absolutely no help from his exalted position to clear the Cavendish name. Richard, of course, knew none of this and she was terrified to think that, face to face with a drunk and vengeful Denham, on his own turf, Antony would reveal their planned assignation.

Richard now gave her shoulder a gentle squeeze.

'He knows you have cut all ties with him,' he said comfortably, 'he would not risk further rejection. We men, you know, we do not like to be rebuffed.' That last remark, meant to be reassuring, was anything but to Eliza. Richard continued. 'Trust me, Eliza, he will be busy impressing the lovely ladies of Yorkshire who are not his fiancée whom he has already snared.' Then his voice lost its teasing tone and took on a serious edge. 'He will have done what I could never do, my love, and that is ... to forget you,' at which he kissed her tenderly and made her doubts and fears disappear at least for that moment. How she longed for him to raise her to her feet and lead her upstairs to her small bedroom and to make love to her. What did it matter if he offered marriage or not? They loved each other, of that she was certain.

Almost on the brink of taking the initiative herself, she attempted to prolong the kiss, but was thwarted by his ending it quite firmly, kissing her briskly on the nose and getting up from the sofa.

As he retrieved his hat from a nearby chair, he said, 'A difficult day tomorrow, my love. I must go and let you get some sleep.'

He bade her goodnight on her doorstep, whispering endearments so as not to wake the baby, and within a minute or so, was striding purposefully down George Street, whistling as he went.

The next morning there was no rehearsal. Backstage and behind the scenes there was chaos as scenery and props not required that night were being collected together, repaired where necessary, ready to be loaded on carts for the journey up the Great North Road. Hampers of costumes stood around ready to transport, with some repairs being carried out hurriedly by Sukey and Peg. Dressing rooms were being tidied and the detritus of the past year removed – damaged hairpieces, odd shoes and bottles. When some of the women had complained bitterly that the mice and cockroaches in the dressing rooms were better fed than they were, Cavendish had promised a top-to-toe cleaning would be done while the theatre was closed.

For those who were in the theatre that morning, which included Eliza, there was a further surprise in store, the next act in the continuing drama of the fortunes of Drury Lane.

Archie the doorkeeper, his florid face dangerously flushed with excitement, let her in, smiling broadly.

'Miss Grahame! Well, there's an unexpected turn of events, and no mistake! Go and see Mr Cavendish soon as you can, Miss. News about Miss Newley – the harpy! Good news!' he called after her as she hurried down the passage, stopping at Richard's open door.

Richard was standing at his desk on which a copy of *The Gazette* lay open. He turned quickly when he heard her hurry inside, his face breaking into a broad grin.

'Here it is, Eliza!' he pointed at the newspaper. 'What we all suspected. Evidence of the treachery of that vile woman.' Eliza came across to the desk, untying her bonnet as she read the headline,

"Sabotage of renowned author's latest play at Drury Lane."

She read avidly, incredulous but overjoyed that the plot had been exposed. The newspaper did not go as far as to name names, but the inferences were clear. No one who knew the fashionable world of the theatre could be in any doubt who was to blame.

Smiling, Eliza turned to Richard, laying a hand on his arm,

'So what we all suspected was true. She paid this man – Rowlands – to get people together to disrupt the performance, to sabotage it. This is not a criminal offence, but will certainly bring down shame and censure on her head.'

'Harries won't like it,' added Richard, 'box office will suffer, assuredly at the Garden. Guilty by association. And they are closing soon for the summer as we are. We are vindicated, Eliza. And,' he turned to her, taking both her hands in his, 'with some time free from my duties here, I can begin to vindicate my father's memory and get to the truth behind these scurrilous rumours of General Allingham. My mother has begged me to clear my father's name.'

Eliza withdrew her hands from Richard's grip and turned to him.

'That will be difficult to do, Richard, will it not? Without the aid of men of influence? Members of Parliament? The aristocracy. It would be very useful for your cause if you had people to fight your corner.'

'It would give me access to documents and records that would be useful so that I could search for the truth. But as you know, my love, I do not have access to these kinds of friends, unless I seek out my father's old associates, though I daresay many of them will be dead by now.' His euphoria at the revelations of *The Gazette* had dissipated as he contemplated the difficulty of the task before him.

Eliza bit her lip, wondering whether the decision she had made a week ago had been the wrong one after all.

Chapter 32

The summer season in Yorkshire was going well. The house that Eliza and Susan shared in York was pleasant, tasteful even, and they had the services of Margaret, a local girl who cleaned and shopped for them as well as looking after Betty. In Pontefract and Leeds they stayed in inns that were generally at least clean and comfortable. Attendances were good, audiences enthusiastic and Eliza was invited out socially for dinner, tea parties and soirees, which she attended when she was able, accompanied by Richard when he was not in London.

Surprisingly perhaps, she had not seen Lord Denham at social functions. When the curtain rose on the first performance of *A Sweet Revenge* in York, Eliza, her heart beating like a caged bird in her chest, looked towards the boxes, but he was not there. The relief almost made her almost cry with gratitude. Later that night after what had been deemed a scintillating performance by the whole cast, Eliza specifically, Susan suggested Denham was probably not even in Yorkshire.

'He'll be sowing more of his aristocratic wild oats in London, you mark my words. Easier to avoid gossip there than here, with his family and the fiancée's family keeping an eye on him. He'll be avoiding her and all the commitments she comes with for as long as possible. Marriage for the gentry seems to be nothing more than a business transaction. I'm glad we don't have to see it like that, Eliza. We can marry for love. No one is concerned about dowries and jointures or whether our estates border someone else's.' Susan chuckled as she put the final touches to Eliza's coiffure ready for the reception at Lady Winters's house in Wakefield. As Richard was in London, Eliza had asked Susan to accompany her to Meadowsfield, Lady Winters's new house.

Mention of marriage had touched that nerve again for Eliza. Five weeks into the Yorkshire season, she and Richard were seen in each other's company whenever he was in Yorkshire. He accompanied her to the theatres she played in where the Drury Lane players socialised with other members of the resident company. Theatre managers made useful contacts, but he had not spoken of future plans or intentions towards Eliza. They tried their best to have some time on their own but that was often impossible. There were passionate embraces, reassuring words of love, but Eliza was increasingly frustrated that he had not suggested marriage. She knew he was determined to overturn the judgement on his father's military reputation, but she still could not understand why this should be reason not to marry her. Yet, he didn't try to make love to her either, which suggested he might be waiting for a formal engagement. Either that, or he didn't desire her, an alternative interpretation she knew for a fact was not the case. There had been many tangible instances of just how difficult they were both finding not to overstep the bounds of propriety.

Only the previous week after a champagne reception at the New Theatre, they had driven back to Eliza's lodgings, both mellow with the wine they had drunk and a rapturous reception they had received. Their kisses grew ever more passionate as his hands explored her breasts. Groaning with desire, his hands pushed under her skirts and petticoats and she shuddered with pleasure. Then the coach pulled up outside The Bear, causing them to quickly adjust their clothing and get out in a daze of thwarted lust and confusion.

Richard escorted her inside the inn, but despite the invitation in her eyes, he merely made a brief bow, kissed her hand and left for his own lodgings.

It was all very puzzling, as she confided to Susan whose advice remained what it had always been; hold out for marriage.

In Wakefield the Drury Lane company were very well received. They were to play three plays from the repertoire, all of which involved Eliza in leading roles. Susan was delighted to find herself promoted to Eliza's understudy in *The Beaux Stratagem* and was busy learning her lines for the role of Melinda, joking with her friend about falling down stairs, or any disabling injury that might give her the chance to shine. Richard had been staying in York but was to come to Wakefield and put up at The Crown where Eliza and Susan were staying. There had been a problem finding someone to mind Betty, so Susan did what many women did; brought her baby to work in the day and left the child with Mrs Cooper, the landlady of The Crown who was more than ready to mind the baby with whom she was openly besotted.

Invited to a reception after *The Heiress*, Eliza pleaded fatigue, but Richard was most anxious for them to attend. He wanted to meet Colonel Hampton, an old army colleague of his father who he knew would be there. His face fell when Eliza told him she wanted to go straight back to the inn after the performance, and he attempted to change her mind.

'I know, my love, how you must be tired, but we won't stay long. Please come with me. I shall be so proud to show you off and bask in your popularity. And I have a few questions to put to the Colonel.' Eliza relented, knowing how much this affair meant to him, and they made the short journey by carriage to Lochhead Manor, a few miles from the town.

Having seen nothing of Denham for the past six weeks and only hearing his name in passing, she had perhaps grown complacent, accepting Susan's idea that he was making the most of his bachelor days in London. It was, therefore, a huge shock when she and Richard were shown into the elegant drawing room of the fine Palladian house, to see Denham, a pretty girl in pink at his elbow, deep in conversation with their host, Sir Henry Richards.

As they both entered, all eyes had turned to look at them, the London stage's most successful couple since David Garrick and Peg Woffington. Sir Henry and Lady Amelia had considered getting them there an enormous coup, one that would enhance their own social standing.

Once Eliza had spotted Denham, suave and handsome in dark green breeches and a well-tailored coat that had Saville Row written all over it, she slipped into actress mode, smiling engagingly at her hosts, and favouring all those close by with her most charming and sociable conversation, even though her stomach churned and her pulse was racing. Richard took longer to adjust to the presence of Denham in the room, responding curtly and off-handedly to other guests while keeping a watchful eye on the insouciant Denham.

Soon Eliza and Richard were furnished with glasses of wine and they began to circulate, at first as a couple, but then Richard noticed that the Colonel was standing alone and took the opportunity to approach him. Quickly excusing himself from Eliza, he moved towards the Colonel, leaving Eliza to be buttonholed by a dowager with several double chins and a lorgnette, who quizzed her on the forthcoming season at Drury Lane.

In the middle of providing the lady with the information, Eliza noticed to her horror that Denham, smiling wolfishly, was making his way towards her.

He bowed coldly to the dowager, then took Eliza's hand, raised it to his lips and said, 'You are looking extremely well this evening,

Miss Grahame. Our Yorkshire air seems to agree with you. I hear you have taken the county by storm.' Excluded, puzzled and exceedingly piqued by the young man's lack of manners, the elderly dowager tutted and moved away from them and went in search of guests with better manners.

Now Denham had Eliza to himself, and he moved closer to her, so close she could see the little nick his valet had given him that morning when he had shaved his master. His distinctive cologne, which he had mixed for him in Floris, Jermyn Street, lime and bergamot, emanated from his handsome person and instantly brought back erotic memories of their time together.

When he spoke, his tone was playfully reproachful.

'You didn't come that day, Eliza. That Sunday. Francis waited an hour for you.' His eyes bored into her, making her feel naked and vulnerable. She needed Richard at her side.

Swallowing hard, she said, 'I could not do it, Antony.' Using his name after all that time made her blush, even though what they had done together in their bed had been beyond intimacy. 'Is that your fiancée, Miss – ?' she asked, glancing across at the pretty girl in pink brocade who was looking at them with undisguised curiosity.

He nodded casually, then continued, 'I thought we had a bargain, Eliza.'

She cast her eyes down to the fine Turkey rug on which they stood. All the confidence with which she had entered the room had evaporated.

'I have kept my part of it,' he continued, his voice getting louder. 'But you will never profit from it … and neither will he,' looking with disdain at Richard who had been deep in conversation with the Colonel, but had now noticed Eliza's plight and moved quickly to her side, his face grave with misgiving.

'Ah Cavendish. Good to see you again. The season is deemed to be a great success I hear. My congratulations.'

Richard inclined his head, saying nothing.

'And do I need to offer congratulations of another kind?' Denham continued in a fulsome tone, after draining his wine glass. 'I myself am engaged to be married as I'm sure you know.' He waved his elegant hand in the general direction of the girl in pink, now chatting to an elderly gent leaning heavily on a walking stick. 'Perhaps you and the lovely Eliza here are similarly pledged. But I suppose,' he continued, noting Eliza's telling crimson blush, 'that you have had family issues to deal with.' Richard looked mutinous, as if he could barely keep his hands from seizing Denham by the front of his elaborately frilled shirt and punching his handsome sneering face. But Denham was turning away from them now, ready to move off as he said, 'By the way, Cavendish, I hope you are more successful at getting Eliza to keep her promises than I have been. She doesn't seem to realise that when you strike a deal, both parties undertake to keep their side of the bargain. Adieu.' And he moved off to where the girl in pink stood, where he touched her arm in a proprietorial way and smiled fondly at her.

Richard was quiet as they were driven back to the inn an hour later. When she asked him about his conversation with the Colonel, he simply said, 'Inconclusive. And the old man's wandering in his mind. Thought I'd served in the Dragoons with his son George.' Then he lapsed into silence and did not take her hand as they sat, side by side, on the plush upholstery of Sir Henry's well-sprung carriage. Eliza was unsure of what to do. Should she raise the subject of Denham? Richard had asked her nothing about what had passed between her and her former protector. Surely, she reasoned, he must wonder what Denham had been alluding to. She knew she could not risk losing Richard by her silence, yet how would he react if she told him she had arranged to sleep with Denham for one final time in order to get his help?

The carriage bumped and rattled its way back the three miles to the inn; the silence inside was palpable. Suddenly Richard said, a cold edge to his voice, 'What did he mean, milord Denham, about striking bargains, Eliza? Have you entered into an agreement with him? It seemed from your embarrassed reaction that you had.' His tone was accusatory and Eliza felt a cold shiver at its frostiness.

Taking a deep breath to steady her nerves, she turned to him, saying, 'He offered to help bring your father's case to Parliament's attention, Richard. He has friends in high places.'

'And in low places too,' he said, darkly.

'Yes, I know well enough. But …'

'Why would he do that, Eliza? What was he to gain? The man despises me. I can see it in his eyes every time he looks at me. It's you he wants, Eliza, Men like that can never take rejection. So what was your bargain then? The one he says you reneged on?'

Eliza was truly frightened now. She hardly recognised Richard in this gimlet-eyed inquisitor. The man who sat beside her now was the man who had treated her with tight-lipped arrogance when he had trodden on the hem of her gown all that time ago in her early days at Drury Lane. 'Well?' he prompted, almost spitting out the word as he leaned towards her.

Now she really had no choice. She had to tell him everything and hope he would understand why she had agreed to do what Denham wanted.

246

She avoided his gaze, saying, 'I was to spend one last night with him in Hanover Square, and in turn he would do everything in his power to bring about the clearing of your father's name – using his influence in the House, his friends, the press.'

'And you believed him?' Richard's voice was incredulous, and he gave a humourless laugh, continuing, 'Eliza, you are so naïve. As if that reprobate could do anything good or charitable in his life!'

Stung, Eliza replied, 'Richard, he is really not a bad person. He is foolish, yes, and irresponsible, but no more so than many young men of his class. I know –'

'Yes, Eliza, you *know,*' he replied sarcastically, 'you *know* him better than most … in the Biblical sense anyway.'

'In the same way as you *knew* Sarah Newley, then Richard? Was it not? You who could have a loveless liaison with a harpy like that to supress rumours you did not want to engage with, just to keep her quiet. Yet no one pointed a finger at you because you are a man and such behaviour is acceptable, no, applauded even.' She turned her face away from him, angry and hurt by his comments and struggling to hold back the tears. Yes, she had made a foolish promise to Antony but had not kept it. And she had done it for the best of reasons; her love for this man beside her who was flinging her past in her face with apparent relish.

'Of course I could not keep my promise,' she said in a small voice, turning her face towards him and noticing the look of abject misery in his eyes as he reached for her hand.

'Why?'

'Do you need to ask me, Richard,' she squeezed his hand gently, continuing, 'because I love you too much to want to belong to another.' He said nothing, and she withdrew her hand and

247

adjusted the thin shawl she wore around her shoulders. His silence was frightening her, but she continued, 'It was wrong of me to agree, wrong of him to ask, but I did the right thing by not keeping the assignation. I am sorry if your father's case is jeopardised, but I have been true to my own feelings and true to you and you are wrong to judge me.'

The horses had slowed to a halt at the command of the coachman who was leaping down to open the door and put down the steps for them. The lights of the inn shone brightly in welcome, but the couple were silent and subdued as they stepped down from the carriage. Richard pressed a coin into the coachman's hand who tipped his hat as Eliza walked ahead to the door of the inn and pushed it open. Turning briefly to Richard, she said, 'I shall see you at breakfast no doubt, Richard. Good night.'

But, in fact, that meeting didn't happen. When Richard, bleary-eyed from lack of sleep and heavy hearted, went into the dining room at eight the next morning, he was informed by Mrs Cooper that Miss Grahame had taken a coach for London at six that morning. Mrs Cooper, leaning on the bar and relishing the drama of her famous guest's departure, was in confiding mode.

'A letter come for her, sir, about four it must have been. Sukey was up and about. Marked urgent it was, so Sukey takes it upstairs for her. Then Miss Grahame comes downstairs and orders bread and some meat and asks us to get hold of a coach for her to London. Then when Jemmy had done that, she pays her reckoning, and a bit more besides – she's a real lady that one. No airs and graces, a real lady. She tells me Miss Susan and the little one are staying on. She had her carpetbag with her, sir, but she was so pale! I think it must have been bad news. Family trouble, I shouldn't wonder. Poor girl. We all has it, sir, don't we?'

Richard didn't bother with breakfast but went up to Susan's room where Betty was crying and Susan wasn't able to settle her, but above the crying of the infant, Susan was able to tell him that Eliza's mother had been badly injured during an attack at her home in which she had stabbed her assailant, and her injuries were life-threatening. Eliza had left for London to see Annie, hoping to reach her while she was still alive.

'She told me to tell you, Mr Cavendish, that she was very sorry to leave like this but asked you to apologise to Mr Shaw for not being able to do the final performance.'

The baby had quietened now and Richard sat on the edge of Susan's bed as she rocked her gently to and fro, saying, 'Of course, she hasn't seen Annie in a long time – you will know that, naturally.'

Richard nodded, his head in his hands now. 'It must have been a dreadful shock for her. I wish she had knocked on my door to tell me. Perhaps I could have helped.' His voice was flat and empty.

'I expect it was that man of hers – Annie's I mean. He was a villain, used to knock her about. And he attacked Flora too. Annie couldn't see any wrong in him, of course,' Susan said sadly.

'We can see no faults in those we love,' Richard replied, but as soon as the words were out of his mouth, he was struck by their hypocrisy. Hadn't he seen many faults in Eliza the night before and chastised her for them? And now she faced with this dreadful ordeal without him.

'What can I do, Susan? I will of course return to London … after informing Mr Shaw at the theatre about Eliza. He'll have to alert the understudy, which is, of course, you, Susan, if it's *The Stratagem*. Are you ready for that?' He had got up from the bed and was doing his best to look purposeful and focused.

'I am indeed. Liza's been hearing my lines and I am ready. I'll be doing it for her – and for my little daughter here,' Susan said, kissing the sleeping child gently on her little cap of golden hair. 'Now Mr Cavendish, we need to get to the theatre and prepare. Eliza will be counting on us.'

Chapter 33

St Thomas's hospital in Southwark was a formidable unnerving place, full of the sounds and smells of disease and death. After a couple of misdirections from harassed nurses, at least one wearing a bloodied apron, Eliza found herself in a large high-ceilinged room where narrow beds were squashed together barely a foot part, though at least the bedding on them looked clean.

A sister, wearing a short blue cloak, directed her to Annie's bed where Eliza found her mother lying, eyes shut, swathed in bandages and dressings up to her neck. Her arms lay on top of the coverlet and both were heavily bandaged too. On her cheeks, deep lacerations, purple with congealed blood, made Eliza gasp in horror and her legs to almost buckle beneath her. She approached the bed, hardly expecting her mother to be breathing, but with relief she noted the slow rise and fall of Annie's chest and, aloud, thanked God to see it.

'Yes, you might well thank 'im,' croaked a voice from the bed next to her, where an old woman lay, her grey eyes rheumy, her red nose the badge of an habitual drinker.

'I wouldn't have give you tuppence for her chances the night they brought her in.' She smiled a grim toothless grin, her hand shaking uncontrollably on the coverlet. 'Your ma is she?'

Eliza nodded, tears in her eyes.

'He took a knife to her they said, after knocking her black and blue. She've lost a lot of blood. They sewed her up best they could, but – well, men, eh? Was he your pa?'

'No!' Eliza was horrified and revolted at the thought. 'I need to see a doctor or a nurse in charge – a sister maybe.' She was scanning the seething ward where the scream and groans of distraught women were a constant accompaniment to the frenzied activities of the few staff visible.

A woman in a nearby bed was thrashing around uncontrollably as two nurses tried to restrain her; another young woman, her hair a cloud of black, was sitting up in bed and shouting obscenities before vomiting violently on the floor, the stench adding to the miasma of the room.

'You'll be lucky, my dear,' the old woman cackled. 'They done what they could. Give her opium. Numb the pain. That's why she's sleeping so sound. Lucky her, I says. Out of it. Best place for us all if you ask me.' And she closed her watery eyes as if to achieve that desired oblivion.

An hour later, with her mother snoring loudly, Eliza had found a nurse who had pieced together a version of the events.

In a drunken fight at Charles Street, John Harkness had used not only his fists and his boots to punish Annie for burning his pork chops, but a kitchen knife as well. He had slashed at her forearms and her face before driving the blade into her chest. Terrified by the amount of blood this attack caused, he dropped the knife on the table where Annie grabbed it and, with the strength of the truly desperate, stabbed him through the heart. Neighbours who were accustomed to their domestic brawls hardly turned a hair until Annie came crawling out of the house bleeding profusely, claiming, quite truthfully that she had killed him. They did their best to staunch her wounds but could see that it was all up with the loathsome John who had done his best to terrorise the dank and fetid courtyard in which they all lived. They bundled her into a cart and took her to St Thomas's. Matthew Carter, who was the most public-spirited of them, reported the assault and murder at Bow Street, anxious to tell the Runners that it was the opinion of all the neighbours that the killing of John had been in self-defence and that the man had been a brute of the worst kind and had finally got his just desserts.

'Your mother escaped death narrowly, Miss Grahame,' the ward sister told Eliza, gazing steadily at her across the narrow desk in her office. 'If your mother survives – and there is considerable doubt about that – she will need careful looking after.' She paused and continued, 'She was herself very inebriated when she came to us and has all the health problems that a drinker of spirits has. She does not have a strong constitution. Can you and your sister take on that care? You are unmarried you say.'

'Yes, I am,' replied Eliza quietly, 'but I have a profession. I am an actress at Drury Lane. I am not without success and therefore means. I shall do everything in my power to look after my mother if she survives.'

As she left the hospital, Eliza was flooded by an overwhelming sense of guilt and remorse. She had known for the past year or more of the destructive abyss into which her mother had fallen and had done nothing to try to extricate her, apart from rescuing Flora from John. She had been so wrapped up in her own life, her own love affairs, that she had completely abandoned Annie.

And now her mother might die: Annie Grahame, aged thirty-nine, a widow, the victim of gin, violence and her daughter's indifference.

Chapter 34

Eliza spent much time at the hospital during the next few days. On the third day, sitting on the edge of her bed, she saw her mother open her eyes for the first time.

'Liza?' Annie said slowly, her voice a croak, 'is that you?' Eliza got up and leaned across the bed to her mother who was looking confused and unsettled.

'I ... what ... where am I? And are you really Eliza?' She had raised her bandaged hand to touch her wounded face and grimaced. Then it seemed memory flooded back, and she said in a fearful voice, 'John? Where is John? Where is he?'

Eliza was struggling with conflicting emotions; relief to see her mother awake, rage at the man who had carried out the attack on her, and an overwhelming sense of helplessness.

'He is dead, Mother. He attacked you with a knife, almost killed you. You – defended yourself. You had to.'

Annie closed her eyes as if to shut out the images that Eliza's words had revived, then in a small voice said, 'I burnt the chops, Eliza. He was so angry with me. He came at me, hitting and pushing me to the floor, then kicking,' her voice rising now, her eyes fixed. 'He took the knife ...'

'Mama! Please don't go through all that again. It will upset you to think of it. Now it is over. He will never hurt you again – or anyone else,' she said, thinking bitterly of what Flora had suffered at his hands.

'But did I kill him with that knife, after he went for me, Liza? Did I ... murder him? I will surely hang for it at Newgate.' Tears were coursing down her cheeks and her voice was piteous. A woman

254

in a nearby bed shouted to her to 'shut up' and Eliza was trying to quieten her and soothe her as she struggled to sit up in the bed, crying out in pain as she disturbed her injuries.

A nurse appeared at the bedside and gently coaxed Annie back into a prone position.

'I can give her a little of the poppy potion to make her calm again. She needs to heal. Agitation like this can only do her more harm. She will need to heal in her mind as well as her body.'

Eliza nodded dumbly. The fashionable drawing rooms of Yorkshire, the curtain calls at Drury Lane, the loving and supportive arms of Richard Cavendish seemed another world to her now, a world that she feared she would never inhabit again.

Eliza went back to St Giles by hackney where she and Flora cleaned the house thoroughly, horrified to see how dirty it had become since they were last there. Now there was little furniture, no doubt because any item of value had been sold or pawned. The kitchen was strewn with dirty pots and there was evidence of rats everywhere. Neighbours had called, ostensibly to see if they could help, but Flora said she though their concern was mostly feigned; they simply wanted to get in on the drama of recent events.

'Things like that go on all the time in St Giles, Liza. You know what it's like here, hardly a caring neighbourhood. People here are too busy struggling to survive. They have nothing left for anything else.'

Flora and Eliza were sitting on two of the remaining old stools drinking coffee that Eliza had brought back in a bag of groceries they were living on while they were staying in the house and working out what they should do next. The Theatre Royal York and even Drury

Lane seemed as far away as the moon to Eliza now as she and her sister decided what course of action to take. Susan who had written to say that the season in Yorkshire was over, that she had acquitted herself well as Melinda, and that Mr Cavendish was anxious to know how Eliza was faring and how Annie was.

But from him she heard nothing. They had parted coldly after their quarrel in the carriage. Whenever she thought of him, there was a dull ache in her heart as if she had suffered a loss from which she would never recover.

Eliza's thoughts were violently interrupted when Flora pulled off her shoe and threw it in the direction of the table.

'Another rat, Eliza! The place is overrun with them. Please let us get out of here. It makes my skin crawl. And Mama? Where is she to go when she leaves St Thomas's?'

'If she leaves, Flora,' Eliza said in a quiet voice, sipping her coffee. 'You know as well as I do there's a strong possibility she will not leave – not alive anyway. Or if she does, she might stand trial for John's murder.'

'No, no, Eliza! There are witnesses to his treatment of her, everyone knows she killed him in self-defence. They would never convict her.' Flora's eyes were blazing with the injustice of any charges against her mother, the victim in all this.

Calm yourself, Flora. I am sure you're right and it will be as you say. If mother survives – come, we must face up to realities. If she survives, and is allowed to go free, we will take her to George Street with us. We can look after her ourselves, make sure she never has to live like that again.' Flora got up from the stool and went to retrieve the shoe.

'Please let us leave this place, Liza. It pains me to think how happy we were here when Papa was alive. And afterwards, how it changed when Mama took up with that ... monster. Please Eliza, we must go. Susan will be back in London in a few days' time – and Mr Cavendish too.' She glanced coyly at her sister, dimpling prettily, waiting for an answering blush. But none came. Eliza merely looked troubled and preoccupied, though she said in a more decisive voice, 'Yes, let us gather together some of Mother's belongings and any objects we might find, though I don't think ...'

Her words trailed away as her glance fell on the hideous space they had once called home.

Chapter 35

As luck would have it, Drury Lane was still closed as renovations and painting were still going on. But the next week, rehearsals for the new season would begin again and Eliza and Susan's lives would once more be constrained by their duties at the theatre.

Annie Grahame was defying all the medical staff at St Thomas's by not only surviving but improving very gradually, though when Flora and Eliza visited, they were still struck by how helpless and wan she looked.

'How can we know, Liza, what she is like under all those bandages?' asked Flora as they walked home after their afternoon visit. The ward had been particularly harrowing with two young women screaming, one tearing at her long black hair and pulling it out in handfuls. Normally the most extreme cases of deranged patients were kept separate from those whose injuries were strictly physical, but clearly there had been problems with accommodating these desperate and violent women and the staff simply had to deal with them. Flora in particular was very distressed, though Annie seemed unmoved by the disturbance the women were creating as two nurses tried to hold them down and quieten them.

'When Mama comes home, we will have to change her dressings and tend her wounds, keep everything as clean as we possibly can so there is no infection.' Flora looked daunted at the prospect, thinking no doubt of all this nursing having to be done in the small front room of George Street. Both sisters knew that their lives would be changing forever, but what were they to do? Once rehearsals began again, much of the nursing, the caring of Annie and the minding of baby Betty would fall to Flora on whose young head major responsibilities would rest. For her, the night of the premiere of *A Sweet Revenge* and the romantic interest of Mr Goodwin already seemed a lifetime away. She had met him and strolled with him several times in St James's Park and found him charming, handsome and attentive, but since Annie's sojourn in St Thomas's, she had had little contact beyond a note. To tell the truth, in her conversations with him, she had played down her connections with St Giles and the rackety way of life of her mother and surrogate father. The young man was, after all, professional, a lawyer – or at least training to be one, in chambers at Lincoln's Inn. One of his favourite pastimes was the theatre, so he was quite dazzled to be walking out with the sister of Eliza Grahame who casually let slip that the eminent playwright/manager Richard Cavendish was a regular visitor to their house. This last claim was perhaps an exaggeration, but on the afternoon when the sisters returned from their hospital visit, it was an actual fact. For as they rounded the corner into their street, strolling arm-in-arm together, they saw Richard on their doorstep, looking as if he were about to leave.

Eliza's heart lurched in her chest and her step faltered.

'Look, Eliza, it's Mr Cavendish come to call. How lovely to see him back here in London.'

It had been eight days since Eliza's hasty departure from Yorkshire, eight days since the meeting with Denham and the silly quarrel in the carriage. Torn between her fear for her mother's life and the conviction that she and Richard had fallen out irrevocably, she had suffered sleepless nights and depression. Susan, as usual, had been her constant support. It was she who had tried to make Eliza see things from Richard's point of view when Eliza had railed against his unreasonable behaviour, pointing out to her friend how matters stood in his eyes; she had, after all, consented to sleep with Denham, even though she professed to love Richard.

'But I didn't go through with it, Susan!' Eliza repeated for what seemed like the hundredth time. 'I couldn't do it. Even though it would have helped Richard's cause. I thought you would understand,' she had said petulantly as Susan laid a hand gently on her sleeve, saying, 'I do, I do Eliza, but men – well, they are all about possession, it seems to me.'

'If he was all about possession, you would have thought that he would make me an offer of marriage then,' said Eliza in a sulky voice, 'if he wanted to keep me solely for himself.'

'Ah, oh, that's it, is it?' Susan burst out in triumph. 'The fact that he hasn't proposed to you … yet.' She chuckled and shook her head in amusement. 'Liza, he loves you. The whole world can see it. Antony Denham can see it. He is waiting for just the right time, when he is free from family obligations, when his career is heading for public, even royal acclaim. All will be well. Have faith.'

But Eliza had been haunted by recent events and was unconvinced by her friend's comforting words as they walked briskly back to their house. And now, as if their earlier conversation had conjured him up, there was the man himself, walking towards her and Flora, smiling and raising his hat to them, his eyes full of concern and – yes, Eliza could see it – love. Taking her hand as they approached, he raised it to his lips.

'Eliza, my love. I came as soon as I could. How are you both? Flora,' he turned towards her, sympathy in his gaze, 'this must have been so difficult for you both.' He bent to kiss Flora on the cheek at which she blushed, fumbling in her reticule for the door key.

'We are coping quite well, thank you sir, though of course concerned for Mother and what is to happen to her.'

'I did ring the bell, but clearly Susan is not at home.'

'Richard, come in, please do.' Eliza ushered him in over the threshold, put his hat and his cane on the stand in the hall and showed him into the sitting room, more untidy and dustier now that she and Flora had been spending so much time at the hospital. While Flora prepared coffee in the kitchen, Eliza told Richard the story of what had happened to Annie. In some parts of her narrative, she stumbled over words due to the emotion that she felt. He leaned forward and took her hand, looking into her eyes and clearly experiencing some of her raw emotion.

'Eliza, my love. How you must have suffered – and are still suffering. If only I could have borne some of this for you. I have thought so often of that silly quarrel we had in Yorkshire. I was at fault. I allowed myself to be goaded by that reprobate Denham. I questioned your judgement. I ...'

She laid a finger gently on his lips to stem the flow of accusations.

'It is all in the past, Richard. There was blame on both sides. What has happened since has thrown all that into perspective.'

'Indeed, my love. And as long as you are still my love, together we can face anything. Does your mother have a good physician? Is she progressing well? How is she in her mind after her ordeal?'

Over the coffee that Flora brought in, all three of them sat and discussed Annie's current situation, the prognosis, and the thorny issue of what was to be done with her in the future when she came out of hospital. Richard insisted on knowing what charges had already been incurred for her treatment, undertaking to pay them all for as long as necessary.

'But Richard, I can pay for my own mother's hospital treatment,' Eliza said, her chin jutting out proudly and steel in her gaze.

'I know you are perfectly able to do that. But I want to do it, for you and Flora. I want to shoulder some of the practical tasks for you. You have had so much to contend with emotionally. The last thing I want is for you to give up the theatre because you are overburdened with difficulties.'

'Richard,' Eliza began, 'dearest, do you take me for one of those little pink and white porcelain women, too delicate, too fragile to withstand life's knocks? I thought you knew me better than that. I and Flora here, we served our apprenticeship in St Giles not Mayfair. We can deal with the slings and arrows, though it gladdens my heart to hear you say you wish to share my burden.'

'If we are to share our lives, Eliza,' Richard said solemnly (at which Flora risked an excited glance at her sister), 'we must do just that. You tried to share my troubles a while ago when you made that arrangement with Antony Denham. You wanted to help me clear my father's name and you took whatever means at your disposal to try and accomplish it. I blamed you for that instead of seeing the sacrifice you were prepared to make. Now I want to help you and share in the difficulties of looking after your mother. Besides,' he continued in a lighter vein, 'I cannot risk losing my leading lady who is the biggest box office draw since Nell Gwynn. Tomorrow I shall call in at the estate agents to inquire about houses to let, larger than this one, so that you will have more room and can live more comfortably. Please allow me to do that for you, Eliza.'

'Thank you, Richard. That would be most helpful,' replied Eliza, smiling and meaning the words. But she noted with some sadness that he said 'so that *you* will have more room' and not 'so that *we* will have more room.'

Chapter 36

Almost immediately the round of daily rehearsals began again as playbills were produced and the final touches were put to the cleaning and painting of the rooms backstage. In St Thomas's hospital, Annie's health declined. Some days she was so sunk in depression that she would not speak to her daughters. They took food in for her but she rarely touched it, just lay, her fingers plucking at the sheet, staring vacantly, tears rolling down her cheeks crisscrossed with deep trenches of scars. The cost of her stay there had been met by Richard, as he had promised Eliza. During that first week of September, life was so busy, so frantic with all the dramas involved in getting the theatre ready for a new season that he had little time and energy for Eliza and her life. Their meetings were brief, cordial but always in the theatre, and though she saw the warmth in his eyes and his smile whenever they did meet, she knew she would have to be patient and to understand the pressures he was under. This she explained to Susan over breakfast on Sunday morning ahead of what was likely to be a very busy week.

'I'm trying hard, Susan, to think of him and how much the whole company depends on him to get this season right, but it is difficult. He did say he would try to find us a larger house. Since then he has said nothing. If we had more room, we might be able to bring Mama home.'

'Perhaps he is waiting … to hear how she will be?' Susan suggested, trying to be tactful.

'If she is going to die, you mean?' Eliza's tone was snappy. 'He has scarcely asked after her.'

'Eliza, be patient. This is a difficult time for all of us – the theatre, his family with the scandal. It will pass, then he will be able to give matters between you and him proper consideration. He loves you, truly he does. All will be well.'

Trying to reassure her friend, Susan laid the sleeping baby gently in the basket, smiling with such obvious love that Eliza felt a dart of pure envy. How could that little bundle generate so much love and adoration? She wished with all her heart that Susan's mother could see the child because, if she could, she would have to fall under her spell. And despite Eliza's own concerns, the germ of an idea began to breed in her head which gave rise to a secret smile.

At the end of Monday's rehearsal for *Much Ado About Nothing*, with Eliza now promoted to the role of Beatrice and Harry Oldfield playing opposite her as Benedict, Richard came to find her as she was sizing up the freshly painted dressing rooms where the women now had further cause for complaint; the smell of the paint.

'Eliza, would you come along to my office, please – nice work in Act 1 by the way,' he said, smiling affably.

Hetty Ames, the most vocal of the critics of the refurbishment, rolled her eyes and grinned at Eliza who coloured slightly. She couldn't quite get used to being the subject of backstage gossip and of innuendo among the company. Doubtless they speculated on what exactly was the state of affairs between her and Richard. Deep down, Eliza wished that matters stood as her colleagues thought they did, but today she gave Hetty a rather superior half-smile and left the room as Richard cheekily said, 'I'm so glad you approve of the redecoration, ladies. The smell of the paint should keep the mice away for a time.'

When they reached his office, he crossed to his desk, littered as usual with sheaves of paper, books and quills. Rummaging for a second or two, he picked up a handful of papers, saying, 'There,

Eliza. At last. Details of some houses that are available for rent. I think there are a few there that might suit you. I can arrange for you to go and have a look if there are some that take your fancy.' She took them from him with a polite 'thank you,' aware once again that he had said 'might suit *you*' and not '*us.*'

'Flora and Susan as well of course, if you would like their opinion. This one,' and he pointed at the paper on the top of the handful, 'this is in Henrietta Street, much bigger than your present place. It has a room which might be ideal for turning into a bedroom, on the ground floor – for your mother, I was thinking.' He jabbed his finger at the paper. 'Just a five-minute walk from the theatre and a more salubrious area altogether. Take a look and tell me what you would like to do.'

He seemed a little deflated by her luke-warm response and glanced at her uncertainly. When she had studied the details a little, she noticed the rental sum and, turning sharply to him, said, 'But Richard. This rent is twice what I have to pay now. It is far too expensive!'

'You are not to think of that for one moment, Eliza. That must not be an issue,' he said vaguely. 'Your comfort and convenience is the greatest consideration. Now,' he continued briskly, 'I think when you and Harry come to the scene in the next act, you must try to show him – very subtly – how Beatrice is beginning to unbend just a little towards Benedict. You were admirably spirited in the first act – I myself would have quailed before you, but now,' he turned towards her, circled her waist with his hands and drew her towards him, 'I think a little more playfulness is called for.' Smiling provocatively at her, he pulled her in for a kiss, murmuring, 'I above everyone know how playful and charming you can be,' and he kissed

266

her deeply so that the very core of her being desired nothing more than to be his.

She was conscious of his heart beating beneath the cambric of his shirt, the scratch of the fabric of his coat, the softness of his lips and the probing of his tongue as it sought hers in pursuit of further pleasure. A sharp rap on the half-open door made them spring apart.

'Mr Cavendish sir. Begging your pardon, sir.' Archie the doorkeeper was holding out an envelope to Richard and looking embarrassed and apologetic at having witnessed the intimate moment between the lovers.

'Sir, a letter just this minute delivered for you. Urgent they says.' Then as an afterthought, he nodded towards Eliza. 'Miss Grahame. Begging your pardon.' The glance he gave her was implicitly approving. 'The Hon Saville's man, sir. Said it was urgent.'

Eliza picked up the house details from Richard's desk as he looked with some puzzlement at the thick cream letter that Archie had handed him.

'Thank you, Archie.' Richard was polite but dismissive, and, though the doorkeeper was itching to know more about the contents of the letter, he left reluctantly.

'What can this be? I know this man's name. He is one of our patrons in a small way but –'

'Perhaps he wants a private performance or a theatre party, Richard. Who knows?'

She moved closer to him once again, emboldened by the passion of their interrupted embrace. She knew that he really did love her and felt instinctively that whatever happened they were going to be together. All would be well as Susan had said it would.

'I must go now. Leave you to find out the contents of your letter.' Her voice was light, her smile teasing. He was hers and nothing would change that.

He was breaking the seal as she kissed him gently on the cheek. Turning towards her, he responded with a deeper and warmer kiss on her mouth. When he released her, he said, 'Tomorrow, my love, I shall tell you what the letter says but whatever news it contains, good or bad, we will face it together.'

The meeting had been arranged for ten o'clock the following morning at White's, a venue agreeable to Richard Cavendish, for although he was not a member, the club had a history of being a useful promoter of Drury Lane Theatre and, on several previous occasions, Richard had been invited to the club before as the guest of George, Duke of Argyll, a keen playgoer and *bon viveur*.

When Richard was ushered into the lounge by a steward who managed to be both obsequious and superior at the same time, the Hon Titus Saville was ensconced in a comfortable chair, a glass of sherry at his elbow and *The Times* spread out across his well-tailored knees. He did not rise to greet his guest, merely nodding a 'Cavendish, your servant, sir,' and indicating a chair to his left. 'So glad you could come. A drink?' Without waiting for an answer, he snapped his fingers at the departing functionary who returned to take his order.

'Coffee. Thank you, sir.' Richard took the seat, glancing round the room where gentlemen sat and dozed, sat and talked, sat and read or just sat. No one here, he was certain, had a rehearsal in an hour, carpenters to chivvy, volatile actors to direct and books to balance.

The Hon began with some preliminary compliments about last season's productions, making shrewd observations about a couple of plays that made Richard warm to him. Then the business of the meeting was broached.

Initially alerted to Richard's father's case by fellow old Harrovian Antony Denham, Saville had become fascinated by its history. He was, he told Richard, from a military family that had served in India who knew the value of reputation and what the blight of dishonour could mean.

Long after Denham had told him drunkenly one night to 'drop the whole Cavendish thing – game's not worth the candle,' he had pursued it tirelessly and turned up, in military records, a quite different account of General Cavendish's behaviour; instead of his actions being taken unwisely, they had been made based on information that General Cavendish considered infallible. He could in no way be blamed for the ambush into which his men were unwittingly led. Based on the information he had received from his scouts, engaging with the enemy would have meant substantial losses, and withdrawal looked like the safest option. It had been discovered later that rebel spies had infiltrated English intelligence at Trenton so that General Cavendish had been given a totally false assessment of the situation in which he acted in good faith. In other words, George Cavendish had made the best decision for his troops as he perceived it at the time and in no way could be considered a general whose judgement was faulty or whose courage was in doubt.

Saville spoke eloquently in his defence of Richard's father and his actions, his voice rising as he warmed to his subject. This caused a few members of Whites to regard him, and Richard too, with

269

attention; one old man broke off his reading of *The Spectator*, wrinkled his brow and listened with undisguised interest; another tutted audibly in the direction of the now animated speaker. But Richard swallowed hard and tried to keep a check on the emotions threatening to overwhelm him.

Of course he had always known his father would have behaved honourably, but for the world to know would mean so much to his mother and his sisters.

Saville had finished and glared at those who had looked at him disapprovingly for disturbing the sacred silence of the lounge. Richard said, 'How can this be conveyed to the public, sir? How is it possible to make the truth known? My desire is to make the truth known. My family want it more than anything. We want this cloud lifted from us, these allegations of Allingham's refuted with the evidence you have uncovered.'

'Of course, and I shall be the one to do so … with your permission of course.'

The politician was pouring coffee from a silver pot into two cups, having finished his sherry. He handed a cup to Richard, continuing, 'I shall raise it in the House when we reconvene, and I am not without influence in Fleet Street and am only too happy to advance your case in the newspapers and periodicals. I am certain that Mr Steele of *The Gazette* would take a lively interest,' he added wryly, adding cream to his coffee. 'Cavendish, I do not pretend to be totally altruistic in my support of your cause.' He paused and Richard raised a quizzical eyebrow.

'No, sir?'

'No, I am recently elected to my seat, eager to make my mark on the House and well aware that I do not have the pedigree of some of my fellow members. If General Cavendish's case becomes a *cause celebre*, it will do my career no harm.'

Richard smiled wryly, acknowledging the ways of the world.

'And if it does not, it will at least take a huge burden off my shoulders, sir. And for that I cannot thank you enough.'

Richard had risen from his seat, as had Saville, and the two men shook hands cordially. 'And please accept seats in the best box for the opening night of all new productions this coming season. I shall personally arrange it.'

As he turned to go, Richard paused, saying, 'So it was Lord Denham who first asked you to interest yourself in my father's cause?'

'Yes, indeed – a conversation we had in Hyde Park some months since. Had it not been for him, the matter would have lain uninvestigated. You owe him so much, Cavendish. Adieu. Leave matters to me. You shall hear from me.'

'It seems, sir, that we have *all* heard from you!' A loud bad-tempered voice came from behind a newspaper in the corner. 'Please endeavour to conduct your business more discreetly in the future.'

Chapter 37

The first week of the season was hectic. There were new players to absorb into the company, a few of whom were proving to be difficult to get to know. Charlotte Gibson, a very glamorous fiery redhead whom Richard had poached from the Garden, appeared to have enough temperament for the whole Drury Lane company and had already had some noisy arguments with Hetty and Susan that ended in slammed doors, tears and a handful of red hair. She was a pretty girl with sparkling emerald eyes, shapely legs and a sweet singing voice. Ned was showing all the tell-tale signs of being besotted with this new arrival. Eliza considered Charlotte might be trouble but couldn't escape the nagging thought that she was simply jealous of this new arrival in their midst.

Harry Oldfield, probably close to forty, had a haughty patrician demeanour and an inflated sense of his own importance. At least all the company agreed on that. But he had been spellbinding as Benedict with Eliza playing opposite him and she felt strongly that he brought out the very best in her performance. He would never be popular with the rest of the company, but the audience loved him in roles that Richard would surely cast him in.

So busy were Eliza, Susan and Richard with the demands of the season, in a theatre redolent of new paint and fresh timber behind the scenes, that there seemed little time or energy for emotional and domestic matters.

Annie had left St Thomas's and was sleeping in a truckle bed in the sitting room of George Street, with Flora doing her utmost to tend to her as well as minding baby Betty when Susan was at the theatre. Annie was a difficult patient, morose and tearful, unwilling to eat.

On Saturday morning when Eliza and Flora were trying to get Annie out of her soiled nightgown, and to make up her bed with fresh linen, Annie scowled at her daughters and clung to the sheet.

'Let me be! I don't want to take off my nightdress. What does it matter if it's dirty? I don't care, do I? John won't see me in it again, will he?' and she burst into tears, tossing her head on the pillow. The sisters looked at each other with a mixture of frustration and disgust. Here was their mother weeping for a man who had repeatedly abused her. Now she was berating herself for having killed him to save her own life. It was all too much for Eliza.

'Mother!' she exclaimed, her voice dangerously controlled, fixing her mother with a steely gaze, 'you are crying for that man, that monster, who treated you so badly. How can you! Look at the injuries on your body. Remember that he beat and kicked you, slashed at you with a knife.' Her voice began to shake with emotion. 'And know now that your lovely daughter here ...' she held a shaking hand in Flora's direction, 'who cleans you and feeds you, empties your slops, was a victim of that monster's violent lust. Your own *daughter*, mother. Why do you think we left Charles Street so suddenly? She was fortunate not to be raped by that vile man, the man you now mourn!'

Annie's face was stricken. Her eyes bulged in disbelief. She looked from one daughter to the other in incredulity.

'Flora! You? He tried to ... to ... force himself on you?' Her voice ended in a croak as she struggled to sit up in bed as a fresh torrent of weeping was released. Flora hastened to her to comfort her.

'Hush, Mama. I was lucky, he did not succeed.'

'I did not know!' Annie's voice had risen to the pitch of hysteria now. 'My own daughter!' she exclaimed in disgust. Eliza took her mother's hand in an attempt to calm her. Thrashing around in the bed would be no good for the dressings that were necessary for her recovery.

'Oh, my poor girl. My little Flora!'

The daughters waited for their mother's outburst to run its course, each of them holding one of her hands, all three women now sobbing. Then Flora released her mother's hand and dropped a small amount of laudanum into a glass of water at her mother's bedside, raising it to her mother's lips.

'Mama, drink this. It will calm you. Please. You have had a dreadful shock.'

A groan escaped Annie's lips as she opened her mouth to accept the drink, keeping her eyes shut firmly as if she could not bear to look at Flora. Eliza touched her sister's arm gently once the opiate had been administered.

'She will sleep now,' said Flora in a flat voice. 'You should get ready to leave for the theatre, you and Susan.'

'Not until later, Flora. I shall help you prepare food. You have already so much to do.' As if to confirm that fact, they heard the baby's thin wail from the room upstairs, and Flora's brow puckered in response. 'We must have some help in the house.'

'And which house, Eliza?' replied Flora snappily. 'Has Richard found another for us as he said he would? We need a room for Mama. If we had more room, maybe we could have someone to live in – just for a while. He did promise he would help, Liza. Has he said nothing about houses?'

'He has been so occupied at the theatre. There is so much to do. He did show me some particulars.'

The look of hope on Flora's face made Eliza feel guilty and she continued, 'He is as good as his word. It will take a little time.'

'If only he would marry you, Eliza! All would be well and would be so convenient!' Flora burst out. 'Why does he not ask you? You love each other – that is clear to everybody. You are both unattached.'

Her pretty face registered her puzzlement and frustration and Eliza sighed and shook her head slowly. Her own pain and anxiety on that score resurfaced, though she tried to combat it. Glancing at her sister, Flora seemed to think that she had gone too far, adding feebly, 'I know he will, Liza. He surely will. I do not mean to hurt you.' They both glanced down at the sleeping form of their mother, her mouth open, still wearing the soiled nightdress, a battle for another day.

'Let us leave her now,' said Eliza softly. 'I will mention the house once more to Richard – however preoccupied he may be.' Giving Flora a watery smile, she made for the door.

'All will be well, I am sure of that.'

Saturday night's play was *The Heiress* and once again Eliza was Lady Heartfort, turning in an electrifying performance, despite Charlotte in her role of Miss Sweet, trying to act Eliza off the stage; the girl would have to be spoken to, thought Eliza, taking her final bow and smiling falsely at this new upstart. While the audience were clapping wildly and on their feet, Richard Cavendish took the unprecedented step of leaving the manager's box and joining the cast on stage. He took Eliza's and Charlotte's hands in his, smiling broadly at the audience. Eliza glanced sideways at him as she could see no reason for this unusual departure from his usual practice. He was not one ordinarily to court public attention usually, the play was not a new one, though he was its author. The audience had not called for him. Then he let Charlotte's hand drop, stepping forward, while holding Eliza's hand more tightly.

The applause died slowly and people resumed their seats, looking at one another in some puzzlement.

Then he began, his voice clear and confident, audible to the back row of the gallery.

'Ladies and gentlemen, your applause is heart-warming. We are pleased and proud that you have enjoyed tonight's performance.' He glanced briefly at Eliza who smiled gamely. Behind them the cast still stood in their curtain call positions, a few shifting their feet, several no doubt wanting to disappear backstage either to slip off home or to change for the afterpiece that was still to come.

'I am proud to have written the piece and gratified by its success, but I am even more proud to have the love of this beautiful leading lady, Miss Eliza Grahame.' He held up her hand in his and Eliza's face burned at this totally unexpected and very public accolade. The audience clapped, whistled and cheered at this pronouncement; some of the more sentimental members simply sighed and smiled at his words. Behind Richard and Eliza, the cast broke into their own bout of applause and calls of "hear hears" as Richard turned to them, smiling and clearly happy.

'So,' he continued, squeezing Eliza's hand, 'I am asking you all to witness tonight,' suddenly he was down on one knee on the stage, 'the moment when I ask this wonderful woman' (now there were gasps and sighs from the audience and people craned forward to see

276

the event more closely) 'to be my wife and make me the happiest man in the world.'

A heartfelt and united 'aah' came from the audience at this romantic gesture, in itself a moment of pure theatricality.

'Go on, love. Have him. If you don't, I will,' came from a woman in the gallery and there was a burst of laughter.

Eliza's mouth was dry, her legs barely supporting her, and her cheeks she felt were burning. Behind her cast members stamped their feet, then Mr Jacobs demanded, 'Let us hear your answer, Eliza,' after which a silence fell.

Taking Richard's hand and raising him to his feet, Eliza beamed at him, nodded and said, 'Yes, Richard, of course I will marry you,' and to applause, whistles and thumping of feet on the floor, the couple kissed.

Chapter 38

The house in Henrietta Street suited everyone. It was close to the theatre for Richard, Eliza and Susan. It had four bedrooms, two large sitting rooms, an elegant dining room, an attic for Mary, their live-in help whose domestic activities Annie Grahame kept a watchful eye on, making sure the girl cleaned thoroughly and brought back the best quality produce from Covent Garden market every day.

'You've got to watch them, you know, Eliza. Servants,' she said, 'they've got their ways. Make sure they don't cut corners or diddle you.' Eliza and Flora often shared smiles at their mother's assiduous watchfulness, concluding that it was a healthy sign and part of her recovery.

Freed of many household chores, Flora could now spend more of her time attending to her clothes. She was showing a remarkable talent for fine embroidery, developing her social life and walking out with Mr Goodwin whenever his legal studies allowed.

He had become a regular visitor at Henrietta Street where he and Richard proved to have a shared passion for Shakespeare and claret.

Eliza had never been so happy. She and Richard had been married that October, on a cloudless golden day when the trees spilled red and ochre leaves on their small group of wedding guests at St Martin's church. By then, Saville had raised the issue of General Cavendish and the false charges levelled against him in the House. As the rising star had predicted, the case became a *cause celebre*. The General was completely exonerated, his name cleared, and Richard's mother and sisters could hold their heads up high once again. *The*

Gazette published a lengthy article about the Cavendish family that did Richard, Eliza and Drury Lane no harm at all.

Antony Denham, much the worse for wear, had shown up at a performance of *A Sweet Revenge* and had gone to the green room where he had flirted with Charlotte. He had spoken slurringly but civilly to Eliza and Richard who had both thanked him for the part he had played in setting Saville onto *The Cavendish Affair*, as the newspapers called it.

His eyes were bloodshot and his cravat was askew, but Charlotte was clearly impressed by the attention milord was giving her; Eliza felt history was repeating itself.

It was the Sunday before Christmas and 25 Henrietta Street was in a state of high excitement. A great deal of cooking had gone on, supervised by Annie, so the house, from basement kitchen to Mary's humble attic bedroom, smelt of cinnamon and roasted meat. Susan had dressed Betty in her finest frock and squeezed herself into a new gown that was designed for fashion not comfort, as she complained to Eliza who had gone to her room to dress her hair.

'What if they don't even come after all, Liza? That's too hard, don't brush so hard!' Eliza moderated her hair brushing and looked at her friend's anxious face in the mirror. This day was so important to her and it had been carefully stage managed by Flora and Annie, drawing heavily on their St Giles contacts.

'They have accepted our invitation, Susan. They will surely come. They will want to see baby Betty more the anything.' Susan nodded wordlessly but didn't look convinced.

'What if my father berates me again about what he calls my "sin"?'

'It is difficult to see Betty as your sin, Susan. With her big brown eyes and mop of fair hair, she looks more like an angel than a sin. Your parents have hearts. They still love you, I am sure of it. And so is my mother. They will surely forgive you when they see her. Time will have softened their rage and hurt. And after all, Flora says your father is not in the best of health. He will want to make his peace with you and see his only grandchild.'

Susan sighed and played with a tendril of hair that was threatening to escape from the arrangement Eliza was making.

'They will never approve of what we do, no matter how successful I become as an actress. They do not hold with the theatre – a den of vice, an anteroom of hell. And actresses the worst of all,' she said gloomily, applying a little colour to her cheeks that were pale with anxiety.

'Well, they are not alone in that,' retorted Eliza cheerily. 'We women have much to overcome if we are to be taken seriously and shown respect for what we do. You and I know it. Which is why I have been trying to get Richard to dismiss Charlotte. She is just the kind of hoyden that gives all actresses a bad name.'

Susan smiled knowingly into the looking glass. The rise and rise of Miss Gibson had been a bone of contention between Eliza and Richard since September; Richard recognised the young woman as excellent box office but Eliza disapproved of her audacious self-promotion and her overtly sexualised performances. No doubt Eliza felt threatened, but Susan could also see justification for Eliza's censure of Charlotte who would never enhance the standing of women in the profession, playing as she did to the men in the audience and inviting their admiration. Only the week before, she had once again tried to upstage Eliza who was playing Portia in *The Merchant of Venice*. In rehearsal, under Richard's direction, as

Nerissa she had appeared to do as he wished; however, on the stage and before an audience, she took her role in quite another direction. When confronted by an angry Eliza and a fuming Richard, she had simply shrugged her shoulders, saying, 'Well, the pit seemed to like it, didn't they?'

Susan could see interesting times ahead for Eliza, Richard and Drury Lane, but at the present moment, she was more concerned with the expected visitors. She patted the ringlets Eliza had created so beautifully and smiled at her reflection in the looking glass. It was Christmas after all, a season for family gatherings, reconciliation, love and forgiveness. Later in the day Mr Mountford was expected and she took some courage from the thought. Even if her parents failed to come or stayed only a short time, Charles would be there with his warmth and his love for her and Betty.

Further thoughts were interrupted by the jangle of the front door bell. Eliza laid a hand gently on her friend's shoulder.

'Come now, Susan. It's time to introduce Betty to her grandparents.'

Reviews on Amazon are so important to us self-published writers. Please take a few minutes to review this book and let me know your thoughts.

If you haven't tried my Foxwood series yet, check it out on Amazon.

To find out more about what else I am writing, take a look at my website and read my blog at **www.janamarsh.com**

28841208R00158

Printed in Great Britain
by Amazon